a no doubt mad idea

By Stephen Minkin

Illustrations by
Christopher Swan

Published by Ross/Back Roads Books

Back Roads Publications
Box 543
Cotati, Calif. 94928

Ross Books
Box 4340
Berkeley, Calif. 94704

Special thanks to my editor and publisher, Stella Monday, for believing in the book in the first place, and for her substantial creative contributions to the manuscript in the course of our collaboration to revise it.

Thanks to illustrator Christopher Swan, who has added another dimension to the book of words.

Thanks to Orlo Spring-Eagle for his distinctive cover calligraphy, and for the expertise of his eyes and hands.

Thanks to Rick Lawson, for helping out an old friend, and to Steve Hirsch, for helping out a new one.

Thanks to Gordon Carrega and Michael Zucaro for their many valuable suggestions.

Thanks to art director Casey Tichenor for the excellence and precision of his artistic judgment, and to Howard Jaroslovsky and Jeff Black for their fine paste-up assistance.

Thanks to attorneys George Lydon, Craig Casebeer, and Sylvan Nathan for their counsel on the legal facets of the plot.

Thanks, Pablo.

Thanks to Jennifer Weil for her impeccable proofreading, to Peter LaDow for the use of his equipment and space, and to our other friends who helped us out as the deadline crept up.

Finally, thanks to Franz and Doug Ross, of Ross Books, our co-publishers, for their invaluable assistance and advice in preparing this manuscript.

And Debbie, of course.

All characters and events in this book are made up. If some of them seem familiar, it's because so many of us grew up playing the same games.

Portions of this book have appeared, in slightly different form, in *Back Roads #7* and *#8, Windmill #1,* and *The Sonoma County Stump.*

Minkin, Stephen

A No Doubt Mad Idea

I. Title

PZ4.M6642No   [PS3563.I4715]

Library of Congress Catalog Card Number:

813'.5'4   78-23602

ISBN: 0-931272-00-9   PBK

CONTENTS

ILLUSTRATIONS

The chapter numeral diagrams are indexed in the *Appendix*.

Three entries from Lerner's notebooks on *Ludics*:

"Play casts a spell over us; is 'enchanting,' 'captivating.' It is invested with the noblest qualities we are capable of perceiving in things: rhythm and harmony."

—*Johan Huizinga*

"I always paint fakes."

—*Pablo Picasso*

"Play as an end means that life itself has intrinsic value."

—*H. H. Brinton*

The Game of Lone Buck Bay

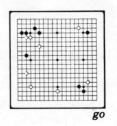

go

1

Grool in his cassock, & Weel in his gown
Dueled all night for a Western town;
The question remains (with Black to play)
In whose dominion is Lone Buck Bay?
        — David Fisher

" . . . back in the days when we were young enough to believe we were something brand new, the invaders from the future." Tom Roebuck stopped to scratch his beard and tilt his microphone a bit, then went on with his speech. "We might think of the child-care center, back up the hill, as representing those salad days. But we outlived our summer of flowers, and watched its blossoms rot. We did the composting, and found that some of its seeds were perennials. Utopian communities, like our own, have been a traditional American folly since long before the sixties.

"We meet here today to celebrate the third anniversary of the signing of the founding charter of our community of Lone Buck Bay -- The Compact of Cooperation. In that remarkable document, we find two prosperous young companies -- Grool's company of music makers and Weel's musical equipment company -- agreeing to pool their substantial resources and build a model community. The Compact articulated the dream of building a new town where none had been before, a town free of all the troubles that inhabited all the other towns." Tom raised his head to the audience. "Did we actually believe that the troubles came out of the places themselves, and not the people who populated them?"

Behind Tom wild shards of land that now belonged more to Ocean than California flung the waves that rammed

5

against them skyward into fifty-foot fans of foam and spray. To his left, on the north side of the bay, an inaccessible peninsula jutted out into the sea, topped by an otherworldly meadow, dotted with gnarled scrub all bent east by the westerlies. To the east, behind the crowd of 150 Tom faced, was the town -- Lone Buck Bay, a low-budget make-do mix of old and new, an old ranch and a new town, another utopian dream gone bust. East of that, the rest of the old sheep-ranch, still a sheep-ranch, soft feminine folds of hills, now in winter's green and amber, turning to emerald in the late spring.

"Joe Weel, one of the community's two main backers," the crowd booed, and Tom waited for the jeers to die down before he continued, "Joe Weel wanted to tear up Lone Buck Bay, and exploit it."

"Let's tear him up!" someone shouted and the rest cheered.

"He still wants that. Today we meet together to play the ritual game of Lone Buck Bay, so we will remember how we got here and where we're headed." There were more loud cheers, and applause. Tom smiled. "The people playing the villains, Weel's team, will be headquartered right here at the reviewing stand, on the beach, by our beautiful bay that Weel wants so much. All of the Weel team's scouts will be issued these black armbands." He held one up.

"As we all know, Weel not only failed to come up with his share of the money, he has also done everything in his power to drive us out of here. And who here doubts for a moment that Weel was the man behind the arson and the terrible double murders of Grool's wife and best friend?"

The crowd fell completely silent. Even after two years, the memory of the shocking tragedies still seemed raw.

"After that crime, for which no one has ever been arrested, the great musician Grool retired from the troubles of the world. He has lived in a cave, ever since. But his founding vision survives in our town of Lone Buck Bay, so Grool's team's home base is The Farmhouse, which is the center of our community."

Tom shifted papers on the rostrum. "The game of Lone Buck Bay is very simple. It has to be -- look who's going to play it!" He gestured to his audience, who laughed.

. . . *we are to enter the play-sphere of the festival, acquiescing in a game of belief,*

"Basically, it's hide-and-seek, one of the oldest games in creation.

"Each of the two teams has one chief, three guardians of the treasures, forty or fifty scouts, and two spies disguised as scouts. The chiefs plan strategy, keep track of which areas have been explored and which ought to be scouted. The guardians hide, and the scouts search for them. Scouts should travel in pairs, as it takes two members of the opposing team to tag a guardian. All guardians can be identified by their treasure disks, which are large enough to be seen from a hundred feet or so. Weel's disks are red, Grool's are blue.

"When the guardian is tagged by two opponents at the same time, he or she is captured and his or her treasure has to be surrendered. First team to capture all three of the opposition's treasure disks wins the game, and occupies the home base of the opposition. Losing team cleans up The Farmhouse after the party tonight. If the game isn't over by sundown, it's a draw.

"Anyone who didn't get an envelope with their team assignment, see Dorothy at the refreshment stand. First-aid station is at the newspaper office. Keep an eye on your own kids; lost kids go to the child care center. OK, let's get going -- all scouts to their home bases." Tom clapped his hands to stir up the movement.

The teams separated. Dozens of people moved closer to the reviewing stand, while Tom along with dozens of others started uphill, toward The Farmhouse. Children got separated from their parents, and began crying and shouting for them. A group of dogs on the north hill panicked when they saw the make-believe armies separating, and began running back and forth, barking wildly. The dogs on the south hill began barking back at them, and some of the people in the middle shouted at the dogs and the children.

One of the Weel team's guardians of the treasure, Mark Lerner, used all the movement and noise like squids use ink, and stole off to a hiding place he had picked out the day before. When he arrived there -- a half-hidden shelf on the southern coastal cliff -- Mark removed his identifying treasure disk from inside his shirt, and displayed it outside

where fun, joy, and rapture rule in ascending series.

— *Joseph Campbell*

his sweater. The disk had a big red $ painted on it -- Weel's treasure. "I feel like a fool," said Mark, and then he looked around to make certain no one was close enough to have heard him.

* * * * *

Mark studied the incoming waves, the way the sharp edges of their crests shredded into white mop heads as they fell. He heard sounds from town -- the occasional shouts and cheers that must have signalled the discovery and capture of one of the other guardians, and the constant beating of the several conga and bongo drums. From behind a rock in the shelf's wall, Mark removed a large bag of peanuts, a bottle of apple juice, a small chess set, and the Fischer-Evans collection of Bobby Fischer's games.

He felt suddenly lonely -- removed from everyone. It was just what he had wanted -- to be away -- not just in this game, but in the larger game of Lone Buck Bay. Mark had resigned his commitments to the town, to go off by himself and resume his studies -- studies in this new, maybe crazy, almost-science of play and play theory -- *ludics*.

But somehow, now, the quiet was too much. The noise of the crowd had been a comfort that he was going to miss. He wanted to run back to town like a child and grab somebody and say, "Please find me, I've hidden myself too well."

"Hey, you!"

Mark spun abruptly around, poised to make a sudden run to avoid capture.

"Let me ask you one thing."

"Where's your armband, brother? Identify yourself."

"My name's Reb," he said nervously. "What's going on around here?"

"Get in here, so you can't be seen. You'll give me away. Get in here -- then I'll tell you."

"OK." Reb crouched down and entered the shelf in the cliff. "Everybody in this town, everybody, is out looking for somebody. Just tell me this -- are they looking for me?"

"No, they're looking for me," said Mark.

He is no player; chess begins where he leaves off.

                                                            — *Buckle*

"What?" Reb backed away. "What did you do? Kill somebody?"

"I didn't do anything. We're playing hide-and-seek. It's the featured event of our third anniversary celebration."

"A game?"

"Yeah. Hide-and-seek."

Reb nodded. He uneasily scanned the wild seascape before them. "Suppose . . . suppose now that some older people, let's say, for argument's sake, that some of these older people wanted to keep an eye on certain other people, maybe because they didn't approve of certain things and activities of these other younger people or maybe because they thought they knew better than these other people what was good for them. You know what I mean?"

"Not exactly."

A stiff grin cut across Reb's face. "Suppose, suppose now that these older people we were talking about, suppose they wanted a way to watch over a lot of people at once. What I want you to tell me is . . . " He shook his head. "I mean do you think . . . do you think it is possible that while a person who has, let's say, for argument's sake, somebody who has been put in the hospital for a minor operation, and while he's there to do all these other things to him . . . " He stopped abruptly, cocked his head as though listening to something. "I can't say too much."

"What are you talking about?"

"Huh?" Then Reb's tone changed. *"Say nothing."* Turning back to Mark, he resumed his earlier voice, "Oh, nothing."

"You mean like putting a radio in your head and making you their slave? They probably could do it, but nobody's supposed to."

"You mean they could do it, though? They actually have the ability to do something like that if they wanted to?" Reb raced on, "Are you actually telling me you actually believe that it is actually possible for these certain unnamed persons to plant a tiny radio inside somebody's head and use it to tell them what to do and what to say? Is that what you're saying?" He covered up his ears with his hands, and whispered, "Do you actually mean to tell me you think it's

No matter how much we seek, we never find anything but ourselves.
— *Anatole France*

possible that while they were operating on you for something else they could put radios and stuff like that inside you so they could talk to you whenever they wanted and whatever you did they would know about?"

"Are you saying they did that to you?"

"*Say no.*" Reb did. "No."

"Is there someone telling you what to say?"

"Yes. *Say no.* I mean no. I mean, suppose these older people we were talking about before, suppose they thought they were older and wiser and more powerful than we were and maybe knew more about what was good for us than we did ourselves, and suppose they fixed up some guy like that, wired with radios and remote control and all that stuff, and then just let him walk around town, talk to people," he pantomimed smoking a joint, "and all the time all this information was being sent back to headquarters. *Don't say headquarters.* Not headquarters. I mean, I . . ." He lost the thread.

Mark took out his pen and pad, and wrote, "Are you and I being listened to, now?"

Reb nodded his head yes and said, *"Say no.* No."

"This is ridiculous. You just blew a fuse, that's all." Mark shrugged. Who knows, though? Who can pick out the paranoids? "But if this is real, why would they pick you? What would they get? A couple of small-time pot busts? Would anyone doing anything heavy do it in front of an obvious nut like you?"

Reb had no answers, but listened intently.

Feeling half scared, half ridiculous, Mark wrote on the pad, "Do you have a transmitter on you?" Why not? Why take chances? He felt he could justify it to himself if he had to. Anyway, he was a person. How else to deal with him except on his own terms. Trust him. Maybe he just wants somebody to talk about his world to, like I do.

"You can write your answers," wrote Mark.

Reb shook his head no.

"Who is doing this to you and why did they pick you?" wrote Mark.

Reb stared, amazed at the question.

"Is there danger to me? Or shall I go on?"

Oh, God, if we are in Thy image, how lonely Thou must be.

— *Rachel Berdach*

Quaking, Reb backed away. Then, "How long have I been talking to you? It doesn't matter. You probably have about ten minutes. OK. So let it be said in my favor that I gave you ten minutes warning. That ought to count for something. Ten percent, maybe." And then he fled.

"That boy is out to lunch," said a woman's voice.

Mark jumped, again ready to run, but relaxed when he recognized who it was. "Joanie. You're on my team, aren't you?"

"Yeah, I'm one of the bad guys too. I was talking to that boy yesterday," said Joanie, who looked like a farm maid in her flowered yellow old-time country dress. "He needs to get away." Joanie crept into Mark's hide-out.

"Away?" Mark looked around them. "We're in the middle of Away. Poor Reb. He thinks his life is being broadcast back to headquarters. How did you find me? I'm supposed to be hidden."

"You brought me here, once," she said. "We were rehearsing 'As You Like It.'"

"Yes, I remember that." Mark remembered. They had played well together, and had stayed late. Joanie was one of his dearest friends. How perfectly like her, to arrive here, now. He wanted to hug her, but felt suddenly shy. "What's happening in the game? You're a scout, aren't you?"

"Scout Joan, that's me." She helped herself to some apple juice.

"Who's your partner? And where?"

"Vivian. And with any luck she's fallen into the sea. Her mouth . . . "

"I know," said Mark.

"And she was also insisting on searching all the worst places -- she wanted to pick through all that thick brush on the north side of Pebble Creek."

"Maybe she's a spy, and wants to throw you off the scent."

"How did you get all this food and junk up here?" she asked.

"I stashed them yesterday, when I picked this place."

"Well, two schoolgirls found one of our guardians, hiding inside an empty garbage bin behind the restaurant."

"Right under their noses! Right outside their

If you can't volley, wear velvet socks.

—*Stephen Potter*

headquarters,'' Mark said. "Did he have one of these dollar signs, too?''

"No, his treasure disk had cartoons of the two Coastal Commissioners Weel controls. We found one of their guardians, too -- Tom-Tom made this great flying tackle. It was right next to the gift-shop on the highway. They stopped traffic. Listen, Mark -- you have to let me stay here. If I go back to the game, they'll assign me to Vivian again.''

"OK.''

"Thanks. Let's play one of your games. It seems only right.''

"Sure. What do you know?''

She shrugged.

"How about twenty questions?'' he suggested. "Everybody knows that one. OK? You think of something, and I'll try to guess. Got it?'' He waited, then asked, "Well, is it animal, vegetable, or mineral?''

"That's a tough question.''

"That's not a question. You're supposed to tell me that. That's the *clue*.''

"I forgot about that. Let's see -- I suppose it must be animal and vegetable, and possibly imaginary.''

"Come on, Joanie! You can't give a clue like that.''

"I just did. Ask your questions.''

"Twentieth century?''

"No.'' She scratched a mark in the ground.

"Since 1750?''

"No.''

"Since the birth of Christ?''

"Yes.''

"European?''

"Yes. Oh, I forgot to tell you -- I met your sweet old friend Larry, at the Weel team meeting,'' she said.

"Forget it. He's not your type at all. Larry can read and write and all that heavy stuff. Besides, what would Woody say?''

"We're no longer seeing each other. I'm sort of with Salugi today.'' She blinked. "I broke it off with Woody for good, last week.''

"Really? Are you going to have a reception?''

. . . *the movements in games are not contrived to serve another end, but are*

"Oh, shut up."

Mark knew she had never been so naive as to think she would have done anything but dump him when he began to weary her, just as she had done with all the other epsilon-minus semi-androids with whom she had mated since her breakup with Mitch. Madonna and Whore, but no longer together, for one man, from one whole Joanie. "You could get a lobotomy. Then you could deal with each other as equals." He couldn't help the jabs. They came from his own frustrated longing for a whole Joanie, who could be more than his friend.

She seemed not to hear. "Well, it's already over, in my head."

"Great. If it works its way down through the rest of your body, you'll have it beat."

"My kind friend," Joanie pinched him so hard in the soft hollow of his elbow he howled in pain.

"Look what you did! You put a crease in my favorite cardigan!"

"Looks like something out of the free box on the Dobie Gillis show."

"This is the modified collegiate look, the look of the future. How many questions is that? I can't see your marks."

"Is that a question?"

"No."

"Four. Sixteen left."

"Is it bigger than a breadbox?" Mark showed her how big with his hands.

"I doubt it."

"That's a good game."

Joanie smirked.

"Is it an object associated with a famous individual?"

"Yes."

He pondered. "European, between zero and 1750 A.D. After 1500?"

"Yes. That's seven."

"Historical figure?"

"We've already said this was a famous person."

"I mean was his fame the result of political power -- like

pursued for their own sake. It is the same with the delights of wisdom.
                                                              — St. Thomas

a king or a revolutionary, rather than a famous painter or composer.''

"I see,'' said Joanie. "In that case, no. But why assume it's a man? We haven't established sex, yet.''

"How many famous women were there, then? Elizabeth, Isabella, Lucretia Borgia . . . of course, *you're* a woman.''

"Twentieth century American,'' said Joanie. "And you know what we're like!''

"All right -- is it a woman?''

"Regrettably, no.''

"What? You set me up for that.''

"You deserve it.'' She cracked a peanut.

"You owe me one. 'Regrettably,' you say -- so you approve of this person. Is it Shakespeare?''

She shook her head and looked indignant, as though the game had been set aside and she was forcing the issue in a deadly serious business deal. "You can't do that.'' She smoothed her dress over her knees, even though she was sitting on a rock. "You only asked that because you know me, not from asking questions.''

"Is it really Shakespeare?''

"Yeah, but I think I ought to at least charge you an extra question on that,'' she said.

"No way!'' Mark insisted. "The art of not giving away extra information is part of every game. If a boxer telegraphs his punches -- say he drops his left before he throws his right -- he's giving everybody else an edge on him, a little extra time to defend.'' She seemed unconvinced, so Mark continued, "Besides, I would never have asked the question in the first place if you hadn't lured me into it so cleverly.''

"OK. As long as you continue to flatter me.''

"How many questions was that?''

"Ten.''

"Some object identified with Shakespeare. I'll take a stab in the dark,'' he said. "In Shakespeare's will, he awards his wife his second-best bed -- is it that bed?''

"No, but as wild guesses go, that's a good one.''

"Is it something written or printed?''

"Very good. Yes, it is,'' she said.

I think work is easier than play. With work there is a certain compulsion to get things

"Is it something written in Shakespeare's own hand?"

"Yes."

"Is it the original manuscript of one of his plays?"

"No."

"Poems?"

"No."

"Hmm." Mark puzzled over it. "A personal document?"

"Yes. That's sixteen."

"It could be his will. But as you said it might be imaginary, and I think they have his will under glass somewhere."

"More extra information I gave you."

"It probably doesn't matter one way or another," said Mark. "I can't think of anything."

Joanie cocked her head and put a finger to her lips. "Listen -- do you hear anything?"

"Yeah. Ssh."

They heard it again.

"Somebody probably saw Reb. Go peek outside," Mark whispered. "And if it's 'our friends, the enemy,' see if you can divert them."

Joanie gave a fake salute, and stuck her head outside. It popped back in with a groan.

"Grool team scouts?" he asked.

"Worse than that. It's Vivian. All's lost."

"Don't be ridiculous. She's on our team."

"I can't accept that," said Joanie. "I'll defect."

"There you are!" Vivian screeched, her voice like fingernails scraping across a slate. Mark hoped it would go away. It never did. Vivian stuck her head inside the hideout. "And Mark, too. Who is one of our guardians, I see! Well, well, what a surprise." She had a face, God help her, that could peel paint. "You've really dropped out of sight, lately, Mark. I don't mean just the game. I mean in real life, around town. Isn't that right, Joanie? Have you noticed that? You don't see Mark in town, and around. Not like you used to."

"Really, Mark." Joanie opted to play along with Vivian. "I'd heard you joined the Peace Corps, teaching contraception to the Patagonians."

done, but when you're playing you have to always be organizing yourself and

"People are talking about you." Vivian seemed eager to tell him. "They're all saying your resignation from the Town Council, and the rest, amount to a massive cop-out on your part."

"That's what a lot of people said about the town, when we started out. If you think back to the planning meetings in San Francisco, you might remember that the activists among us argued against the move to the country. They claimed that by abandoning the urban poor, we were forfeiting our political responsibility and integrity. But it seemed to me, as a student of play, that a small Utopian town could be a very effective tool for political change."

"That has nothing to do with your resignation," Vivian said irritably.

Mark was remembering his argument: Erik Erikson's idea of play as a *model reality* within which the child's skills can be developed, in relative safety; and his own idea, that some playspaces ought to function in the same way in adult life, as testing laboratories where we construct prototypes, practice dry runs, and float trial balloons. Setting up small utopian towns, a very sensible and natural approach to social experimentation and progress. Changing the world, an impossibly big job. But building a small scale model of a more perfect society, within which people could practice living in the future, and discovering what works -- that might be possible. The argument had worked. People had repeated it to themselves and others. They had come to Lone Buck Bay. Mark realized that Vivian was staring at him, waiting for something more, so he told her, "Now all I'm asking for is the same kind of place apart, as an individual, to experiment with my own models. I want 'the right to be left alone.' "

Vivian scowled.

"Well, rest easy, Vivian. Before I vanish completely, I'll turn over to the town my complete sets of diplomatic portfolios and dossiers, the secret bank accounts, the codes to control my personal international network of underground operatives . . . "

"The only thing you're passing is the buck," Vivian interrupted.

perpetuating activities. If you don't have anything to do there is a tendency to mope

"You know where that comes from?" he asked.

"What?"

"Passing the buck. It's from poker. The dealer used to set a buckhorn knife in front of him so everyone could keep track of who was dealing, and when he passed the deal, he also passed the buck."

"Boy, you're a regular fountain of that kind of, uh, tidbit," Vivian said. "Hey Joanie, let's go back to the game."

"I have a devastating headache," Joanie lied. "Would you mind terribly if I stayed here?"

"No, that's all right, honey. Well, see you both at the party, later." And, shoving a half-dozen peanuts into her jeans pocket, Vivian left.

Mark and Joanie poured some apple juice and toasted each other.

"I didn't think she'd take no for an answer, so easily," said Joanie.

"I figured if I bored her badly enough, she'd leave," said Mark. "Getting back to the important issue at hand, though -- am I to understand that this is a personal document in Shakespeare's own handwriting that may or may not have existed -- is that right?"

"Is that a question?"

"No, it's a clarification."

"OK. That's correct."

"Is it a personal communication concerning love or money?"

"You could say so."

"Well, would you say so?"

Joanie made a face. "Not much room for ambiguity and subtlety in this game, is there? OK, I'll say so."

Mark shook his head in defeat. "Give me a clue. How many questions do I have left?"

"Three. Love, kind of, rather than money," she said.

"A love letter?"

"No."

"Tell me who it was written to?"

"If I tell you, you'll know," said Joanie.

"No, I won't."

around.

—H. Salt

"Richard Burbage."

"See," said Mark.

"You don't know that story? Richard Burbage was one of the Globe's leading actors, and he once made a rendezvous with some hot lady for after the play. So, following the performance, Burbage goes over to her house, and there he finds, tacked to the door, the very same note from Shakespeare that was the answer to the twenty questions game."

"And what, pray tell, did this note, which may or may not have existed, say?"

" 'William the Conqueror came before Richard the First.' "

Mark laughed, but then disapproved. "You can't ask something like that. Nobody knows that."

"Common knowledge," said Joanie.

"Yeah. That's not how the game goes. You're supposed to make it possible."

"Are you supposed to make it possible in chess?" asked Joanie.

"No, that's different. You're worse than Vivan. Look at it the other way. Did you know that the Russian composer Aram Katchaturian described his 'Sabre Dance' as no more than a button on the shirt on the body of his work? No? You're not alone. Suppose my twenty-questions answer was that metaphorical button -- would that be fair? No one would have a chance!"

"So? That would just go to show what good players you and I are -- nobody *ever* guesses what we're thinking."

Mark shook his head.

"And," Joanie continued, grabbing his shirt, "if you ever make another comparison between me and -- oh, Jesus!"

Suddenly, three of the Grool's team scouts entered the shelf on the left. Mark scrambled out on the right, and scurried along the narrow cliff path until he reached the open grassy crest above the shelf, where he broke into a sprint. The three opposition scouts took after him, and chased Mark toward the highway.

As he ran across the south hill, Mark heard shouts from

Don't look back. Something might be gaining on you.

—Satchel Page

town, as scouts in the valley spotted the chase. Several people started running uphill, toward him. He backtracked toward the ocean, but had to circle south to avoid his original trio of pursuing scouts, who were closing on him from the west.

As he neared the southern boundary of the town, Mark felt that his legs and lungs had been pushed to their limits. Mark turned and saw that the scouts from town had closed in on him fast. They were fresh and they had not had to circle around the scouts closing on him from the west. The scouts from the town began to fan out. Mark realized they would be able to seal off the northern and eastern escape routes before he could get loose.

They've got me, he realized. He removed the treasure disk from around his neck and, true to the spirit of the game, waved it around his head while shouting, "Money, money, money!" in an evil and maniacal voice. He fell to the ground, to cushion the shock of the five scouts who fell on him immediately with cries of triumph.

When they peeled off, and let him up, the first face he saw was Vivian's. "I'm a spy, baby," she told him, and winked.

*   *   *   *   *

As the last of the bad guys to be caught, the crowd showered Mark with hoots and catcalls when he was led back in defeat. "Let's hope we're this successful in handling Weel in real life," Tom Roebuck said. Tom congratulated the winners, and declared the anniversary party officially begun.

The people spread themselves out in the day's remaining sunshine. Like the town itself, the party was more or less centered around The Farmhouse, a huge white Victorian, with a fine wide west veranda, facing the ocean. The house was built by José Lopez y Garcia in 1874 to house three generations of Garcias, who were the first settlers to actually own and live on the land. The building was ample enough to house the thriving Pleasant Peasant Restaurant's dining

The trick is not to arrange a festival, but rather to find the people who can enjoy it.
— Nietzsche

hall, kitchen, and pantry, the Community Hall, the Cooperative Food Store, the Town Office (originally, Señor Garcia's chapel), and still leave a dozen other .ooms for other uses. The restaurant, which occupied the old south wing, was painted blue and red, and lit by floodlights at night. A recent addition to local custom encouraged everyone to make a string of sticks, pebbles, feathers, shells, souvenirs, and what-have-you, and hang it somewhere on The Farmhouse, so the building would always have a kind of music of its own. In the spring, the flower-boxes would bloom, again -- azaleas and irises and, on the sheltered side, the lilies-of-the-valley, brought out from Michigan by somebody's sister.

Mark looked over the dozens of people partying, drinking, smoking -- all the country dresses, beards, blue jeans, saris, guitars, jugs -- until he spotted the friendly face of EZ Beazly, and sat next to him.

EZ passed Mark a pipe and asked, "Wanna buy a dog?"

Still panting from the chase, Mark's hyperventilated world spun like a top. He made loose fists, pressed the bottom thirds of his index fingers against his eyelids, and stared with closed eyes at the pattern of contiguous and concentric squares, expanding into diffusion, new ones originating from each square's center, a marvelously inventive interior kaleidoscope whose source was an even greater mystery than its productions. Cheap thrills, right? From somewhere, seemingly neither within nor without him, came a voice, a voice not unlike his own voice heard from a great distance, saying, "Wanna trade a joint of this for a frog and two dead mice?"

EZ returned to the original offer. "He's an exceptionally intelligent animal. Sancho -- show the man your best tricks." The puppy rose, raised his ears and lowered his tail as though he had been caught in some condemnable act, cringed counter clockwise, whimpered once, and finally crumpled on his paws. "The letter *C*, by Sancho Panza."

Abruptly, a young auto mechanic walked up to Mark, and pointed at his chest, "Now that your bullshit facade of wishy-washy liberalism has been peeled away by your

. . . serious things are intrinsically better than funny and amusing things . . .
— Aristotle

resignations, you have proven to us all that hiding behind it was nothing but the egotistical tap-dancing of a spoiled-child pig from the intellectual bourgeoisie!'' This was Tom Price, known as Tom-Tom, to distinguish him from Tom Roebuck, the newspaper's editor and the day's emcee. Suddenly Tom-Tom's attention was diverted by a remarkable sight, passing not ten feet away from the group, heading toward the ocean. With an uncharacteristically softened voice, he said, "Look at this beautiful woman.''

All did. No more than 18, she was made up with heavy blue mascara, two-inch earrings, an eggshell gown with a train, long white gloves, a silver lorgnette, and a brass ankh on a chain around her waist.

"In Los Angeles,'' EZ confided to Mark, "this would pass for reality.''

"I have never been so taken at first sight,'' Tom-Tom whispered.

Even the man known as Wince, the Mumbler, who was rarely aware of his own existence, much less anybody else's, stirred as she sashayed past. Then, to the utter astonishment of all, Wince rose to his feet and actually gestured towards her. In a voice obviously suffering from extended neglect, he asked, "Did you see her?''

"Indeed we did, man!'' Mark rallied. "Every mother's son of us.''

Wince, still slightly reeling from his unfamiliarity with the fully erect standing position, wondered, "Do I look halfway together?'' The words jumped out like a recitative from a twelve-tone opera's mad scene.

"My man, that depends entirely upon what you look like when you're entirely together,'' EZ calculated.

"I can't let that degenerate get to her,'' Tom-Tom spat, and took off after them.

The man behind Mark was telling someone else, "When my old lady had her first baby, she used to sell bottles of her piss to chicks for $50, so they could get welfare. You can't do that now, they changed the rules.''

The belly dancing troupe began their show and the music, legs, colored silks, coins, breasts, finger cymbals, tambourines slamming into bare thighs, shoulders, earrings,

The opposite of play is not what is serious but what is real.

— *Sigmund Freud*

and smooth swaying skins succeeded in casting their spell over Mark.

He toyed with the perception of this party as an enchanted theater, filled with bright costumes, broad performances, the decorative play of flirtations and courtesies, the music, the dance, all the implicit backstage dramas, the clowns, and the sideshow freaks.

Someone tapped Mark on his shoulder and said, "Do us all a favor, Mark." It was Tom Roebuck. "Pay Grool's cave one last visit, before you go off into your own cave. The lawyers need him to sign these papers."

Mark took them. "I'll see him tomorrow, after the crafts guilds meeting. And Tom -- I'm not moving anywhere, I'll be around."

EZ passed a bottle of wine to him, but Mark declined, saying, "I'm going to take a walk on the beach." He stayed out until long after the sun set.

* * * * *

When the beach became too cold, Mark headed back to the party. The town looked deserted, everyone being inside The Farmhouse. Mark headed there, too.

It was even more crowded than he expected. "What's the music?" he asked of a man who looked as though he knew something.

"Bootleg tape of Coltrane, made in Tracy in '68, the year after he died."

Mark spotted Joanie, who looked distressed. "What's wrong?"

"Mitch is here," she said. Mitch was her ex-husband, her "dreaded wuzband," as she called him. She loathed him. "I'm leaving."

"We have to clean up," said Mark. "We were on the losing team, remember?"

"I did it already. I did a load of dishes."

"Does that count?"

"Sure. Talk to the chief."

"That's a good idea. Why don't you wait just a bit while

When a man marries, dies, or turns Hindoo/His best friends hear no more of him.
— Shelley

I talk to the chief and do some dishes, and then I can go home with you, tonight?" Mark asked.

"No." It was her seventh consecutive rebuff. He expected it. "I told you, Mark -- I'm kind of with Salugi. But even if I weren't . . . " Cupping her hands on his face, "It's too risky. I'd be too scared to lose you as a friend. How many times do I have to say these things to you? Why don't you come by for breakfast, before the meeting?"

"OK," said Mark.

"Are you going to the crafts guild meeting, tomorrow?" she asked. "It's at Pearl's house."

"Yes. I'm going."

"Good. Are you and Pearl seeing each other again?" Joanie teased.

"No! What the hell is that about?"

"I won't say. You and I gossip far too much, Mark. That's because we're such good friends, I know, but this time I'm going to practice discretion, and not blab. I can use the practice."

"Good. I don't want to know."

"You'll know." She picked up her coat. "Here comes Salugi. Will you come by for breakfast? Around ten?"

"I will."

She gave him a parting kiss, gathered her belongings, cast a parting scowl at her ex, turned to the party as a whole and announced, " 'Fortune,' and the rest of you slobs, 'Good night. Smile once more. Turn thy wheel.' "

Mark scanned the chaos of the party, then crossed the big Community Hall to the pay phone, singing in soft falsetto The Velours' oldie, "Can I Come Over Tonight?" -- exceptional bass line and one of the more memorably off key lead lines in the history of our indigenous contemporary pop-folk-art genre -- rock'n'roll.

Folva Thoolman was finishing her phone call. Folva had huge breasts, like a nursing nanny goat, and she wore a blouse that was so tight she was compelled to leave its top seven buttons undone. Mark played with a momentary fantasy of being a shepherd on a grassy hillside covered with such simple, gentle creatures as Folva, all grazing peacefully, bleating softly, once in a while, for his kind

For you may imagine what kind of faith theirs was, when their chief doctors, and

attentions.

After a minute or so, Mark realized that Folva had completed her call. She simply had not moved. Mark called Angela.

"Hello."

"Hi. Want to play spin the bottle?"

"Are you drunk?"

"No, but men of my kidney are in the rapidly dwindling minority."

"OK. Pick up some kindling on you way over, and we'll make a fire."

She was so sweet. If he loved her nearly as much as she did him, life would be simpler. "Me and the sticks'll be over in an hour or so. I have a load of dishes, first."

"Bye."

fathers of their church, were the poets.

— Francis Bacon, about the heathens

Bed
& Breakfast

tangram

2

> *"Are you not scared by seeing that the Gypsies are more attractive to us than the Apostles? For though we love goodness and not stealing, yet also we love freedom and not preaching."*
> — *Ralph Waldo Emerson*

Angela's room was a space unlike any Mark could conceivably create for himself. The "look" of his rooms was always the unintentional byproduct of a nonvisual process. Papers, books, folders, staplers, scissors, pads, pens, none of it arranged by design. His eyes were focussed on too small a space to notice anything as human-sized as a whole room.

But Angela was a painter, and her room was so rich in visual nuances and tactile pleasures that every time he visited her he made a new discovery. Paintings, paints, brushes -- her whole work corner had a look not unlike Mark's. The signal difference was that hers had been contained to a corner, whereas Mark's tapered off, but never entirely vanished. There were plants and prints in hers, and fabrics -- hung, draped, one red-patterned remnant tied, with a length of wool, into a crumpled ball and suspended from the ceiling -- knotty blue spruce walls . . .

"What's that?"

"Hadn't you seen that before?"

"No." It was a large acrylic on canvas, an immense daddy-longlegs dominating the foreground, alley weeds big as redwoods. Through the spider's legs, set far in the background, stood a street gang, leather jacketed, flanked by garbage cans. "I like it. I really like this one. In fact, I think I like this better than anything else I've seen of yours, except maybe 'Peacock In The Tumbleweed'. You had that incredible color-play in that one. Conceptually, though, this one's even more interesting. What do you call it?''

'' 'Daddy.' ''

They laughed. She was prettier when she laughed, he thought. Not actually pretty, but prettier. ''You must have done this incredibly fast. I never even saw you working on this.''

''Oh, I finished this one a long time ago. Before we started seeing each other.'' That had been only two months ago. But they had known each other over a year, having met through Joanie, who was Angela's business representative for children's book illustrations. ''My gynecologist bought it, and it's been hanging in his house. Last week his nephew scribbled over part of it, so for another $25 I'm repainting that corner, cleaning it up.''

From a pillow's width away, he reminded himself, her face crossed the threshold into prettiness. And of course her skin was wired directly to his sexual circuitry and their relationship between the sheets (and in Ramblers, meadows, beaches, and once on a bench in a booth in a basement level restaurant in Chinatown) was very good. Her yellow robe, ruffled with white lace, rustled softly.

Angela told him, ''I had kind of a disappointing afternoon. I spoke to my mother, and found out that the $18,000 she had put away for me and my two sisters was spent, last year, to help bail my father out of his business troubles.''

''Well, that's not all that much,'' grunted Mark.

''A third of $18,000 is a *lot* of money to me,'' Angela retorted.

''That ain't a lot of money,'' he grumbled. ''A million dollars -- now, that's a lot of money. I don't want to talk about money. Let's talk about something else.''

''OK,'' said Angela. ''Let's talk about what a prick you are.''

''Me? I'm not a prick. Darth Vader -- *he's* a prick.''

She laughed and they were easy with each other. Angela. He knew her face by name now, instinctively, and its name was the same as this woman's name; he knew her now,

Art seduces us into the struggle against repression.

— Norman O. Brown

too -- their names were Angela.

. "How's your work going?" she asked.

He thought, it's only beginning, not yet out of sight of the docks. It's completely untested, and I'm afraid for it. He said, "Not much, really."

In a soft voice off the same spool as the warm tea she served, she advised, "Don't fret about it."

"And with you? How's your work going?"

"Oh, I haven't had time for much this week except the drawings for that job Joanie got me, the English-as-a-second-language readers."

"I like that book you lent me. Love that story about the painter who covered up the naked Christ and apostles on Michaelangelo's *Last Judgment* in the Sistine Chapel."

"Who has been known ever since as 'Il Brachettone,' Big Underwear."

They laughed, and he said, "What do *those* eyes mean?"

"Only I know."

"OK, be mysterious. Just come over here." She joined him on the couch. He drew her face to his, kissed her, canoodled her, and before long there was no place left to go but to bed.

She touched him, and trembled. "I'm the only person who has erogenous zones on other people." She went to the bathroom, took longer than usual.

He ignored her when she got back.

She said, "Well, put the book away, light the candle, and shut off the lamp, stupid."

"Say pretty please, bitch."

"Pretty please, bitch."

"That's better."

Afterwards, they held each other, wordlessly, for a long time. Then, softly, they began talking again, less concerned with what they were saying than that the way they said what they said left their lovemaking special and whole.

"Hey, Angela?"

"What?"

"Where's the alarm clock?"

"Oh, come on."

"No, really. I need it."

If you can't think of anything nice to say about anybody, come sit here by me.
— Alice Roosevelt Longworth

"What for?"

"I want to make your clock tick."

She rolled over.

"I have to be up for breakfast, at Joanie's. We have a morning meeting to go to."

"It's on the dresser. Keep a secret?"

" 'Promises and pie-crusts,' writes Swift, 'are made to be broken.' "

"The way Joanie and Lily first met is that Joanie was hot for this greaser-type who was staying at Lily's, so she snuck into Lily's house, in San Francisco, when nobody was there, and put on Lily's clothes and jewelry, and waited in Lily's bed for the guy to come home. But Lily came home first, so Joanie seduced her, instead."

At a loss for an acceptable snappy comeback, one of Mark's robot selves responded with a weak, "Really?"

Angela, seeing him forced to bare his own vulnerability, risked hers. "Do you ever think of settling down into a domestic relationship again?" There was a kind of unspoken agreement between them to talk abstractly whenever they wanted to talk about the two of them, a code designed to avoid talking about "the relationship." They had both seen too many instances in which the entrance of the word "relationship" signaled the beginning of "the relationship's post-mortem phase."

"I don't know. I have so much work to do now. Maybe it would have to be somebody I knew for years before I would settle down with her." This was part philosophy and part string-along number three, and he hoped she knew it, too.

"I suppose I'm still hoping for a man to show up who'll tell me I am what he has been searching for all his life."

"Now what the hell would you be doing with some fool who thinks you're the answer to what he's been looking for all his life?" She laughed, bless her, he thought. Please understand me, Angela, before you make me spell it out for you. I like you, I admire you, I even love you in a way. But not in *that* way.

If it came to it, he would simply tell her he had not yet bagged his tiger, to prove his manhood, and he had to make a mark for himself in the world before he could begin to

But for my dear Monet, we would all have given up.

— *Renoir*

consider a close live-in relationship, again. That was true, or mostly so.

The past year, after the break-up with Pearl, he had spent living alone, and usually loverless. He was no longer terrified by his loneliness, and no longer frightened by the thought that he might remain single for the rest of his life, or for much of it. He had buried and mourned one of the quests of his childhood and youth -- true love, two hearts that beat as one, someone made in Heaven for him alone. He had learned to live by himself, after thirty years of uninterrupted domesticity, learning that it was inevitable that his I-don't-need-nobody-strut would sometimes collapse into the I-don't-love-nobody-and-ain't-nobody-love-me shuffle. It was sad, it was sad, he would slobber in his beer if he were more of a beer-drinking man. And yet, all things considered, sentimentality played a less crucial role in his life, and the woe-oh-lonesome-me blues no longer weighed as heavily as they once did.

She had fallen asleep on his arm, and by now her head had grown heavy. He moved it over to her pillow, thinking that even the most gregarious people lived their inner lives solitarily, within themselves. And yet since everybody inhabits that same kind of aloneness, even our isolation was but another of the many things we shared. What a mystery, what a mystery.

He looked at her. He just wasn't in love with her. She wasn't pretty enough for him to like looking at her. He felt ashamed of himself for not being able to look past that, to her fine, admirable inner qualities. But there was no getting around it -- he could never say, "I love you" to her, not even once.

Is falling in love with love really a feeling of make-believe? Long-time one of the only games in town worth playing. So take a chance, fall in love, ante up, bet a heart, play the game, pick a part, take a chance, take a chance . . . He risked little here, with Angela. He was The House in a craps game -- a safe, small, no-thrill sure thing. Nothing ventured, nothing drained -- and from these threadbare thoughts it was but a fraction of an inch into unconsciousness, and Mark slipped the rest of the way into it. He lay beside

. . . there is no sanctuary in one bed from another.

— *Cyril Connolly*

Angela, dreaming of Pearl.

*　*　*　*　*

She lay beside him. "Jay noo poo valoo," he quipped, trying to impress her with his wide command of nonexistent languages. He would have liked to have spoken directly to the subject of the pentagonal dodecahedrons, and The Tertiary Manacle, but to do so too quickly would have been, as they say, *non don va don*.

It was getting very cold, and Mark began shivering. His teeth chattered. He was adrift on a giant slab of ice in Hudson's Bay, freezing to death. Christ, what happens when the last of the dogs is gone? What then? he cursed. He fought passing out.

Angela turned on the heater, in the real world. She thought of waking him, saying she wanted to put more covers on them, make love again. But she was shyer with him than she was with most, and didn't.

He left the Arctic. He was in downtown New York. It was deserted. Hurricane winds were blowing everything that wasn't set in concrete. It was dangerous to be outside, impossible to stand or walk.

A blind beggar, with a dog and a cup, stood calmly in the storm. He was the only person in sight.

"How do you do it?" Mark shouted above the howls of wind.

"Like this," explained the blind man, explaining nothing.

Mark was blown against a building, then into the street. He clutched an overturned car, and dove through the nearest door. Breathless, he staggered to an easy chair, and crumpled into it like a deflated beachball.

The others at the cocktail party stared. How else was he supposed to look, having just stepped in from the hurricane? He looked out through the large picture window at a serene summer's day in a modern industrial park.

He began running down the steps. The burglar alarm went off. He stopped, moved outside, through walls, to a

. . . personal God quaquaquaqua with white beard quaquaquaqua outside time without

cross-section view of the whole building. The alarm bell was on the eighth floor. He rose, and as he neared the eighth floor he realized that the alarm sounded just like an alarm clock. He opened his eyes, shut off Angela's clock.

She rolled over. "Going?" She kissed him goodbye, rolled over, fell back to sleep. Mark left, heading into the streets, deserted now except for a few cats, and a couple of dogs. Between the street and the river, the quiet grove of redwoods had the air of a cathedral carpeted with trillium, oxalis, and ferns. The branches crackled, while a hidden critter scampered through and crunched dry leaves. The fog skated effortlessly up river.

From up river: "Don't be so rough with each other!"

"We're only playing."

Lido Grande (ten miles inland from the coast, a beach and a bridge on a bend in the Russian River) had three seasons: pretourist, tourist, and posttourist. This was still winter, the off-season.

"Every fucking day!" somebody down river shouted. "Every fucking day and every fucking night and every fucking morning! I can't take it any more. Do you hear me! I'm fucking cracking up!"

"The whole goddamn town hears you! Now shut the hell up," a neighboring voice shouted back.

Angela lived on River Way, but Joanie lived on the other side of town, on the hill over the firehouse. It was covered with old houses that had been built to host the summer and weekend vacations of city-people. But most of the houses now served as low-rent quarters for the newer, younger residents of the old resort town. Like the settlers of Lone Buck Bay, most of them had moved north from San Francisco, in the late sixties and early seventies, because there was no place west to go, and they were still searching for their homes and their communities. Some of these tenants rented with the understanding that they would have to leave in the spring and return in the fall, so the owner could spend his vacation there; or, often, so the owner could rent the place out to vacationers willing to pay the monthly rent weekly. There was a blatant temporariness to it all, even more so than to the rest of California, and the whole hillside

extension who from the heights . . . loves us dearly with some exceptions . . .
— Samuel Beckett

looked like it might quietly slip out of town one morning.

Smoke rose like a genie from Joanie's chimney. Joanie, in a purple robe, gave Mark a quick hug at the door, and turned back in.

There were two others at her round dining table.

"Mark!"

"Salugi! What the hell are you doing here?" Then Mark remembered Joanie had left the party with him. Astonishing that he had forgotten that, he judged.

"What am I doing here? What the hell you think?"

Mark nodded his greetings to Lily, pretty Lily, looking uncannily virginal, precious, and a bit brittle, even, this morning, in white lace and white makeup to make her face look fragile as a cameo. Mark smiled and winked at her, to win her blush, but her dissonant, steely stare cut grooves through his wink like sled trails on an untouched hillside.

"Where do you guys know each other from?" asked Joanie from the stove. "Originally, I mean."

Recovering quickly from the double jolt of Salugi and Lily, Mark narrated, "In the days of my debauched youth I used to visit a notorious speedfreak crashpad and lamastery called The Greta Garbo Hotel. The origins of its name are lost in antiquity, or worse. Salugi was one of the resident specimens, and also the greatest of the Italian kalimba players. And one of my good friends, a marijuana dealer of limited earnings but boundless grace named Grasshopper, was an impassioned jew's harpist who used to go to the hotel to play music with Salugi."

"Yeah. Heavy." Salugi was aloof. "So what have you been doing?"

Mark considered. "Making up my mind."

"Don't be a chump. Keep them both!"

"Not women. I'm trying to decide what to do with my life. Before long, I'll be dead."

"For real? What have you got?"

"Just a figure of speech, Salugi."

Joanie stared at him. Above her, the kitchen cat-clock swished its tail, tick-tock. She turned over the egg-timer, reached for the bowl of eggs.

Chessplayers are people who believe they are doing something very clever when they

Salugi railed at Mark. "You know what your biggest trouble is?" (Look at this! thought Mark.) "You *think* too much. It's not good for you. Really. This is not some off-the-wall riff I'm making up. I read this. This has been proved by science, and medicine. Too much thinking depletes the body of certain essential mineral nutrients. And women can't relate to you if you think too much."

"But it is only by thinking that we can create artificial spinach, and conquer the charley horse."

"You don't even know how to think right! You only *think* you can think. You can't really think. You spend all your time trying to think, and you *still* can't think! Give it up. Take up pool."

"Play pool. Maybe. Thirty's not really old. I mean, baseball's a young man's game, but Dazzy Vance didn't win his first major league game until he was thirty-one, and he went on to lead the league in strikeouts seven years in a row." When Salugi omitted the quick comeback, Mark moved on to, "Seen Buzzy lately?"

"Buzzy, man. Fucking Buzzy! Did you hear what happened? No? Listen to this shit. About two weeks ago me and Buzzy are both completely wasted as usual, maybe even a little more so, and we had his car parked up on this hill in South City, you know?, both of us completely fucked up behind reds and yellows and wine, I mean . . ." Salugi shook his head at the past wondrousness of it all, and downed some more breakfast beer in tribute to its memory.

Joanie was unimpressed,and left the room, returning a few minutes later, dressed for the business of the day.

"Now Buzzy," Salugi continued, "he's even more fucked up than I am. I mean, at least I had it together to stand up and get out of the car and start walking down the hill. Buzzy's still nodding, he can't even make it out of the car. Anyway, I'm going down the hill, you know?, and about halfway down I start to feel loops, like I'm losing it, you know, so I sit down on the curb, for a bit, so in case I fall it won't be that far. Right? So I look up the hill, and I can see Buzzy starting to move around in the car, he gets behind the wheel, releases the emergency brake, leans over to turn the

are only wasting their time.

— *G.B. Shaw*

key . . . and the fucking dude nods out again! I couldn't fucking believe it! This car is rolling down the street, straight at me! Man, by the time my mind registers that I'm supposed to get out of the gutter, and let the car go by, it's too late already. It runs over my feet, man, all the way down the hill, and crashes into a fire hydrant. Wow. So I'm so fucking ripped, right, that I don't feel a thing. I can't stand up, you know, but I can't figure out if I can't stand up because my feet are broken or because I'm just too wiped out. I couldn't tell.

"OK. So now Willy -- see, we were visiting Willy, in South City -- and when Willy hears the crash he comes charging out of his house, to see what fuck was going down. All right. Meantime, Buzzy sobers up as soon as the car hits the pole, and he's so freaked out by this he gets out of the car and starts motivating in a southerly direction. And me, I'm crawling on my hands and knees, and Willy of course is a pretty heavy coke freak, and a little paranoid to begin with, so when he sees me crawling around he starts going bananas, asking me what's wrong. I can't say anything, and Willy's yelling at me, 'What's wrong with you?' He's looking around, but Buzzy's gone, and there's nobody else on the street. And then, like a weird delayed reaction, I say, 'Buzzy ran me over.'

"Willy goes absolutely crazy! He goes, I'll kill him!' See, he was thinking Buzzy did it on purpose, and I'm too wrecked to tell him I'm talking and walking so weird because I'm drugged out of my skull, not in pain, not any I could feel, anyway. So Willy goes home, and gets a pipe wrench, but Buzzy's long gone by then. Then Willy took me to the hospital. They gave me some more reds. I woke up under this freeway exit ramp in Oakland."

Joanie slapped a platter -- an avocado, cheese, and mushroom omelet -- noisily on the table in front of Salugi, segueing abruptly into the cyclical modality of the edible. Lily laid the baked bananas on the table so very delicately that everyone felt her sense that it all might shatter like glass and balsa wood unless everyone moved and talked very lightly.

The only way to have a friend is to be one.

— Ralph Waldo Emerson

True to type, Salugi bulled in with, "Rub-a-dub-dub, thanks for the grub. All right, now let me ask you a serious question, Mark -- what would you do if you went to fuck this girl and she had no cunt?"

Lily coughed Victorianly. Joanie, from the kitchen counter, looked disgusted; then, with a resigned snort, remembered that she had expected no better, and went on with the drinks for the breakfast. With both Mark and Salugi present, the interior walls between Joanie's split selves shook with pounding, but held. The men alive in her mind must be kept out of her body, and vice-versa. Mark threatened the system, but she had been successful in keeping him from knowing how much.

"No cunt? You mean she was smooth?" Mark decided to play. Maybe if he talked dirtier and acted more like the idiots Joanie took as lovers, she'd change her mind about him, he thought. "Well, as long as she has tits and hands and a mouth, we could probably work something out."

"What if she didn't?" hypothesized Salugi.

"Hey, man!" protested Mark. "What the hell am I doing with some woman without no cunt, no tits, no hands, and no mouth?"

"Don't ask me, man. She's your date."

Joanie poured some cold water on Salugi, sending him leaping to his feet and unfurling as extensive string of profanities all artfully woven together as though they were a single word. But Salugi was a domesticated barbarian, and when he finished howling he sat back down again and went on, as though virtually nothing had happened. "Do you remember old number 43? From the Greta Garbo?" Salugi turned to Joanie, offering her this modest measure of gallantry. "This guy is a college jock who just shows up one day, wearing this football jersey that says 43. And this guy used to do a trip he called The Safety Blitz, where he would get as fucked up as he could with whatever was around, usually pot and speed, and then he would have one of the needlefreaks shoot him up with Novocaine in his hands and feet. And then this dude would go outside, play basketball, football, padding around with these gigantic Novocaine

I read in the newspapers they are going to have 30 minutes of intellectual stuff on t.v.

mittens. Dude was fucking out there!"

"He's an accountant now." Mark assured the disbelieving Salugi that this was true, "He gave me a ride hitching, about a year ago."

A knock at the door, that Joanie answered. She returned to Lily. "Tom-Tom wants to see you."

"God." Lily's voice had matched her look. Tell him to go away. Tell him I don't want to see him at all."

Joanie passed the message, returned with a new one, "He says he'll wait on the porch until you change your mind."

Mark asked if Joanie was about ready to go. She was. She blew Salugi a kiss, and went through the front door.

Mark followed, almost tripped over Tom-Tom on the porch. Mark stopped, while Joanie went down the steps. "What are you doing? Loitering?"

"I am examining myself, searching to see if these powerful personal feelings in me are real, or if they're contradictory to revolutionary thought. I'm not just dabbling in revolutionary change -- I am committed to it. So there is only so much time I can give to rhapsodizing about pretty breasts in the moonlight and so forth. Why doesn't she want to see me?"

"My guess is she's enjoying watching you fawn and squirm."

Reaffirming his priorities, Tom-Tom said that after had left the party at the Farmhouse, Charlie had told a stirring story about a northern California utopian experiment, from the turn of the century. "The Kaweah Cooperative Commonwealth, which was a socialist commune that worked hard for five years to build a road up the side of some mountain, into virgin timber country. Nobody else had tried to build the road, because everybody thought it would be impossible. And this socialist commune *did* it! And *then*, after five years of living in a tent city and working so hard, just when they got the lumber mill set up and were about to cash in on their collective investment, that son-of-a-bitch McKinley sent in the marines to take over the whole place, and threw the Kaweah people off their land. And that's the

every Monday from 7:30 to 8. They're going to educate America. They couldn't educate

true story of how Sequoia National Forest came to be! Even the townspeople, who weren't all that sympathetic to the socialists, denounced the government siezure as criminal.''

"Come on!'' called Joanie from the car.

"That's right,'' Mark replied to Tom-Tom. "The government acted like pigs. And yet the man who started Kaweah, who sacrificed all he had to that community, who took the rap and went bankrupt and to prison because of the community -- a good man -- he wound up quite disillusioned with the improvability of man. When it was all over, and he evaluated it, he concluded that his people had been lazy and selfish, and that, perhaps, people needed such things as greed to spur them on to hard work.''

"Whose side are you on? You always emphasize the wrong contradictions.''

"Mark! Come on.''

"Coming.'' Back to Tom-Tom, "I'm not just playing word-chess. It's just that oversimplifying things doesn't really help. Complexity only *seems* confusing. Deceptions are what's really confusing, and too-easy clarities deceive us worst of all.''

"Yes, Father Bullshit. See if you can find out from Joanie where Lily's head's at.''

"Ask her yourself.''

"I did.''

"Mark!''

"In a minute! What did she say?''

"She said, 'Don't worry. You know what Shakespeare says.' She's so strange, man.''

"What did she say Shakespeare said?''

"Some jive about worms and death,'' Tom-Tom tried to remember, "and love ain't for shit.''

"Love ain't for shit, huh? Doesn't ring a bell. Maybe Troilus, by the color of the language. Well, I'll see you later on.'' Mark started down the steps. The bell rang on the fifth one, and he turned to remind Tom-Tom, " 'Men have died from time to time, and worms have eaten them; but not for love.' *As You Like It.*'' Holding on to the bannister, Mark took two steps at a time, all the way down to the car.

America if they started at 6:30.

—*Groucho Marx*

He slid in next to Joanie, and started the engine. "You know, Joanie, among all the many other reasons I'm fond of you is that you're one of the very few politically active people in this town who haven't been haranguing me about my resignations."

"Would it do any good? How much of a must is doing your play-work to you?"

"I must eat. I must sleep. I must do *that*."

"That's what I thought."

He took her cheeks in his palms and kissed her lips, filching a moment apart together to mark the truth of what the regular course of their relationship would never plainly acknowledge -- that they were in a way that mattered much to both of them -- in love with each other. "Oh Joanie, Joanie, my Oberon's Titania, my Higgin's Miss Doolittle, my George's Martha -- run away with me, swim with me to Tahiti and we'll live in a tree and fuck each other into insensibility."

Success has always been a great liar.

— Nietzsche

The Coastal Courier

3

Monopoly

> *"I have a plan: to go insane."*
> — *Fyodor Dostoyevsky*

Mark and Joanie met Dieter and Larry at The Farmhouse, on the eastern veranda that faced the soft hills through which Pebble Creek meandered. In the far northern corner of the huge porch, two four-month old Golden Labrador puppies played at being in a fight-to-the-death. One of the young musicians, new in town, guzzling ale with three others on the porch steps, called Joanie over for a word in private. Mark asked Larry if he wanted a ride to Gumpers Corners, to the guild meeting. "Everyone else has a special town council meeting to attend first, at the newspaper office." Mark smiled. "The first one in years I will not have to attend."

Joanie broke away from the teen-aged drummer with the safety-pins all over him, to tell Dieter that the pottery shop's chief distributor in Santa Clara County wanted twice as many mugs and half as many pots, next time. Dieter, as usual, wore his tan jump suit, spattered with clay, and his clay-covered work shoes.

Larry slid into Mark's car, and they bumped slowly down the rough road to the old sheep-shearing shed, the improbable newspaper office by the sea. Although it had been refreshed by little more than an occasional letter, over the last eight years, Mark's friendship with Larry had once been very important to both of them. They went on with the

41

calling of the roll. "Barry Maris? Let's see, Barry married Iris, from Gino's crowd. They both work for welfare, live on 637th Street, between Morose and Depression. Did you hear about Frannie?"

"I heard." Frannie had been the brightest, most spirited and most redheaded woman in their college class. She had overdosed on heroin the year before. For Mark, it had been a season of the deaths of beautiful women -- only a month or two before Frannie OD'd, Patti Humphries, one of the original front-office dynamos of Grool's troupe, Joanie's dearest friend, and an old lover of Mark's, took two weeks to travel around the state to hug or fuck everyone she knew, and then threw herself from the roof of the San Francisco hospital where she was born.

"Did you see Ralph Winter, when he came through?"

"Briefly. Did he make it to South America?"

"Nobody knows. But what happened with you and Michelle? The two of you married even younger than we did."

"We gave up on our eight-year running argument as to which one of us was ultimately right, in the final analysis. What happened to Phil and Dolores? We used to play bridge together."

"Very straight. Two kids, sells furniture on Jerome with his uncle. Ernie's managing a bubble-packaging plant on the Island," Larry plowed on. "This is one of those conversations that would leave anybody who didn't know all these people staring at their feet."

"Maybe not. Do you know the story of the Zen master who died quieting his students' eulogies so he could listen to his neighbors swapping gossip?"

Larry smiled. "And you, what is it exactly that you're doing?"

"I'm being ludicrous," said Mark. "It means ridiculous. But up until a few hundred years ago it meant playful. And the word changed meaning, I think, due to the decline of the play element in western culture. The Renaissance and Baroque were *ludicrus,* loved the arts, the graces, ornamentation. But that spirit got buried by the rise of the

What is middle class morality? Just an excuse for never giving me anything.
— G. B. Shaw

industrial age: efficiency and materialism. Which brings me, somehow, to wonder what you've been doing? I think you went into child psychology, actually, didn't you?''

"A poor relation of child psychology," said Larry. "I've been working in child care -- residential homes for emotionally disturbed adolescent boys. I like working with kids. I like the kids. I like the work.''

"That's a lot -- to like your work," said Mark, and he parked his car near the office of the bimonthly Common Coastal Courier based in Lone Buck Bay and serving the coast from Tomales Bay to Gualala.

"Doesn't look like a newspaper office," said Larry, squinting critically at the old livestock shed.

"Sure don't, but then you can't go by appearances. There's a story about the time the grandmaster Efin Bogolyubov game an exhibition at a small Swiss chess club. Bogo played their ten players simultaneously and blindfolded, and won all ten games.'' Mark motioned for Larry to go up the sheep ramp that surrealistically led into the newspaper office. "Well, the village photographer took a picture of the event, but when the photograph was published, the grandmaster wasn't in it. They asked the photographer, but he said he didn't know anything about it. They didn't mean that fat guy with the beery face, did they? He looked so out of place among all those chess players, the photographer explained, that he cropped him out of the print.''

"Looks like a newspaper from the inside," Larry admitted.

Tom Roebuck passed a sheet of contact prints across the front desk, pointing to three prints in one corner. "Look at these -- would you believe that this man is taking foxtails out of a rug that he is about to take to the dump! I asked him why, and he said, 'Hell, that's just the way I am.' '' Tom took the sheet back, put it with two others, and asked Mark, "What do you have?''

"This." Mark handed over to Tom a manila envelope, containing Mark's private notes on two committees of the town council -- the Community Development Committee and the Water Resources Committee, which Mark had chaired

We have become the tools of our tools.

— *Henry David Thoreau*

and which oversaw the problems of the physical bodies of Pebble Creek and Lone Buck Bay. The water committee was crucial -- the bay and the creek had become the principal points of contention between the town and Weel. The settlement on the original contract between Grool and Weel was still in the courts, and Weel expected to have to pay a settlement. But the rights governing the exploitation of the bay and the creek were still being actively contested.

Weel had been attracted to the town in the first place because he discovered that all the local gravel dredging companies had been trying for years to acquire the rights to dredge Lone Buck Bay and Pebble Creek, and tear up Goat Hill, east of the town. There was a small fortune in gravel there, merely waiting to be scooped up. Weel also knew that dredging the bay for gravel would deepen it enough to open a commercial boat harbor. Weel had had big plans for Lone Buck Bay right from the start, although none of them had anything to do with music or utopian communities.

"Anything new on gravel I ought to know?" asked Tom.

"I haven't heard anything since the last meeting," said Mark. "What do you have for the paper, this week?"

"A humorous editorial."

"What?" Mark feigned shock, incredulity, and finally indignation. "In times like these, when we are locked in a life-and-death struggle for survival, you have the ill-conceived audacity to serve up jokes to pacify the masses? Come the revolution, we will not look kindly upon this."

Tom grinned. "That supposed to sound like anybody we know?"

"Go on, read it aloud to us -- out with it."

" 'The Last CHP Report.' " Tom perched himself on a layout stool, sipped some coffee, and read:

" 'It is with a curious blend of regret and pleasure that we announce the termination of the most widely acclaimed regular column in the Courier's checkered history, the California Highway Patrol's Inspection Site List. As you no doubt know, the inspections themselves have been cut from the state budget.

" 'Our regret is, of course, that we are losing our most

Put your trust in God, but mind to keep your powder dry.

— Oliver Cromwell

popular feature. Nobody ever had a bad word to say about the columns, and some people liked them so much they hung them on their walls, up there with the batiks, the Van Gogh prints, and the Fritz Perls quotations. Though the author of the column chose to remain selflessly anonymous throughout his career, his stark and gothic prose was deathless -- "Thursday, May 29 -- River Road and Fulton." The influence of Kafka is unmistakable.

" 'How did the Courier get the column? You may well wonder. Simplicity itself. The California Highway Patrol considered it a public service for newspapers to print the site locations, so anybody who was looking to get their car inspected would know right where to go. Do you believe that? We requested that they send it to us, and it came regularly in the mail. Then Dorothy would lose it and her rapidograph pen, find the pen, and ask Janet to call the CHP and have it read to her over the phone.

" 'Although we will miss the column itself, it must be admitted that it is a twofold pleasure to bid goodbye to the inspections. Firstly, it should give the CHP more manpower to chase down some of those clowns who come north to visit our incomparably beautiful coastline and drive around it as though they were on Mars, and all the laws of gods and men had been suspended.

" 'Secondly, it will make life simpler for me and my friends. No longer will we be required to execute split-second U turns on River Road, between Korbel's lush fields of champagne grapes, because we didn't look at the list that morning and remember to go through Pocket Canyon instead. No longer need we slip into Santa Rosa semi-deviously, via Piner Road. No longer will we be compelled to stay on top of the latest developments in the baroque pattern of strategies and conter-strategies that arose in connection with the inspection station of River Road between Lido Grande and Gumpers Corners -- as likely a stretch of road to look for cars in need of inspection as any this side of Tijuana. First the CHP set up their station on the long Gumpers Corners straightaway. That was a piece of cake to slip -- Gumpers Lane, River Crescent, and Old Lido Grande

All problems are divided into two classes, soluble questions, which are trivial,

Roads all did the trick. After a while, the CHP caught on to the fact that there weren't much but late model cars going back and forth, so they moved down the road a couple of miles. This didn't help them much, since Old Lido Grande Road still got you around them, and you could even turn up at Cnopius and save some time. Eventually the CHP must have figured out which road the more mature automobiles were taking -- no fools, they -- and moved the station to just beyond where Old Lido Grande Road lets out at River Road. That one had me baffled, initially, and once caused me to drive from Lido Grande to Gumperstown via Lido del Rìo and Sawmill Road, which is about fifteen miles out of the way, but I later learned it was common knowledge that you could get around that one by taking the road behind the golf course, which lets out past the motel.

" 'I went through an inspection once, with a car I had just bought -- a spiffy '62 Ford Galaxie 500 with a T-bird engine, stickshift, and overdrive. Got as much as 3½-4 miles a gallon on downhill stretches of freeway. The inspection crew were amiable chaps, and the cordially cited me for a couple of insignificant irregularities: an expired and mutilated driver's license, overdue registration, two bald tires, excessively noisy and illegal dual glasspacks (I had never heard of glasspacks before, except the rock'n'roll group. My neighbor later told me that the first time I started the car her husband ran to the window because he thought there was a helicopter landing outside.), one high beam out, both headlights in need of adjustment, one defective stoplight, and a gas leak at the pump. Picky, picky, picky! Fortunately, the car gave up the ghost before I had time to worry about how I was going to pay to fix all that stuff.

" 'And so we wave farewell to the CHP inspection stations. We will never forget them -- the plotting of alternate routes, the adrenalin rushes at seeing one rise unexpectedly on the road ahead, the surrealistic ambience of the inspections themselves, the pathos, the laughter and the tears. All gone. Adieu.' "

Larry said he liked it and Mark smirked and said Madame Defarge would receive a tearsheet.

and important questions, which are insoluble.

— Santayana

Tom fidgeted a moment with the sheets of his article, and looked up to find Dorothy smiling fondly at him. They both blushed.

"I still have a lot of work left, in the darkroom," Dorothy told Tom. "If I'm not out by the time you leave, would you stop off at Crotchky's and get his ad fixed."

"Sure," he said. Dorothy returned to the darkroom, and Tom asked Larry if he had had the pleasure of meeting Crotchky yet.

"The guy with the mutton chops and the striped apron, in the store on the highway?" Larry asked. "Yeah. I was talking to him yesterday. He says he hates it here and he wants to sell the store. Was he with the original group?"

"No, he's a renter, from L.A., " Tom said. "Let me give you an idea of what Crotchky's like -- a couple of days ago I go to his store to talk to him about his ad. He didn't hear a word I said. He tells me, 'They sent me the wrong box. They must have sent me the wrong box.' So I asked him if he ever saw the movie of the same name, based on a Robert Louis Stevenson story, and Crotchky says, 'Wait a minute! They didn't. They sent me the right box. I *ordered* the wrong box!' "

They laughed, and heard other laughter outside. Mark poked his head through the door and reported back, "It's Joanie and Dieter and Amy."

"Amy?" murmured Tom. "I wonder why she's here."

"Who's Amy?" Larry asked.

"A maverick witch," said Mark.

"Grool's girlfriend," said Tom, "and the only person who still sees him regularly. Her husband died in the arson, along with Grool's wife."

Joanie came in, looking as bright as her yellow print dress with soft puffy shoulders, followed by Dieter. And finally Amy, wrapped in a hypnotically patterned white crocheted shawl, a white and green peasant blouse, and a green and brown skirt with a scarlet pentagram sewn into its seat.

"Are you here for the meeting, Amy?" Tom asked.

Amy laughed and shook her head. "You mean like a

Work expands so as to fill the time available for its completion.
— *Parkinson's First Law*

surprise nomination?'' She laughed again, the warm laugh of the old soul that lived in Amy. "No, I was just discussing business with Joanie.''

Tom shook his head. "This is only the second time a member of the original town council has been replaced -- not since Dieter replaced Paul Kenner -- and *nobody* shows up to see it.''

"There aren't many political animals in this town,'' said Mark. Besides, everybody assumes it's a foregone conclusion that Dorothy's got it.''

A pickup truck drove up to the shed, and Charlie Speer joined the meeting. He wore a freshly cleaned and pressed copy of his garage's new uniforms -- blue jeans, pin striped work shirt with "Charlie'' embroidered in script over the left pocket and "CHARLIE'S GARAGE'' in iron-on letters on the back, and over that, one of the four finished jeans jackets with colored embroidery on the back, identifying the garage. Charlie greeted everyone with a genial smile, even the ones he knew despised him. He was a businessman, and a good one. There were customers and there were suppliers -- liking and disliking had nothing to do with business. It was good business to be pleasant, and good politics, too, Charlie believed. "I have a formal letter from Vivian,'' he announced. "She'd like to endorse Tom-Tom.''

As there was no response, he put the letter away. "I have a special request, of the council, before we turn to that crucial vote. Since the outgoing councilman Lerner is here, I think a few words by him, on his resignations would be in order.''

"A retreat from political activity can also be an advance into another realm,'' said Mark. "We're amphibious animals, and a wise government appreciates the vitality of diversity and individuality.''

Mark's words hung in the air like a punching bag waiting to be walloped.

"Individuality.'' Charlie repeated it as though it were the name of a particularly repulsive disease. "Individuality is a capitalist cover word for selfishness. I'm not being personal in this case, though. We all know that Mark is not

We will reach greater and greater platitudes of achievement.
— Mayor Richard Daley

greedy. No, my friends, what has happened to Mark, you see, is that he's had a vision. Mark has seen, with a prophet's eye, how hidden deep within the enigmatic mysticisms of mah-jongg and bowling lie the solutions to the problems of poverty, oppression, and war."

"Nothing that grand, Charlie," said Mark, "but a contribution nevertheless."

"Mark, your self-indulgences are so far beside the point as to be a betrayal. We've been victimized. It's our obligation to set it right."

"Time's done a lot of that, and it'll probably finish the job. Weel's idea was evil and faulty, and ours was noble and faulty. We'll all get just about what we deserve."

"Us? It was *our* fault our town got burned down and our people killed?"

"We led our friends and colleagues to build their homes on the flood plain of a river. We were too self-absorbed to do our own work. We thought Weel would look after us. We were children, pretending to be grown ups, presumptuous enough to think we were a better batch than all the generations of utopian failures before us, while understanding nothing about contracts, checks and controls. It was all love and confidence. Nice feelings, but not enough to generate half a million dollars from our big daddy."

"Yes, and to punish us for our faults, Mark is going to walk off by himself, and make for himself a little fantasy world, like our exalted absentee landlord -- Grool."

"You've got no right to use Grool's name as though he owed you something," Amy said angrily. "He bought the very land we're standing on. And the lawyers he's been paying for are about to get the rest of the town built. He's given more to this town than all of you put together, and now he just wants to be left alone."

"I'm sorry, Amy. It's just my frustration at seeing this turkey give up on us. Grool has certainly given more than his share. We all hope he'll return, someday. Maybe when the court action is concluded?"

Amy was the only one who still saw Grool. "No, he won't ever be back." Amy Greco closed her eyes, rocked

Amusement is the happiness of those who cannot think.

— *Alexander Pope*

slowly. "Do you know the story of Merlin's retirement? He went home to The Enchanted Forest, where he taught his apprentice one of the two spells he had withheld from her -- how to bewitch Merlin himself. Grool, by now, can make his music do that."

"What was the one Merlin never taught her?" Joanie asked.

"How to undo the spell."

*　*　*　*　*

Mark and Larry left before the vote, and drove to a small roadside restaurant in Gumper's Corners.

"I like your friend, Joanie," Larry said. "Are the two of you involved?"

"Intimately," Mark chuckled. "But not sexually. We're in second place, behind Tom Roebuck and Dorothy, for the town's longest and most intense unconsummated flirtation."

"What?" Larry chose to drop it. "You know, everybody in this town wants you to explain why you're leaving active politics. But I knew you in college, and you were never much of a joiner, then. What I wonder is how you came to join this town in the first place."

"I needed to join a group. For the first time in my life, after too many years of going to school, I was free to work alone. I had as much trouble teaching me discipline as my teachers had. And after about a year, I'd lost perspective on the work, and I was no longer sure if what I was doing was worthwhile or as useless as a cargo cult's landing strip."

"What's that?"

"Cargo cults? During World War II, the United States used some of the primitive islands in the Pacific for landing bases. The natives, on some of these islands, thought the cargo planes were birds sent from heaven, bring them all that otherworldly booty. And when the war ended, and the cargo planes filled with candy and bright toys and cigarettes stopped coming, the natives created dummy landing strips out of wood, lit by fire beacons, believing these were nests that would entice the great birds back to their islands. Well,

Only the hand that erases can write the true thing.

— *Meister Eckhardt*

I began to feel as though my independent scholarship was as futile as that. So when the town came along, and presented the opportunity to throw off the burden of having to be somebody special, and allowed me to be just one of the easy anybodies, I jumped at the chance to participate in a communal project and be part of a group. And, intellectually, I still believe in the soundness of the idea and in its relationship to my studies of play and games."

"How so?"

"I believe in the value of models, and I see utopian communities as social laboratories within which experiments in living could be fleshed out."

"Do you think Lone Buck Bay's been a valuable experiment?"

"I'm sure it has," said Mark, "both as an example to inspire and as an instructive failure. Reading its lessons, though, will be no easy task."

"And now? Now you're returning to what you were studying before, and what you were studying when I knew you in college? Play and games?"

"That's right. I transferred to a school in the midwest, to study the later writings of Johan Huizinga with Professor John Ross." Professor Ross: Mark could see him plainly -- a short, wiry man in a brown three-piece suit, with a face that seemed to challenge any man or idea he looked at. "Huizinga's theory is that play is what makes human culture possible; and, that all cultural forms are permeated with the play element."

"I can't see it," said Larry. "Why didn't you study the psychologists, on play. Piaget and Erikson and Freud -- seems more logical."

"I have studied them. Freud thinks play is an activity generated by the pleasure principle, but not a consummatory activity, like fucking or eating."

"That's right."

"No," said Mark, "that's wrong. Play *is* an end in itself. For Freud, play is basically erotic, and governed by the instincts for pleasure. But for Huizinga, play is ungoverned and free."

"Free of what?"

Growing up consists in finding new toys, new symbolic equivalants.
— Norman O. Brown

"Free from compulsion. Free from inevitable sequence, cause and effect, natural selection. Free of the kinds of laws that govern the apparently mindless physical world.

"But the field has grown far beyond Huizinga. There are now dozens of different studies that touch on various aspects of play and games, though there's still no unifying science. That's what I'm hoping to find.

"I'm studying everything about play and games -- psychology, mathematics, cultural history; all of it, from all the angles. I'm looking for connections, for the relationships between sequences of children's play and the play element in sacred rituals, and between poker strategies and the dynamics of social freedom. They've already researched many of the connections between poker strategies and waging war."

They pulled into the parking lot of the little restaurant in Gumpers Corners.

Larry looked around in disbelief. "This is where you want to eat? This place looks pathetic. It has surprisingly good food, though -- right?"

"You'll be surprised," said Mark.

* * * * *

When the town meeting ended, Tom and Dorothy stayed behind to finish up some chores in the office. Tom stared at the darkroom door. He was a brave man, in most ways. But not with Dorothy. He had been secretly in love with her for a year -- which is to say that although it was obvious to the whole town, including Dorothy, everybody kept their knowledge of it secret from Tom, hoping for the day he told her himself.

He had tried. Many times. They worked together on the paper, most days of the week. But he cared too much, and always got a bad case of stage fright whenever a suitable opportunity presented itself. Between the passion and its occasion fell the shadow of the rebuff.

How hard could it be? he thought. I'll walk in and say, "Hi!

All music is in the understanding of one note.

— *Ali Akbhar Khan*

blah blah blah, and let's go somewhere Saturday night." What could be simpler than that? That goes on all the time. Why do I even have to ask her out? I've seen this woman every day for the last two years. Am I programmed to date the ones I like? How ridiculous. We know each other, already. Look -- she either feels this way about me, too, or she doesn't. Right? She must know by now. Musn't she? So why don't I just say, "Dorothy, I really like you?"

Rolling himself into a determined lump in his throat, Tom went into the darkroom to confess his love.

"Hi," she said.

He experienced the sensation that his head was being elongated into a dunce-shaped cone. Do it now! he screamed to himself, but he was too embarassed to do anything. She asked him if he thought Mark was himself, these days, and Tom said he thought so. And he thought, oh my god, look how beautiful she is, and he wanted to say: I love you, I love your face, what you say, your ass, how you walk, your breasts, everything. I love everything about you. And then he caught himself, for the thousandth time, staring at her, and he panicked, and thought, I've waited too long. If I say something now, she'll know I've been trying to say something from the beginning, and it's taken me all this time to get it up to say it. That was true but it embarassed him, and he said nothing about how he felt about her, only that he had better get going so he could speak to Crotchky about this week's ad and then get over to Pearl's in time for the Crafts Guild meeting.

He took off on his bike and halfway up the hill he screamed as loud as he could for as long as he could. And then he cursed himself, "You whimpy fucking yo-yo. You gutless turd!"

A child who was never kissed will never kiss anyone.

— *Theodor Reik*

Pearl's Patch

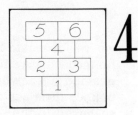

hopscotch

"When I say I know women, I mean I know that I don't know them."
— *William Makepeace Thackaray*

Pearl was still saying her goodbyes to her last night's lover, when Mark and Larry arrived. "A charity fuck," she whispered to Mark. Embarrassment became her, he thought. Everything became her. This morning, she chose to look like the schoolmarmish madame of a frontier town. She was so pretty she made Mark wonder if a woman who lacked Pearl's kind of beauty could ever fully make up for it in any other way. But why should she have been embarrassed at my having seen her last night's lover? he wondered. The obvious reason, of course, was that she was interested in him again, although that was a reason that was itself a greater cipher than the question.

The previous week, Pearl had passed Mark in the streets of Santa Rosa, while his head was still swimming with saddle points, mini-max solutions, the St. Petersburg Game, mixed strategies, and the other rudiments of game theory he was dusting off. Perversely, but true to form, which is to say upsidedown and backwards, his relative indiffererence excited her, for she was as irresistibly drawn to the inaccessible man as a scientist to the inexplicable phenomenon of a spoiled child to the unbought toy.

Pearl whisked Joanie into her sewing room, with news of the fabrics she had bought in San Francisco, afloat again on her familiar fantasy of travelling the world in search of fabulous prints, rare buttons of bone and gold, exotic bazaars

55

where she would bargain with silk thieves, and so forth. Pearl flounced back into the living room. Joanie, trailing her, beamed a knowing smile at Mark, as if to say that Pearl's bouncy little act was transparently for Mark's benefit. Pearl sashayed to the full length mirror placed prominently in the kitchen hallway, to admire the fresh blouse she was still in the process of putting on. Like squirrels, her hands scuttled, button by button, up the back of her blouse to the the top button, while her onyx pendant bounced across her breasts. She primped and posed. She spent more time in front of mirrors than anyone Mark had ever known.

Dieter, Joy, and Dorothy arrived from Lone Buck Bay together; and Joanie was relieved to see that the Sebastopol group had sent Vern, instead of her ex-husband, Mitch.

Pearl was an ideal hostess during all these arrivals and preparations, serving fruit and cookies, coffee and tea, flirting at least a little with them all, and a lot with Mark. Mark had by now witnessed enough of Pearl's flirtateousness to know that it was by no means entirely erotic. Much of it was social style, and economic instinct. Early in life she had learned that her beauty was not a *passe-partout,* but only a commodity. Walk, wink, smile, pout, and all -- each had a fluctuating market value. Not always as negotiable as money itself, but it hardly ever hurt, almost always helped. And, she would be the first to argue, she sure could use help, couldn't she? She was just as ambitious as Mark, but not for the nebulous kind of God-knew-what he was chasing. She wanted cash, and the good things money could buy.

Mighty and pervasive though Pearl's magic was, the most powerful single stroke of a female's eyelid came from Dorothy, in greeting Tom's arrival. It practically floored him. Mark guided him to the room where the jackets were put, distracting him from present fancies by explaining that he had just heard, from Dieter, that "Dieter's girlfriend's roommate says Weel is working hard on pressuring that pivotal coastal commissioner to give him the go-ahead to tear up Goat Hill." Goat Hill was just east of the sheep ranch just to the east of Lone Buck Bay. Weel had recently bought the hill, planning not only to make money from the gravel, but also to ruin the clear winter stream, Pebble Creek, that ran down the hill

Seek ye first the Kingdom of God, and all things shall come to you. I'll make $14 million

through the town. And then to dredge Pebble Creek, and then to dredge the Bay itself. "Scuttlebutt around the county office building is that nobody's ready to make the necessary accommodations for Weel, especially as long as the dam issue is still a hot potato."

Pearl girlishly grabbed Mark's arm, and said, "Hello. I thought you were supposed to come by." She smiled, as though to say . . . Who knew what Pearl's smiles meant? Not Mark, certainly, although he was as helpless before them as a fawn transfixed in a car's headlights.

There was, however, no time to pursue this for the moment, since all the private conversations finally yielded to the scheduled business at hand -- the often talked about plan to form a cooperative guild of the craftspeople on the river, the sea, and inland. The guild had held one previous meeting and had developed a list of priorities, including: the development of a sales staff that could do a better job of marketing their products than the craftspeople could; and coordinating their supply and delivery trucking runs.

"Can you work this into your regular runs to San Francisco, Charlie? Or is this going to mean a whole new set of schedules?" Vern asked.

"Can't tell yet," Charlie answered. "We'll have to see what the loads are like, how many stops are involved, how many miles; and a lot of other things we won't know until we actually start to do it."

They discussed formalizing the structure of the guild, but decided that there were too few of them in attendance to do that. They agreed to a date for a next meeting, and appointed Dorothy to handle the publicity -- ads in the local papers and flyers for the public walls.

"Tell them to come out and vote!"

"Tell them to exercise their franchise!" Pearl feathered her warm breasts softly across Mark's back. "Nobody wants nobody with a flabby franchise."

Joanie was to begin work on finding a sales force, and to collaborate with Dorothy on outlines for an ad campaign and a promotion catalogue.

"You could use a patch for your pants," invited Pearl.

"Sweet of you to notice," Mark replied, almost in spite of

himself.

"Why don't you stay after the meeting? I'll fix it for you."

"Well . . . I have to see Grool today."

"It won't take long."

What the hell, he thought. "OK."

* * * * *

"I can't very well patch your pants if they're wrapped around your legs."

He took them off.

"I'd forgotten what strong legs you had."

He pretended the dust tumbling through the sunlight was incredibly fascinating.

"Are you still mad at me?"

"I could throw you through a fucking window."

"You ought to wait until I finish the patch, at least. I hear Lily and Tom-Tom are making romantic history."

"Yes. He's her dog, and she beats him and makes him sleep outside."

She laughed.

Fluids sped. He wished they didn't. Wishes and fluids swam into each other, whirling the waters.

Pearl ran the sewing machine. She worked with such expert quickness that by the time Mark could make out just what her hands and fingers were doing, and why, she was done. "Come here and let's see if it's going to fit."

"Should I put them on?"

"I want to take a look at them first. Come here." She put her arms around his hips and held the pants against his farther leg, leaning across him to examine it. Her cheek grazed the front of his underpants. "Hmm." She moved the pants around, as though to see how they would look in the front. She stared a moment at the swelling outlined by his briefs, gave it a light squeeze and flipped its head. "Now put this thing away. We'll never get an accurate fitting with it sticking up like that." By now he was hard and smiling, and she grabbed him. "It'll push your pants up and forward. We won't be able to tell if it's a good fit."

He reached for her, and she put her arms around his

Love is all a woman needs to be content,/But the bonds of love are best at 6%.
— Cole Porter

neck, and he carried her to the bed while she affectionately rubbed her face and head against his. And they made love for the first time in almost eight months.

She fell asleep, a wild maiden in a green toga, tossing straws into the wind and polishing the stones in a winter creek's bed.

He watched her. She was beautiful. No getting around it. Pearl, Pearl, prettiest of them all. His golden *shiksa* cheerleader, burned him to a cinder, like frostbite. Mirrors for the bed, mirrors for the door, mirrors on the closet -- the house of a woman who loves to look at herself. She turned in her sleep, pressed a thigh against his.

Ah, when will I ever get over dear old what's-her-name? And where oh where is my sweet reciprocation? O Come All Ye Faithful! That let's her out. Free Love Incarnate -- the great open cunt of the Aquarian Age! He smirked for thinking that, knew it only mattered because, in spite of himself, he still cared. He had loved her and she had hurt him and he needed to continue explaining her to himself until the subject lost its juice and he grew bored with it.

There was a safety in it, in her ways. Like a dilettante, dabbling in this and that, never investing enough of herself in any one thing to risk failing at it. Of course, none of this would have mattered had he not fallen in love with her more than pretty face.

Well, no point dwelling on it. No way you're going to give it another serious go 'round, he preached to himself. Quite a trick, willing a rational 'no' to her while his whole body screamed, "gimme!" Like trying not to scratch, when you have poison oak -- the certainty that scratching will only worsen the histaminic reaction doesn't make it itch less. No, she was his irresistible distraction, and doing his work would become more problematical than ever. But look: isn't she beautiful?

She opened her eyes, five-foot-wide blue stars, and whispered, "Penny for your thoughts."

"When Sophocles was eighty years old, he said of sex, 'I am at last free of a cruel and insane master.'"

"Oh! You're a real son-of-a-bitch! What a thing to say, right after we make love again for the first time in so long."

The Sanksrit word **Kridaratnam** *translates literally as "the jewel of games." It*

"Was I supposed to be all gushy and precious after being detained and seduced?"

"*Seduced?* You initiated everything. You carried me to the bed!"

"*I* initiated? You know something -- one of us is just plain fucking crazy."

"Yes, and I know which one, too. If you live to be a million you will never understand women like me." She was up and pacing, her yellow robe on, cigarette lit.

"You know what one of the basic flaws in this relationship is?"

"Explain it all to me, I am trembling with anticipation."

"We're both in love with the idea of the other one being in love with us, but neither of us trusts the other enough to actually let it happen. It's hopeless."

"You're hopeless. You intellectualize everything so much you don't talk about anything. You just talk talk."

"Maybe you're right. It's kind of sad, you know. I think if I hadn't fallen in love with you last year we might have stayed great friends."

She was softened by his saying that, and asked, "Did you eat lunch yet?"

"I have to go."

"Now?"

"Yeah."

"Why?"

"I have to meet with Grool. Part town business, part personal."

"Come back for dinner, at least."

"No."

"When, then?"

"I hadn't thought about it."

"Why don't you come Saturday, at six. I'll make us chicken, like I used to, and you can bring some wine, and then we'll go someplace, or noplace, if you want."

"No."

"Why not?"

"Pearl, I just can't handle you now."

"You don't want me?"

means making love.

"We all want you. But at this point, in particular, with all the other stuff going on in my life, I can't take you. I won't."

"Why?"

"Seeing you is bad for me, so I don't want to."

"How can what you want be not what you want?"

"It's common. Classic approach-avoidance bind. With approach-approach complications, in my case, considering also the pull of my work."

"You are so unreal. Everything you know is memorized, by Dewey Decimal number."

"You will never understand men like me."

"I think I heard a line like that, recently."

His eyes moist, he finished tying his shoes, got his jacket. "Bye, Pearl."

Her tears falling, she said, "Just like that. He gets his pants patched, screws me, and splits."

"Yeah, old fuck-'em-and-forget-'em Mark."

"Come by soon, if just to chat."

"OK."

"Promise?"

"Promise."

"Promise to keep your promise?"

"To hell with you."

"Why? Does that mean you won't come?"

"You're like an octopus. Listen: " He raised his right hand, and pledged, "I swear that I, Mark, will visit you, Pearl, sometime in the indefinite but not-too-distant future, by the memory of my mother's mother, may she rest in peace, by the mother of The Holy Mother Queen of Martyrs, by Mother Cabrini's mother, by the All-Seeing Eye of Agamotto, and by the All-Seeing Eye of Agamotto's mother. OK?"

It was, it was OK, at least for now. They hugged. "Goodbye, Pearl. Thanks."

"Bye, love."

Take no notice of what is said on the pillow.

— Chinese proverb

Saint Barnabas

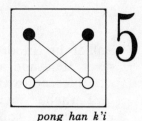

pong han k'i

5

*"I have very little of Mr. Blake's company.
He is always in Paradise."
— Mrs. William Blake, Catherine Boucher*

Two travellers stood at the long redwood log north of the Lido Grande bridge, where hitchhikers heading for the coast always station themselves. One carried a large pack on his back and a sign reading, "Anywhere but here." The other wore a white robe. Mark had seen him around town before, and Tom had once pointed him out to Mark, said his name was Barnabas and that he had read too much philosophy, or had, in some other way, mutilated his mind. His thumb asked for a ride, but his eyes stared silently into a space he alone could see.

Mark pulled over and told the two of them, "I'm going up into the hills west of Cazadero."

"I'll pass," said the backpacker. "I want to get to the coast."

Barnabas got in. "Do you know where Duncan Road is? Good. I live on a little dirt road off that."

"OK. Fine day we got today, isn't it?"

"Sure is," Barnabas agreed. "Why on a day like this you can actually *see* the slow but inevitable formation of the Messiah before your very own mortal eyes."

"Yes, indeed -- that's sure seeing some."

"My name is Saint Barnabas."

"*Saint* Barnabas, is it?"

"I wouldn't use the title lightly. It was given to me last month by the Archangel Gabriel when I was knighted in The

Hall of the Hundred Wonders, after witnessing the descent of seven thousand angels from a spaceship."

"Pleased to meetchya. My name is Mark."

Barnabas invited Mark to join him for a minute's talk and a cup of coffee; and Mark, eager for a change of pace after the scene with Pearl, agreed. Barnabas showed Mark where to park, and pointed to a small wooden cabin, up a steep hillside, perched precariously on stilts. They walked to the cabin by a narrow path, gutted, like the hillside flanking it, by erosion. Excessive logging had abused the hill into defeat. Tree roots and weeds stuck out of the steep sandy slope, but nothing new and substantial grew there.

Saint Barnabas carried two small books with him. The smaller was a Bible, "HOLY SCRIPTURES" embossed in gold on its black leather cover. Beneath that, a large book wrapped in a white cloth. "It isn't good to let the general population even know this book is around. Very high esoteric Entipling prophecies," he confided to Mark. "That's why I keep it covered with this cloth."

Why tell me then? Mark wondered. Why do the flipouts pick me to talk to? Do I look like one of them? Am I?

Barnabas' eyes glinted conspiratorially. "This particular cloth is part of it, too. It was given to me by a Puerto Rican Sister who found me in New Mexico, after I'd been wandering in the desert for four days, man, having visions and experiences on the levels of very high astral beings and demons."

"Sounds incredibly heavy."

"It was, man. I was tempted by seven devils on the third day, and returned to my body on the twelfth. Are you hip to the significance of those numbers? And the nun who found me, Sister Theresa -- I haven't told you about her, but she's part of this whole thing, too."

"Who isn't?" Mark asked amiably.

Barnabas stopped abruptly at the stump of what had once been a large oak, and pointed to the ground. "Know then that this is where I do my deepest meditations? This is holy ground upon which ye trod." His eyes tested Mark's.

"I'll try to trod lightly then. But tell me, is humility no longer fashionable among the saintly?"

Myths are things which never happen but always are.

— *Salustius*

"Although humility is righteous, it is also the good calling of this age that a man exalt any true light given him, so the world may know its saints, and seek to understand them. And I say unto you that anyone who tries to ridicule such a man and seeks to confound him is Death's lover and will reap a bitter harvest of the mischief-seed he sows."

A ragged gray poodle-terrier appeared and, evidently mistaking Barnabas' passion for a threat, began barking. "Dogs always get freaked when they're around vibrations like mine. Cats aren't like that, though -- cats are higher, and they can handle this kind of astral weather. But the dogs always blow it."

"Hey, Muff! I know this dog! Yes, girl. What have you been doing?" Mark scratched her ears, and the mutt was at peace.

Barnabas' one room was cluttered with pictures of saints and gurus; a framed photograph of Saint Barnabas, looking perfectly straight, at a carnival; a newspaper clipping about the likelihood of life in outer space; and a dozen striking mixed-media shoeboxes. Mark was astonished -- the boxes were something special. Primitive art. Crude, rapid strokes, unadorned, without artifice, without a trace of civilized tradition, very stark, and very strong. "I like these boxes, very much."

"Those things?" There was a box filled with candy wrappers and stones that portrayed ducks floating on a pond beneath a green rise where sheep grazed. "I used to sell them on Fisherman's Wharf. Got as much as ten bucks apiece for them, sometimes." There was a series of boxes depicting the Stations of the Cross, with stick figure Christs of dried twigs. "But the boxes ain't where it's at." There was a box with Cracker-Jacks toys and trick-mirrors, and images flashed wildly through it as you looked at it from different angles. "This is where it's at!" He handed Mark a book entitled, *Christ's Legacy To The Living Elect: The Deathbed Revelations Of A Tibetan Lama.* Then Barnabas picked up the box depicting the Crucifixion of Christ, and explained, "See how the walls of it are covered with that unknown writing. While I was writing it, these angels were trying to slip me these symbols, but it was hard to do, man,

Eternity is in love with the productions of time.

— *William Blake*

because we were trying to communicate across all these dimensional barriers."

"Do you mind if I make myself some coffee?"

"What is your story, man? I make an extremely rare exception for you, and invite you into my house, which is more than a house, it's a shrine, so I have a right to know. Where are you at?"

"Here, mostly," Mark offered good-naturedly.

"I see. I made a terrible mistake with you. You're not part of this at all. You're on a whole, lower level."

"How is it lower?" A moth, brown, mottled, stuck sideways to the pale yellow door.

"You don't seem to realize who you're dealing with. I process primary level stuff! Is your mind intimately and exclusively involved at all times with the fundamental spiritual transformations of the Cosmos into Godhead?"

"No. I have to confess my mortal frailties, and admit that, from time to time, other thoughts do cross my mind."

"That's what I'm saying. You're nowhere near as high as I am. My mind is fixed. I am pure spirit, powered entirely by the energy of my eternal essence. Do you have any idea what I'm talking about?"

Yes, Mark might have said, truthfully and from experience. But instead, he said nothing.

"This is too bad. This whole meeting between us was not really supposed to have happened. This should be a valuable lesson for me."

"For me, too," Mark encouraged him. "Tell me more about yourself. Tell me who you really are."

Barnabas, eyes shut, rocked in his chair in a trance. "Perhaps this meeting was supposed to have happened, after all. That would explain why it actually happened. I see." He opened his eyes, spoke with a new calm to Mark, "When I was a child we had a crucifix on the wall, and the Christ on it kept falling off. The same thing happened in my fifth-grade class, with Brother Theodore. He's part of all this, too."

"The four-leggedism guy?" Mark couldn't believe it.

"Quiet," commanded the Saint.

"Must be another one," Mark assured himself. "Shake

. . . the serpent said that every dream could be willed into creation by those strong

it off.''

"All my life has been filled with such signs. Only last week, in San Francisco, a voice from a thundercloud spoke to me, saying, 'One will follow.' And the next morning a man came to the door of the house I was staying at, and he said he was Saint Martin of Tours and was looking for Him whom he must follow. You can't ignore signs like that!''

"Of course not. Did you say you had coffee or not?''

Barnabas looked compassionately at Mark. "Is the intensity freaking you out? Like the dog?''

"Well, not quite like the dog,'' hedged Mark, "but I would like a cup of coffee.''

"Don't get upset,'' Barnabas replied with exaggerated reassurance. "I didn't mean to heavy you out. I'm not trying to be heavy. In fact, I can do nothing by myself. Everything I do is really being done by the spirits sent by God to operate through me to further the reappearance of the Christ. But the people, they do not believe.''

"I know what you mean.''

"That's because none of them are as sensitive as I am to the mysterious spiritual processes now in progress. Last night I saw the air part before me and show behind it a blue flower that bloomed, then caught fire and burned. And this I knew at once was the sign that I'd been invited to enter the inner halls of the temple of God. Great God Almighty! There were times I fasted and prayed for days on end, wondering if I'd ever get an answer. And when I was imperfect, and doubted, then the petty distraction of the material mud would wash in, and darken my mind. But now I know that the Godhead is truly about to enter its timeless time again; that what we call the Aquarian Age is only a tiny part of this whole vast transformation being generated by the reappearance of the Christ.''

"Oh,'' said Mark slowly, "*that's* what's happening.''

"Late, very late last night I woke from a dream in which an archangel and one of Satan's main demons were battling for my soul. I ran to the window, lit my prayer candle, and opened my Bible. It fell open to the story of The Seven Seals in the Book of Revelations, and the sky flashed with light and the thunder spoke to me again.'' Barnabas raised his

enough to believe in it.

— *G. B. Shaw*

face to the ceiling, and beyond. Speaking for The Ages, he said, "This must be the time of which You have spoken to me, my heavenly Father, my master, for the signs are now too heavy for me to bear alone, in secret, any longer. The season of the spirit is ripe for the masses to know The Sacred Heart beats again in vulnerable human flesh. Thus do I trumpet and fulfill the coming age, here do I first reveal myself to the world of men and women, and now do I begin my work to fulfill the promises and prophecies that my Father revealed to the prophets and to Christ, that Christ would come and then come again, for He has, for I am He, I am the Christ, and I have come again."

Mark said he would drive to Lido Grande at once, and tell the others.

This is what God would have done if He'd had money.

—George Kaufmann

Exiled from The Sixties

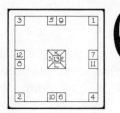

skelly

"For instance, if I ask myself, 'Will the social ideal, as such ever become a reality?' I cannot tell, I only know that whatever may be in my power to make it so, I shall do; beyond that, I can count upon nothing."

— *John Paul Sartre*

That afternoon Larry had an interview for a child care counseling job at a Santa Rosa group home. When he arrived at the office the secretary told him that the director had just called, and said to apologize, but she was tied up in Petaluma and would not be back for another hour.

"I'll come back," said Larry. "I haven't taken a good look at Santa Rosa yet."

"There's a park two blocks that way," the secretary told him.

Larry went there, stopping only to buy a fast-fried chicken. When he finished his lunch, he took a small book from his portfolio. It sported, on its cover, a striking aerial photograph of Lone Buck Bay, along with the unwieldy title: *The Northern California Council of Cooperative Communities' Handbook of Members.* Larry had taken it from the free rack at the newspaper office.

He flipped to the *L*'s:

Lone Buck Bay

"Lone Buck Bay is a cooperative community on the Sonoma Coast four miles north of the mouth of the Russian River, with a population of just under 200. We are now employed in a variety of occupations, although we were all connected with the music business when we moved here in late 1968. The story of how we changed, and why -- the little history of our village -- is worth retelling:

69

"By 1968, Grool was universally recognized as the most innovative and influential percussionist in the jazz-rock fusion. His last four albums had made a small fortune, and his professional family (of accompanying musicians, front-office people, sound engineers, technicians, equipment handlers, OM-peace-love-granola hippies, beatniks, neoindo ascetics with packs on their backs, and other assorted what-have-you's) were all enjoying a comfortable post-hippie standard of living.

"And yet Grool and many of the others thought of nothing as much as moving out of the city, to try to build again yet another new world.

"The search for enough capital to buy and build a town led them, naturally enough, to Weel. Weel had recorded Grool's last three albums, all of which were huge successes, as were many other records made at Weel's studio. Weel also owned a profitable sound equipment factory, and had begun to invest in real estate. 'Grool's dream town,' as Weel called it, held little attraction for the businessman, and he told Grool he would not consider getting involved in such a project.

"Grool's company debated the wisdom of such a move for several months. A utopian broadside published by Grool's lyricist, Tom, set down the majority view that 'Our greatest need now is not for more money, more politics, or more people; but for a restoration of our lost sense of community. The destructive impact of technology on our long-standing social forms have left us groping for someplace to call home. Our most basic need now is to build a human-sized community in which we know and are known by others.'

"Only two relatively small groups within Grool's troupe objected to the move. Most of the managerial and technical people, headed by Grool's chief sound technician Paul, were not interested in leaving San Francisco. They liked the briar-patches of city life, the opportunities for making money, the dress-up scenes and the parties, the pavement and the cigarettes. But since Grool paid well, they did not object too vehemently. The second and far more vocal dissenting faction consisted of the half-dozen or so political activists and radicals scattered throughout the organization. Led by Grool's road

I find it hard to believe that the way to run the world has been revealed to a

manager Charlie, this group fought the move on political grounds.

"The conflict between those who wanted to stay and the majority may have been most sharply articulated during a debate between a Marxist professor, invited by Charlie, and Mark, who printed concert and dance posters for Grool-Weel Enterprises. The professor charged that their planned retreat to the country was a soft, self-indulgent, cowardly betrayal of their true priorities. He argued that it was far too early to build cooperative villages, that such decentralization could come about only after the nation's system was changed, and its imperialism curbed. He contended that their plan was a bourgeois copout, that a town such as they envisioned would be insulated from reality and without value as an agent of social change. But Mark countered the professor's line with Huizinga's theory of play spaces as worlds set apart, and with Erikson's theory of model realities, within which new skills were perfected in the safety of play; that the planned community was a kind of social laboratory within which specific experiments in living could be fleshed out. It was inevitable, Mark argued, that their results would be of value to future communards -- either as examples to inspire or as instructive failures. Although the professor remained unconvinced, Mark's theories made good sense to many at the meeting.

"After a four-month search in Marin, Sonoma, Napa, and Mendocino counties, Grool's land committee announced that they were recommending a 327-acre sheep ranch on the Sonoma coast. The last three owners had called it Lone Buck Bay Ranch.

"Shortly after Grool's entire troupe approved the land committee's choice, Weel changed his mind about the project. At the time, it seemed like a great stroke of luck. Weel's investment in the town would insure that it got off to a fast start, with a solid economic base. At first, Grool later told us, Weel simply wanted to buy him out and acquire the property for himself. Grool assured him that we were serious about building our town there and were not looking to sell the land; but if Weel wanted to reconsider our earlier invitation to join us, he was still welcome. This time Weel agreed. 'Just

minority of pushy youngsters and middle-aged malcontents.

— Spiro T. Agnew

as long as Grool's great music continues to grow,' he told us at the next meeting. The truth of the matter, as we later learned, was that Weel changed his mind because he discovered that Lone Buck Bay could be dredged for gravel at a great profit. The local gravel companies have been trying to sink their teeth into it for years, and were prevented from doing so only by a ban handed down by the Coastal Commission. And getting the ban lifted, although not easy, would not be altogether impossible. At the time we were all so happy to have Weel with us, nobody stopped to question his motives.

"The overall agreement between Grool and Weel was for Grool to purchase the land, which would cost about half a million dollars, after which Weel would develop the town with houses, businesses, roads, and the rest, until he had paid as much into the town in development as Grool had paid for the land. Weel's one major reservation about the project, he said, was his fear that Grool and his friends would slip into a laid-back, unproductive, country-hippie life style. As a guarantee against that, Weel and his lawyers included a condition subsequent in the contract. Such a condition establishes certain circumstances that must be met following the signing of the contract, or the entire contract is void. Weel's condition subsequent required that Grool and his troupe construct a recording studio from materials provided by Weel, by such and such a date, or Weel was released from his obligation to help develop the town. 'My interest in Lone Buck Bay is in seeing that Grool's music remains alive,' Weel told us. 'If you build the studio promptly, I'll know you mean business. As soon as the studio's built, I'll come right in and build the rest of the town. But you're going to have to show me that this move to the country doesn't mean Grool and the rest of you are retiring.' It seemed like reasonable self-interest on Weel's part, we thought. Since we intended to build a studio and carry on with the music and recordings anyway, we readily agreed.

"Grool put up the money for the land, and we all moved up there. The physical beauty of the place impressed all of us. Being there made it easier to believe in. We were all eager to get going, to start building our town. Some of us set up tents and lean-tos, while others lived out of their trucks. And there

Kill what you cut off. Four corners win a game. Make territory while attacking. Stay

we waited for Weel to show up with the materials for the studio.

"After a week of waiting, we began to worry. Grool called Weel at his manufacturing plant in San Francisco, and Weel assured him that he had been busy all that week purchasing materials and renting the heavy equipment. None of that was true.

"After another week, a delegation from Lone Buck Bay went to San Francisco to see Weel. The delegation consisted of Grool, Joanie, who managed Grool's bookings and publicity, and Paul, who engineered Grool's recording sessions and live shows.

"Weel had the police eject them for trespassing.

"At this point, Grool and the rest of us began to see the situation for what it was. Weel was delaying intentionally, to prevent us from meeting the deadline. We did what we should have done long before then -- hired a lawyer to protect our interests in the case. In fairness to us, however, it had not seemed like a case before. We thought Weel's attorneys had been working for us too.

"Since the deadline for the condition subsequent had not yet passed, Paul and Joanie convinced Grool that he should put up the money for materials to construct the recording studio, so that Weel would have to honor the rest of the contract. The studio would be used to release a new album, and the money it generated put into paying Grool back. Also, by involving everyone in the construction of the studio, we could help keep the original dream alive and well, despite Weel's efforts.

"Grool agreed, put up another $55,000, and all 122 men, women, and children in the Lone Buck Bay group began work on the new recording studio. We worked with conviction. We worked quickly, and yet there were so many of us with so many diverse skills that the building was filled with beautiful touches. Wherever one looked in the new studio, one saw something fine and distinctive -- the signatures of all the hands that loved the building and what it represented.

"A few days before the roof went on the central part of the building, the new studio was burned to the ground. It is likely that whoever torched it had no idea that Grool's wife Belle

away from thickness.   — go *proverbs*

and his graphics artist Phil Greco were inside it at the time, completing work on their mural celebrating the joys of music. Both died in the blaze.

"The sheriff's office said they had no clues. They had one. A tipster sold police in San Francisco the information that a professional arsonist had bought a new car with some crisp big bills the day after the fire. Many months later, the car turned up on a lot in Cleveland. The Ohio police put out a bulletin, but nothing ever came of it.

"Although we have never been able to prove anything, many of the people of Lone Buck Bay are convinced that Weel was the man behind the arson and murders. From the very beginning down to the present moment, Weel's entire involvement in Lone Buck Bay has been designed to drive out our community, which would leave him free to exploit the bay for his own purposes. In light of all that has happened since, it seems obvious to many in Lone Buck Bay that the arson fits right in with the overall strategy used by Weel in his ongoing war to drive us off the land.

"The fire and deaths were too horrible for us to take in stride. Weel's actions had stunned us, but we had not lost heart. But the deaths by burning of Belle and Greco were too real. None of us ever imagined it would come to killings. The town spirit of creative cooperation gave way to desolation. Only a day before the fire, out little tent village had looked to us like a frontier camp of courageous pioneers; after the nightmare, the same view was of a defeated army's last stand.

"Grool himself left the town the day after the fire. The police spoke to him, discovered nothing. Weeks later it was learned through Paul Greco's widow Amy that Grool had bought some land in the hills above Cazadero and was living in seclusion in a cave.

"With Grool and the studio both gone, Paul and most of the technical staff returned to San Francisco. Charlie and some of the other vocal radicals denounced them as traitors. But Paul and his assistants gave no signs of caring. They replied that they were simply professionals in the music business, and had no flags to wave and no scores to settle. All they wanted, Paul explained, was to return to work and go on with the day to day business of living.

Experience is the best of schoolmasters, only the school-fees are heavy.
— Thomas Carlyle

"Most of the rest of Grool's troupe stayed.

"Grool's lawyers produced witnesses who testified that shortly after Grool's troupe decided on Lone Buck Bay, Weel conducted an intensive investigation into the feasibility of a gravel dredging operation at Lone Buck Bay. Grool's lawyers seemed confident that this testimony would prove that Weel never intended to help Grool build a town, but was after gravel right from the start. And that meant that Weel would be found guilty of fraud, said the lawyers. We are now involved in a civil case -- Grool vs. Weel -- in which we are suing Weel for $500,000, his promised share, plus damages. However, with the civil courts and Weel's lawyers being what they are, it might take a couple of years before the courts award their judgment.

"Several months after the arson, Weel succeeded in pressuring the county building inspector into 'red tagging' the new makeshift housing that was going up in Lone Buck Bay. But Grool's lawyers won a restraining order from the court, directing the agency not to issue the citations until the relevant court cases had been concluded.

"After that, Weel concentrated on wooing votes on the Coastal Commission, to get them to reverse their previous decision to retain the ban on gravel dredging in Lone Buck Bay. He reportedly won over two of the five commissioners, and is believed to be working hard on the swing vote. He has also acquired two parcels of land adjacent to Lone Buck Bay, and has tried on several occasions to buy us out.

"Many of us who stayed at Lone Buck Bay staggered through the early months on pure pluck and food stamps. But over the next couple of years, the community proved to be enterprising, establishing several small businesses and cottage industries. Charlie's gas station and garage replaced Wingate's Garage, and Charlie proved to be such a better mechanic than his predecessor that the shop flourished. Dieter's pottery shop, after many delays and a disastrous first year, has begun doing reasonably well. The Coastal Courier has enough advertising to almost support four people. Wes and Laurie's Pleasant Peasant Restaurant, in the Farmhouse, has built up a well-deserved reputation for a small but excellent menu of low-priced dishes. The restaurant employs

. . . I and my companions suffer from a disease of the heart which can be cured only by

two cooks, two kitchen helpers, two dishwashers, six waitresses, and provides Charlie's trucking service with a good
share of its business. The gift shop has now had two
profit-making years, in a row, selling work by our town's
craftspeople.

"Joanie manages the country punk band Botulistic
Mucilage, the belly-dancing troupe, the magician and his
clown, the juggler, and the dog act, all of whom live in Lone
Buck Bay. The Cooperative Food Store breaks even by design.

"Most of the town's income, of necessity, comes in from
outside employment. A dozen women work as waitresses in
restaurants along the coast; half that many men work the
fishing boats out of Bodega Bay. One couple works at a group
home for emotionally disturbed adolescent boys, and another
sells real estate for Sea Ranch. One woman does topless
dancing in Santa Rosa, another edits textbooks, a third is
secretary to the president of a vineyard, a fourth lives off a
sculpting stipend from Grool, a fifth strings beads and
earrings, a sixth makes stained glass windows and hangings,
and so forth. One man is a partner in a lucrative landscaping
service, another cooks for a restaurant in Petaluma, a third
works for a print shop north of Santa Rosa, a fourth carves
wood, and a fifth washes dishes in Timber Cove, just up the
coast from Lone Buck Bay.

"The town is hopeful that the court will render its
judgment this year, and that it will be substantial enough to
help us generate more income and employ more of the
community in the town itself."

gold.

— *Hernando Cortez*

Grool,
The Troll

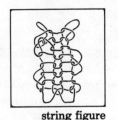

string figure

"Music is a place in the ear."
— *Harry Partch*

Mark fumbled his way through the cave's outer chambers, irregularly lit by flickering torches mounted in fissures in the cave's walls. He heard the flapping of bats. His "hello" reverberated through a dozen unseen chambers.

He saw the light of Grool's main chamber, and crawled into it through the immense, asymmetrical spider web made of piano, harp, and guitar strings that stretched from the floor to the cave's highest ceiling. The web sparkled in the torchlight like silk spangled with dewdrops. Flanking it were devil's masks made of crabshells; a cave-painting of a man eating his own heart; a dummy with ping-pong balls for eyes, impaled on two sharp stalactites, playing a black bugle; and scores of drums, gongs, and percussion instruments that existed nowhere else on earth, many made of jetsam Grool had found along the beaches.

In the corner of the chamber farthest from the entrance was a nook housing an ancient, splendidly carved sea monster with a face that might have come from crossbreeding an oriental dragon with a deranged hen. It had once been the prow of a proud Pacific Islander's fishing canoe, smashed by a Spanish galleon's forecannons (come to spread the gospel and save the damned natives). It had made a tour up the Japanese current, washing up in California, weathered for centuries by the salty westerlies, and was now Grool's altarpiece. Above the prow glowed a soft blue white pearl. All the cave's grotesques belonged to Grool, the musician; but only the pearl belonged to what survived of Grool, the man. It had been his wife's necklace jewel. Sometimes he cried so hard that he had to put cool pebbles on his eyelids to make the throbbing stop, and then he would become a troll again, and trolls feel no pain.

Mark joined him around the fire in the pit, gave him the papers, told him how soon they were needed in court.

"Amy told me the lawyers were sending you here," said Grool. He was a very short man, made even shorter because he was stooped forward from years of playing drums. He had lost his hearing in one ear in a childhood bicycle accident, and his head turned to one side, from habitually putting his good ear toward the music he was making.

"I've talked to some of our old people in San Francisco," Mark told him. "Guys who are still in the music business. They say, if you came back, you could get whatever you wanted, from any of them."

"None of them ever had what I wanted. You know what I want, I want to be left alone."

"Don't you miss living with people?"

Grool shook his head. "What place do you imagine my music -- and my life, which I give to it -- can have in a world of people?"

That's just what I've been saying! thought Mark. And it sounds right. Very odd, that to play the good man now, I must speak for both sides.

"Come back and work with us again, Grool. It would galvanize everybody. We're sure to win the final court decision soon, and Weel will be forced to pay, and we'll build the homes, and equip the studio. We'll make the town work the way we dreamed it, back in the beginning."

"What do they want? You can't *use* music. It's not rhetoric. It's no good trying to fit it into some plot."

"Doesn't your music have a context?"

"Sure. My life. I make music. I hear music. I stop making music. I hear silence. I make music again. Very simple."

"And doesn't your life have a context?" Mark plodded on.

"What good did my do-gooding every really do any of us?

Between grief and nothing, I'll take grief.

—*William Faulkner*

I've lost too many battles. No more. From now on, I'm staying home with my drums." He nervously poked at the fire with a piece of iron so old and rusted that its original use was a mystery. "Tell them that I am just not their boy. Tell them I am not the key to their puzzles. I am not The Man. I do not save worlds. I do not build cities. I do not fulfill prophecies. I just play music." He quieted himself, tried a new tack. "I've got it. Tell them that the past year-and-a-half has been so hard on me that I am no longer able to put out professional quality music. Tell them my mind is decaying. It's true. It is. This isn't an easy thing for me to admit, but I'm going fast. My creative period is over. You can't control these things. It's not like turning a faucet on and off. I can only recombine the old elements now, and as the combinations grow increasingly familiar, they dry up completely. I have played all the riffs I know. It's all repetition now. All old songs. My music is so trite I might be ready for top-forty. Don't tell them that, though; they might like that."

Grool got up. "Want to hear a new tune? I call it 'Sweet Wendy Twinkle, Young By Silver Moonbeams, Never So Again As Much In Love -- Part Five.' " He sprang like a bent cat to a ledge, began beating out a patchanga on some hand drums, jumped to the tympani and shook the cave with its eerie harplike tones, to the snare drums, to the wood blocks, the metal gongs, the bass marimba, the instruments with no names, to one new sound after another, buzzing and humming, bouncing off walls, hopping and dancing from rock to ledge to ground to shaft, dazzling music blazing from his hands while his long multi-colored scarf jiggled around his shoulders like the tail of a comet.

Mark sat gaping like a monkey in the middle. The red ear painted on the floor where he sat marked the place where all the sounds echoing off the cave's walls converged, and every note Grool played crossed this spot at least three times. One high gong near the ceiling came to the red ear eleven times per note played, and when Grool hit it seven times quickly it sounded like one impossibly long, thick, high-pitched gong, instead of seventy-seven little ones.

He who has a why to live can bear almost any how.

— *Nietzsche*

GROL'S
CAVE~
NO DOUBT
MAD
IDEA

CS·78

Everything was brand new, and it was all too much for Mark to take in.

Suddenly, Grool stopped playing. The cave seemed to vibrate with the absence of the music, just as it had been shaken by its presence.

Mark could say nothing. Grool's creativity was about as played out as an exploding volcano. His music had grown elemental, fierce, and untameable. Far beyond what he had done before, and probably far beyond caring about making phonograph records. But his music was no longer beautiful. It was an inhuman kind of music -- music an ocean might compose, or a forest. Its sorrows seemed so deep and dispassionate as to be not merely the sorrows of a man, but the sorrows of man. His music explained everything about him. What wouldn't it explain? The politics seemed irrelevant.

The music set off so many associations in Mark that he was overwhelmed by all the images pouring through him. In a fleeting moment of sobriety, he realized that he probably should not trust himself to speak for a pondful of rubber ducks, much less a town, and he rose to leave. "Did you sign the papers?"

Grool nodded, smiled, handed the papers to Mark. "Tell them my hands went bad from the dampness in here, and I can't hold the drumsticks any more," Grool called after him.

When Mark left, Grool stared seriously at a candle for a long time. Although he had argued so forcibly against returning to the real world out there, to Lone Buck Bay and the music business, there was a part of him that wanted to do just that. He rarely faced this in himself, and so in some strange, secret, and unreal way, life out there had become luminous and legendary to him. Solitude and socialization constellate their opposites, each other. Grool secretly hungered for the whole catastrophe of the usual, the daily banalities, the cooked and overcooked insipidities of comfort. He had severed almost all his strands with the world, and yet its felt ghost continued to haunt him. Only Amy was part of his world, and she was as crazy as he was.

God is fire in the head.

— Nijinsky

The day before the night of the arson and the murders, Carmody visited Grool at the recording studio with a message from Weel. If Grool did not leave town immediately, they would destroy everyone and everything in Lone Buck Bay . . . except him. Grool had never told anybody about this -- not Amy, not Mark, not the police, not anyone.

When one tugs at a single thing in nature, he finds it attached to the rest of the world.
— John Muir

Play

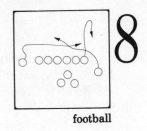

football

8

He would go through all the old notes -- superficially at first, with an eye to both future projects and the basic, overall organization. Then he would go through them again, more carefully, working with them attentively, reviving his lost facility with their details. Great Blake had said, " . . . Art and Science cannot exist but in minutely organized particulars . . . " and Mark had reams and reams of particulars. It was like trying to sort out a truckload of sand, by shape and color, grain by grain. Where to begin?

He paused, took a deep breath, gave his quieter, contemplative selves a moment or two to consider things. He quoted Harry Pillsbury to himself, "I want to be quiet; I mean to win this tournament." That was before the strong international chess tournament at Hastings, 1895, which Pillsbury won. Mark stilled.

Mark did not know exactly where he was going, or even if it was possible to get there at all. He had no unifying theory to test, yet; only perceptions, intuitions. The *proofs* of his as yet unconstructed theories lay further in the future. He was a beginner in a primitive field -- a medicine man experimenting with wild herbs, not a technician operating with laboratory tested materials. But he was willing to take the wild chance of living as though his best hopes were, in fact, true. It was far from a sure thing. It was a ritual gamble, a holy make-believe, a leap into the fog, an act of faith.

83

The phone rang. Once. Stopped. Mark took it off the hook, before it tried something else.

How to begin? Separating the baseball anecdotes from the unpaired socks? There was too much, too many notes, the filing cabinet, the boxes, and in them the folders and mailing envelopes, all the old notes, the old notes. Entropy had beat them into a thicket. A brief layoff from ludics would have responded to a simple tidying up; but these years of prolonged neglect had allowed the whole body of his work to sink into a new level of decay, and slums need more than streetcleaning to bring them back to health.

He skimmed file after file, envelope after envelope, note after note. And cautiously, he began making notes and sketches for their divisions into useful working categories. He outlined the salient family resemblances, the theoretical congruences, and the cross referencing strategies that seemed serviceable. His contemplative tentativeness stemmed from an intuition that the way he sliced it all up to begin with would in itself exert strong influences on the development of the work to come, would affect the shapes of new ideas in ways he could never fully know.

Mark had been a Californian long enough to be able to distinguish between the itch of an old flea bite and that of a bite-in-progress. Slyly raising his foot to his chair, and slowly raising his pants leg, he spotted the beast in the thicket of hair on the ankle-calf cusp. He pushed a thumb into it, pressed and rolled, mangled and smothered. He knew how merciless he had to be, how often he had been sure he had killed one of the little bloodsuckers only to watch it take a wounded hop safely out of sight, and strike again on the thigh. This one he got, and examined a moment. The insect by lamplight, dead and bent. Yes, and it's a miracle it's there at all, he thought. A miracle the gap between nothing and something had already been bridged.

He worked, and worked more, and after two days of work broken only by a three-hour nap, he felt very tired. But Mark now feared indolence far more than he feared over-work, so he stood at attention at his desk and shouted,

There is so much that has not been said or thought.

— *Nietzsche*

"Emulate Arjuna, conqueror of Sloth!" He worked until he
fell asleep.

* * * * *

He slept for ten hours, and when he woke he was fully
refreshed. He remembered no dreams. He began to work at
once, and it took off into work as work might be. This was
work that sang, work that played with him, who played with
it. He participated happily in the revival of romances of
thoughts within himself, their secret rendezvous, their
ecstatic matings, and their reluctant breakups. He glimpsed,
in all their mental play, the organism of ludics, the body of
that unmapped science. He saw that it was not a mass of
unrelated data he was trying to squeeze together into a box,
but an organism, with complicated interchanges of blood
vessels and nerve axions, tissues and muscles, and a
character uniquely its own.

He worked on, straight as an arrow, bent as a maze. He
dabbled in twenty things, toyed with three, stared blankly at
one, and, on the brink of despairing and calling it quits for
the session, burst through the blocks while the by-now-
familiar problem practically solved itself for him. Truly, as
his mother's teacher had told her, "What one fool can do,
any fool can do."

The food began running out, along with Mark's
exuberance. Progress now, he knew, would depend upon the
kind of sustained struggle he had spent much of his life trying,
through cunning, to avoid.

He thought ahead, to what he was preparing for. The
further ahead he thought, the less real and more fantastical
his thoughts became -- monumental theoretical
breakthroughs, the valued recognitions by the best minds,
and all the honors and accolades. He rehearsed an ac-
ceptance speech, glad of the reemergence of these day-
dreams native to ludicians. These fantasies gave him pep,
like vitamins for his will. Their unreality did not bother him.
Mathematicians use imaginary numbers -- like the square

. . . *a piece of creative writing, like a day-dream, is a continuation of, and*

root of a negative number, which is axiomatically impossible -- to help solve equations with practical applications.

*　*　*　*　*

Staring bleary-eyed at the congenitally rumpled intellectual looking back at him in the mirror, facial-lines deepening like Death's fingerprints, Mark preached, "they always said you'd wind up like that." He grabbed an apple from the kitchen, boiled water for coffee. God help him, he thought, that one there in the mirror. His eyes wandered without focus over a week-old newspaper, reread the passage on the pad next to the phone from Stefan Zweig's "The Royal Game." He was so inefficient, with all his warmups and little rituals, leisurely circling around the work itself, until he arrived at that particular place from which he performed his special work. The fencings-off before the goings-on within the worlds-apart.

He thought he might continue with the nature of play-spaces, or the psychology of play -- something big and difficult. But instead he decided he was better off beginning with something fairly routine and mechanical. That seemed to him the natural way to proceed. Like remembering how to play the piano -- one first had to practice scales, note by note, left-hemispherically, even though one once had known all the Mozart concertos. Only after this could he switch to autopilot, coordinating all the details automatically, and freeing his consciousness for playing and experimenting.

First, then, the idiot work. He started with captures, in all the board games -- the races, the wars, the spatial games, the *mancala* group, some card games, too.

Sub-category outline, needs more articulation, what do we have? Replacement captures, like chess. Jumping, like checkers. (Need a section on the difference between the opportunity to capture and the compulsion to capture. What about huffing -- taking you for not taking me? Not unlike the way the cop in the B-movie disarms the girl, because she couldn't bring herself to gun him down.) Then there's flanking, as in Reversi -- playing pieces on both ends of the line to capture the pieces in between. (Add *Othello* to Reversi

a substitute for, what was once the play of childhood.
— Sigmund Freud

identification -- that's the name of the hit version of its current revival.) Flanking in *seega* as well. *Seega* boards were scratched into the great pyramids by the Arab tour guides. In both *seega* and Reversi, the outer squares are the most crucial because of the flanking. Interception. Interception? That's when a piece is played in between two opponent's pieces and captures them both. In what? Chinese game, Sixteen Soldiers. The Romans used the intercepting tactic of the wedge to split enemy lines.

What about kill moves in *go*? Are they a special class of flanking? Could I call it 'suffocation?' Not quite right. Suffocation sounds right for fox-and-geese, and games with that cornering or backing into a wall feature. Cross reference fox-and-geese to that whole family, it's a global feature, a team of several limited pieces battling a solitary opponent with special powers. Think of a *karate* champion attacked by four juvenile delinquents. The fox is like the fighting master, able to execute many more kinds of moves than all his attackers put together. The delinquents, like the geese, have only a few options and moves, but they have the numbers on their side. They can force the *karate* master into a blind alley, and cut his moves down to zero by backing him into a corner. Also cross reference fox-and-geese to puzzles, since it's not really a game, it's a puzzle, like tic-tac-toe, you can solve it.

Nullo games -- get back to that, reversal of losing and winning, like hearts, losing chess, nature of the mirror image distortions and compensations for that.

Mancala games, special class. Wonder if Africans are looking into it? Ought to, it's up there with the best of them, and it's unique. Ugandans play a four-row variation, probably still do, *Idi Dada* notwithstanding. Unique movement of *seeding*, and the most complicated of all counting games.

South Indian and Ceylonese variation of *mancala*, certain numbers of stones appearing in one of your cups wins them for you, bizarre new variable in already complicated game; plus, as if they weren't bad enough, dead holes, they call them rubbish holes, which aren't used, except under certain circumstances when they spring magically back to life. Like dead groups in *go*, just pop right up. This element of games -- the 'apparently' dead returning to life -- this had some

I know at sight what a position contains. What could happen? What is going to happen?

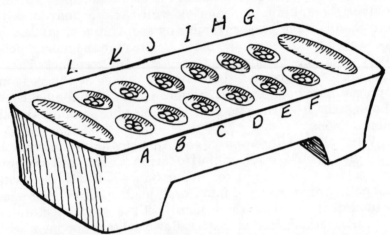

There are many individual games within the family of *mancala*, or *wari*, games. This is a simple, representative type.

Board: Usually made of wood or ceramics, as pictured above, but may be dug into the ground, or consist of a layout of bowls and cups.

Pieces: Pebbles or seeds. In this variation, we start with four in each hole, not counting the large capture holes at the ends.

Players: Two.

Plays: Each player alternately removes all the stones from one of the six holes on his side of the board. He seeds them, one by one, into each hole, going counterclockwise around the board. For instance, South might open the game by picking up the four stones in *d* and sowing them, one by one, into *e, f, g* (the capture pits are skipped) and *h*.

If a player has no stones on his side of the board, he must pass, and must continue to pass until he can play again.

Captures: If a player seeds the final stone of his play into an empty cup, he wins that stone and all the stones in the cup opposite. In the example above, after South opens with *d* to *efgh*, North can win five stones by playing *l* to *abcd*. Because his final stone falls into the empty *d* cup, North captures that stone and the four stones in his *i* cup. He scoops these stones out of their holes and stores them in his capture hole. The game ends when all the stones are gone. Player with the most captured stones wins.

connection, Mark felt, to something that had nothing to do with board games. It was like, what? Like feelings you thought were gone, until they came back to you; like thinking you can't love anymore and then you see *her,* and realize it's not going to be that simple.

Is *pallanguli* still played? Write the embassy, what's it called now? Sri Lanka.

All those West Indian *mancala* games, too. Probably all came over with the slaves, one of the elements of African culture the white man permitted them to practice openly, since it was only sowing pebbles in holes in the ground. It was only a game, even though it was as African as their names.

Now the trouble is that most games without a body of literature, like *mancala,* have been picked up by anthropologists or explorers or newspapermen with no special interest or training in games, so they take pictures, copy diagrams, ask whoever's around about how to play, make notes like a naturalist logging a tufted puffin sighting. So the difficulty with these primitive games is that we don't know who to ask for instructions. If you want to study chess, do you go to a playground and find two little kids? They'll tell you the main thing is don't throw your queen away and the knight is the best piece. Like Bergman's "Seventh Seal," where the Good Knight plays Death for the fate of them all, and both of them play the game like a couple of rank rookies. Death stupidly opens his knight-file in front of the castled king for a tremendous rook check by the good guy, who not only fails to follow it up but blows the whole game by leaving his queen *en pris. Mon Dieu!* Best part was the little kid in the movie house, last time I went, who wanted to know where the seals were.

Wonder if Harmon can get his machines to calculate the complexity of *mancala* games? What size? Six-stone-a-cup-two-lines and twelve-stone-a-cup-four-lines, see how it stacks up against chess, which is twenty-five times ten to the 120-something power. Africans better get going on *mancala* before some jive you-ess-of-ay corp moves in, takes out copyrights on it, changes the name to Tycoon, sells it back to them. Happens all the time. Look at those two great

You figure it out. I know it!

— Capablanca

games of Victorian England -- Halma and Reversi. Halma
faded away, then an American company, during the depression, brought it back, changed the board to a colored star
and the name to Chinese Checkers, had a big hit.

Reversi attracted some serious attention and analysis, but
never really caught on when it came out in the 1880's. Went
unappreciated until the 1970's, when a modified version was
released under the name *Othello*, and found a worldwide
following. The book by *Othello's* inventor of record, Gero
Hasegawa, advises the player to capture the corners, which
are stable, and the relatively stable edges, early in the game,
which seems to be the strategy natural to the game. All good
Othello players have always played that way, until the revolutionary system of the Japanese champion Hiroshi Inoue was
sprung on his unsuspecting rivals at the recent World
Championship tournament, in Tokyo. Inoue won the title by
being the first *Othello* master to discover how to exploit the
structural weaknesses in early edge occupation. It seemed to
Mark that Inoue's strategy paralleled the hypermodern revolution in chess in the 1920's, which challenged the premise
of the classical school that early occupation of the center
squares was advantageous. The hypermodernists demonstrated that an early center occupation can often be under-
mined from the flanks, transformed into an inviting target.

He took a fast look through his folder on how the basic
cultural differences between eastern and western civilizations
are expressed in their two great board games -- *go* and chess.
In chess, different kinds of pieces have distinctive abilities,
and vary in value; in *go*, there is only one kind of piece, a
stone, which is valuable only in terms of its value to the group.
In chess, pieces *invade* the adversary's forces; in *go*, they
surround them. Erik Erikson claims that little girls will play
with blocks by making enclosures surrounding an innerspace,
like a womb, like the Great Wall of China, like a group of
stones in *go*. Little boys, Erikson found, tend to use the blocks
to build towers, like a penis, like a rocketship at Cape
Kennedy, like an attacking thrust on the chessboard. In chess,
forces converge and *time* is crucial, and each game unfolds a
history. In *go*, *space* matters most, and each game explores
a *geography*, and ends with a completed map. Mark filed

According to the 17th Chapter of the Egyptian Ritual of the Dead, playing board

the folder for another day.

He changed radio stations. It had the impact that changing clothes had for some men and women. The soulful black blues yielded to the moving brilliance of Bach's *Magnificat in D*, followed by some forgivably overdone bit of Dvorakian bathos.

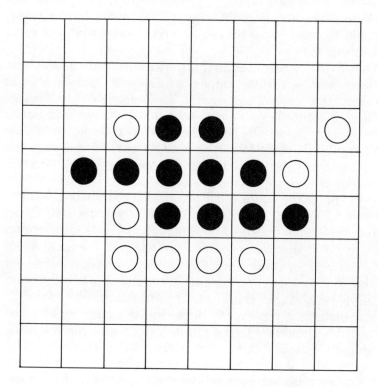

games is one of the promised delights of the afterlife.

What about safety? Don't I have a safety category? Safety from capture? Out to lunch, last time I worked on this. Safe squares, where pieces are immune from capture, like castles in Parchesi, home in *Sorry*, the corners in Reversi, and so forth. Where's mine? he wondered.

And Japanese chess, *shogi*, have to have a category for that, where captured pieces are enlisted for service on the other side. Great feature and realistic, too, since in battle you turn around the captured tanks. They use that in some of those battle simulation games. And in espionage, if a spy is caught and made to work as a double agent against his original side, he is said to have been turned around. Check that out some more, make a note.

What's this? Just did something with this, nullo variations, here's the rest -- misere games, yeah, yeah, possible tie-in to Taoism here? Is that too weird? Well, probably not for this fool. Run it through your head a couple of times and see if anything sticks to it. Oh Hell, that's a good game, modified nullo factor, a *de facto* factor, one might say, if one were not above that sort of thing -- bonus for making exactly the bid number of tricks.

Sports notes too -- but this needs much more work. What's here now? Tagging, tackling, striking out, forcing out, flying out, recovering the fumble, knocking out . . . no, that's wrong. Knocking out is the whole contest, but capturing is an element within the play of the game. Ejection by officials? Pinning a man, no, but look at that, pinning a man means two different but clearly related things in chess and wrestling.

In wrestling, a pin means defeating the opponent by forcing both his shoulders to the ground; in chess a pin is a tactic that immobilizes a knight, for example, by threatening to capture the king the knight is shielding. The former is like the overthrow of a leader by a military coup, as in Cuba, Chile, Ethiopia, Fredonia. What happened in the Watergate scandal is like the chess pin. The minor figures, shielding the principals, were pinned by the prosecution's attack. Sloan moved, exposing CRP; Butterfield moved, exposing the tapes. Dean moved, exposing the Oval Office.

He savored a moment's rest, and smiled, glad to have recovered the joy of loving his work, and of wanting to work as

Once get a knight firmly posted on king six and you may go to sleep. Your

long and as hard as he could. He stretched.

Seated again, he contemplated the still center of his clock, all three hands spinning clockwise, and his attention seemed to fill the room with the glow of human concentration, and everything in it appeared to be charged with life and intelligence.

What about solitaires, the orthagonal jump and capture in that peg game where you try to wind up with one in the middle, big market item, years back, in plastic, but I saw a picture, find that, in Bell's book, I think, same game as a beautiful French salon item, eighteenth century, silver pieces on silver pegs and platter.

With card solitaire now, moving piles in Canfield or Klondike, or Accordian or Pyramid solitaires. I don't know, that may be stretching it to call that a capture. More likely that it's useless information, that all the solitaire stuff is merely variant forms of simple board game captures. Can't tell what's trivial or not until I have enough of it together to see what it is, where the congruences and variations are, what comes to mind. Can't even tell yet if *capturing* is worth studying or if it's trivial to the overall study. Can't really tell if the whole overall study is trivial in the whole Overall in terms of the me qua me and the me as participant in the human overall process, blah qua blah.

What about Marcus' *Lord of the Rings* game, with its unique invisible piece, which reveals itself upon capture, changes sides, and vanishes again? What the hell is this? This doesn't even belong here. Wrong goddamn envelope completely. Just a plain two-mover, by who? Russian named Maximovski. Set it up on the peg set, as long as it's out. Let's see, black king on KR1, rook on KN1, pawns on KN2 and KR2; white to move and win has king on QN1, witch on QN2, rook on KN1. So how's R-R1, N-pawn pinned and if he pushes on rook pawn, rook takes pawn is mate. No, he just moves the rook. Maybe the only way to keep the rook there is with threat of queen takes knight-pawn mate, but then what's to stop him from pushing the rook pawn. Aha! Very pretty, yes, rook to knight six, very elegant, put it in the To File pile, it would be a pity to lose that one.

An insistent knock. An unhesitating, uninvited entrance.

game will then play itself.

— Anderssen

"Mr. Peterson?"

Mark's employer stared at him the way one might eye a rodent emerging from an abandoned house. "What the hell are you doing, sitting around playing checkers with yourself? You were supposed to be in yesterday."

"Yesterday? Is that Thursday?"

"That was Thursday!"

"Sorry, I lost track."

"Let's go. There's a shitload of work backed up for you. You got magazine covers to score, and this ridiculous fucking job, these tickets, with perforations and two numbering machines apiece. Embossed business cards, and . . . there's one more. There's another one, too, I forgot."

"On the Heidelburg?"

"No. Everything's on the old C and P. The Heidelburg's tied up for another week. I still got a billion more wine labels for that idiot Martocelli. He had a vintage year, a few years ago so he held back, to age it more, and he's marketing it this year, along with his regular juice. Come on, kid! Time is money, and you've been costing me. Let's go."

"You got any coffee there?"

"Gallons. Vats of it. Just let's go make some money."

"Money? Don't you know what Weiss said?"

"Weiss who?"

"He said, 'The poorest chessplayer is more to be envied than the most favored servant of the Golden Calf; for the latter grovels all his life long in the mire of materialism; while the former dwells high aloft, in the bright realms of imagination and poetry.' "

* * * * *

When Mark and his ex-wife Michelle moved to San Francisco, he got a job at her Uncle David's print shop. Uncle David was not really an uncle at all, but a second cousin. He was also a first-rate pressman. Mark could not have had a better teacher. Uncle David taught Mark the subtleties of the split fountain technique of offset printing, where different colors are put next to each other in the ink fountain and allowed to run into each other. Split fountain printing was then

He was part of my dream, of course -- but then I was part of his dream, too.
— Lewis Carroll

in vogue in San Francisco's psychedelic poster business, to publicize concerts, dances, and celebrations. Mark's ability with this technique led him to switch jobs in 1968 to Sitting Bull Poster Printing Company, a wholly owned subsidiary of Grool-Weel Enterprises, which specialized in such work. By the time he moved to Lone Buck Bay, the style had begun to fade from popularity, and Mark was rarely called upon to use it at Peterson's shop. Most of the work Mark did for Peterson were specialty jobs on the two letterpresses -- the Heidelberg and the Chandler and Price platen press.

Peterson climbed into his delivery van, and told Mark, "Ride with me. We'll drop this stuff off at Timber Cove first." He flipped on the radio, and a quasi-hysterical tenor screamed back at him, " 'Tears in My Ears,' by Francois and the Touch-Tones. Next, two rifles, three blondes, a redhead, and dope in a motel room -- that story and other news right after this message for headache sufferers!"

"Holy Jesus motherfucking Christ!" Peterson screamed back at it, and turned to some vapid arrangement of "Why Try To Change Me Now."

"Saddle stitching! That's the other job. After you score the magazine covers, you got to insert and stitch them. That's supposed to go tomorrow morning."

They stopped at Lone Buck Bay on their way back, and Mark followed in his own car. In Gumperstown, he spotted Pearl's car. He observed with an emotional ambivalence but undeniable obsessiveness that he was excited.

Peterson's shop was north of Santa Rosa. His outer office was furnished with chrome and black vinyl chairs. Mark thought it looked like the waiting room of some banana republic's fourth best airport. "Here they are. Score them straight down the middle. That's all. Nothing fancy."

Nothing fancy. That was the great virtue of the job, as far as Mark was concerned. He counted himself lucky to have an employer like Peterson, who could be so tolerant of his eccentricity and unreliability. On the other hand, he knew Peterson counted himself lucky to get as good a pressman as Mark at such subunion wages. Nothing fancy. Mark reasoned that while he did his ludics, blue-collar work suited him much

I do not hope for anything. I do not fear anything. I am free.

Kazantzakis

better than white. Working-class bosses just bought labor; white-collar positions were paid for with your personality as well as your sweat.

He washed up the first job, locked up the second, changed the packing. Peterson drifted by with a sandwich and nodded a muted OK to the scoring on the covers. Mark had always marvelled at how fastidiously prepared and wrapped Peterson's sandwiches were, and had long ago deduced the existence of a small and still shrinking wife, accustomed to cowering in corners from years of avoiding Peterson's bullish fits.

Above the press, the fan whirled, its spinning blades generating an illusion of solidity. Mark worked all day, late into the night, thousands of repetitions of the same motions, then the new lock-up and make-ready, and then more repetition, through the next morning. Twenty-four hours out of twenty-six.

He could see the indentations in the air, and feel the spiders tip-toeing over his shoulders. The great chessplayer Akiba Rubenstein developed the delusion that his enemies were commanding remote control flies, which were sent to distract him at key moments in his games. I can understand that, thought Mark. Probably true. I ought to get into the play element in drinking contests, and sleep-loss psychosis, and drowning. I ought to be asleep.

Shortly before noon, Mark told Peterson he had finished it all, done three working days all in a row, promised he would work the following Tuesday and Wednesday, and thanked Peterson for the paycheck.

Just north of Santa Rosa, Mark drove past a huge round barn lettered "FOUNTAINGROVE." It was the only surviving building of one of the country's more bizarre and extraordinary utopian experiments, fifty years ago. It had centered around a mad-eyed mystic named Thomas Lake Harris, who fancied the place was filled with fairy sprites, and that all his people had 'counterparts' of the opposite sex in the spiritual kingdom, who were their true lovers. What really got him into trouble was that he also fancied that the counterparts could slip into human bodies, and that it was fated to mate with them when they did. Each month, Harris would tell one of his fine young

To the eyes of a man of imagination,/nature is imagination itself.
— *William Blake*

devotees that his fairy realm counterpart had entered her body, and that she was his chosen spiritual mate. It was a powerful sexual mysticism; unfortunately, the rest of the world called it adultery, and rocked the place with scandals. One can still see the landscaping from the Japanese gardeners who joined Harris. Hewlett-Packard owns the place now.

He parked near the downtown freeway exit and smiled at the pretty woman on the bicycle, who immediately broke into a song about Jesus. Mercy on us all.

Look at this! He entered the second-hand shop. "How much for the die in the window?"

"With the bell and the blank sides? Three bucks."

"How 'bout a buck and a half?"

"Three. Firm. Interesting conversation piece for the window, even if I can't peddle it."

"Two-fifty."

"Three. Firm. Really."

"OK. Three."

"You know what it is?"

"Yeah. You?"

"Not really. I bought it as a favor from an old German woman, lives down the block."

"They use it in a very interesting gambling game called Schimmel, or Bell and Hammer. Do you have the other one? There are more dice, and cards. You bid for cards, which determine your roles, then you throw the dice, and different combinations mean different payoffs for different roles, and then everything changes, you get new roles, new payoffs, I forget the particulars."

The shopkeeper shrugged. "Play chess?"

"Yes."

Opening glass encased bookshelves, he removed a slim volume. "A first edition." He handed it to Mark.

"Two and three movers by Lloyd." Mark looked inside, saw that the book was in good shape and that $12.50 was the asking price. "This is very nice. But I'm not in the market."

"Tell you what. I'll let you have it for ten."

"Problems really aren't my specialty. Not even for seven-fifty."

"I couldn't do it for seven-fifty."

Casey Stengel once tried to catch a softball dropped from a helicopter. His

"Me neither." He wrapped the die in his handkerchief. "Thanks for the Schimmel bell. See you."

On to the library. And all through his time at the card catalog, combing the shelves, filling out the request cards, he danced a silent, flirtatious minuet of the eyes with a rosy-cheeked redhead in the biology section, pages of notes spread before her. All his life, he had had a yen for women in libraries. In a cerebral setting, the physical becomes irresistible. Also, he figured he was really more likely to meet a better or at least more compatible woman in a library than in a saloon. Ought to have singles libraries, with soups and salads, Bach and Mozart, Montaignes bound in morocco; place to sip, smoke, and seduce in a classical setting, noon to midnight. Chaucer's Salons, call them, franchise chain.

Back to Gumperstown. The bank. "What's my balance? I think I'm overdrawn." Foxes to the right of him, foxes to the left of him. Goddamn branch hires tellers the way restaurants hire waitresses. Sell some tit with the sausages to stimulate appetites, better tips, return trade. But a bank?

"You're not OD'd."

"I beg your pardon."

"You're not overdrawn. This is your balance." She passed him a slip of paper that read $126.23.

"Absolutely ridiculous, madam. I haven't had that much in there in months. Why do I give you my money to play with?"

The teller took it personally, counted his cash icily.

"Tom!"

"How are you doing? Have a cup of coffee with me."

Mark went with him, sped ahead to dodge a beer truck, the instinctive New Yorker in him responding to the challenge.

"You look a little tired, Tom." They slid into the stuffed vinyl seats of the luncheonette's booth.

"Metabolism's still fighting to adjust to my new job. Graveyard shift at the cannery. My Monday morning is everybody else's Friday night. No, just coffee."

"Same. What's new?"

"Still care?"

"Of course I do."

"Jim and Tom-Tom are up in Mendocino. United Stand meeting with county officials. They're trying to get the codes

buddies in the air dropped a grapefruit instead, and when it splattered all over him,

changed to allow individuals to build noncode houses and outhouses, if it's just for their own family's use. Governor's for it. Building and health code people claim outhouses and kerosene lamps are hazardous to the neighbors. United Stand says six American presidents were born in log cabins without structural engineers." He paused. "Hey, Mark. How have things been going? Really?."

"Really? Great. Could use a little more exercise. I was doing good on my bicycle, but I spaced out on it and stopped. I ought to cut down on cigarettes, and coffee, make a few other adjustments to the fine tuning. Could definitely stand getting laid more. But all in all, I've been fine."

* * * * *

Two hours back into his work, the phone rang. He, re-entering the tin-can, ignored it. Why risk tampering with it? He ought to take the damn thing off the hook again. What's-his-name's corollary. Murphy's Law -- states that if something *can* go wrong, it *will*. And what's-his-name's corollary to Murphy's Law is, if a system works, leave it alone. And his did. Tired and overtired as he was, a few minutes work rallied his energies, returned him to the interior centerland from which his best work issued. Like a king in chess, its value was the worth of the whole game, too costly to risk parading around on a busy board, far better castled away with a knight at the gate. The opportunity of internal order was only passing through, and vulnerable to invasions, so it was best used while he could.

Little can be done, however, if somebody simply opens the door and barges in. "Hello, Reb!"

Reb fell into the easy chair, beer-can in hand, and looked at his host with a ridiculous grin that seemed to say, send me away or let me sit, but please, don't ask me to explain myself. He mumbled something.

"What's that?"

"I said I didn't think I would be here long. Teddy says I ain't been here yet. I think I'm on the nerve of a vergeous breakdown. Teddy says I don't have it together enough to

Stengel thought it had busted his head open.

listen to the radio. But I think I pretty much got my feet on the ground, as far as my head is concerned. Of course, what if and who asked you and don't be too sure about it, you know what I mean?''

Mark ignored him. Next envelope. Let's see, a little mess, that's what it is. These are the kinds of areas that will give the most trouble and are potentially the richest -- very abstract, fragmentary, indistinct definitions, and so forth. This one's on the relationship between risk and safety in play. Intense play offers the maximum of thrills and challenge without exceeding the boundaries and venturing into real life. Sailing to Hawaii in a good boat is fun, but floating around on a life-preserver in the middle of the Pacific with nobody in sight is not. Death is not to be toyed with. Mystery lives in the mean, in the play between excitement and safety. Put the whole deal into the psychology box, for now. That's where most of the citations come from, and it's too boring for the arts.

Boredom! Cross reference it . . . no, put it *with* boredom, with that section in Kierkegaard about God creating Adam because he was bored and creating Eve from Adam because Adam was bored and creating their children because the couple was bored, and then they were bored *en famille,* and then *en masse,* and so on. Not at all outrageous. Essentially the motive of the Creator in the Hindu version. Cross reference it to that, which is in the hide-and-seek section. Boredom, yes, boredom at the poles of randomness and inevitability; interest is in the potential for intelligence sparking between the known patterns and the apparently unpatterned.

Broadcasting into the beer can, Reb called the play-by-play: ''It has to happen, so it could just as easily be this one as another. Right? It's close to happening, that's obvious, and this wouldn't be anything like the first time, that's obvious, although it's really hard to know just when it actually does happen since sometimes it seems afterwards that it has when it hasn't or it did when it didn't, and sometimes after it did it seemed like it didn't. I mean close, Charlie, but no cigar. And then there's this whole other level, of course, and from there it's the same thing, although then the question comes up about if it's the same thing, is that new level itself the same thing, if

As far as the laws of mathematics refer to reality, they are not certain; and as far as

you see what I mean, and so maybe that other level isn't really that at all, maybe it's the same as the others, only in mirror, maybe, in which case how can it speak for the others? But see then again maybe this whole thing is before the first level where there even *are* levels in the first place, if you get my point, and that would make the same thing, too, and then *that's* the same thing, and so's that and so's that, or did the levels get switched? I'm asking you? Did the levels get switched? I'm asking you, man, listen, I'm asking you." Reb struggled to express . . . "There's got to be a better way than this. Am I right?"

"I wouldn't be at all surprised."

Raising his head slowly, a strange smile of recognition now spread across Reb's face, as he looked around Mark's room. "Existentialism!" He pronounced it lengthily and cryptically. "Right? I knew this wino professor from Florida, steamer trunks filled with theories. Am I right?"

"I'm sworn to secrecy," Mark said. "What do you do?"

"What?" Reb shrugged. He squinted at Mark, recoiled when Mark fixed him with a stare. "I play the sitar," Reb lied. "I'm only nineteen," he lied again. He looked, now genuinely and openly, at Mark. "Hey, I'm asking you -- there's got to be a better way than this. Am I right?"

they are certain, they do not refer to reality.

— Albert Einstein

We Are Here
To Weep

9

Chinese chess

*"One way or another the no doubt mad idea
entered my mind that my own actions had
historical importance, and this (fantasy?)
made it appear that people who harmed me
were interfering with an important
experiment."*

— *Saul Bellow*

Mark slept late, and was astonished to find that Reb was
still outside his house the next morning. "Are you going to
Lido Grande?"

"What are you doing here?"

"Looking for a ride."

"Where did you sleep?"

"Over there."

"In the drainage ditch?"

"There ain't any water in it. Hardly."

"Oh, the humanity . . . Hey, I'm going into Lido Grande.
I'll drop you in the street over there, see which way you roll."

Mark stopped first at Crotchky's, to buy innumerable
prunes. He paused for the view, no less beautiful for being
familiar. Pebble Creek wriggled quietly through the gulch
below him. Twigs. A bird. Its call. The scratching of some
small animal. The patterns of the grain of the telephone pole
shone in the sun like the charged symbols of a totem pole. On
the hill across the Coastal Highway, Mark watched two pintos
suddenly sprint to the next fence north. There had been a
whistle, he half-remembered, having screened it out. See!
Reduction, again. The sculptor's chisel. See how basic it is to
consciousness, how before we can think about anything we
have to dismiss almost everything else. No one came for the
horses. The whistle was probably for a dog in another field.
But the whistle was the whistle of the pintos' authority, so they

103

stood, tall, proud and ridiculous at the north fence, waiting.

He drove, thinking, reversing that habitual reducing process is much of what traditional mysticism's about. Reinvesting significance in what we learn to screen out as infants. Staring at our fingerprints. Feeling the air going in and out of us as if by itself. Watching waves of unfocussed light. What just *being* amounted to. Reduction -- like trading pieces in chess when you're ahead -- to simplify and clarify.

"You're under arrest," said Reb. Mark kept driving.

And yet there was something new, too, some other kind of mysticism emerging in him. Gautama's exit line was -- all complex things are subject to simplification. This new vector was a Chardinesque inclination to subject all simple things to complexification. That was alchemy, the crystallization of the vaguely simple into minutely organized particulars, the revelation of the more active and detailed world embedded in the obvious one.

He left Reb off on the Lido Grande Bridge, both of them scowling at the puddle of gas floating on the river, spilled by a sloppy boatsman, suspending in its toxic slime all the dust and dirt that normally sank. Mark turned into town. A delivery man spat into the street through the open door of his panel truck. And with fitful chugs and belly laughter, Abruzio and Mimi and their brood burst out of the door of their peeling sedan and into the Food Co-op. In front of the Co-op, on display, Tom-Tom passionately plighted his troth to Lily. She was decked out as a vampy flapper, effervescent and flirtatious; wouldn't give him the time of day. Beside them stood Folva Thoolman, conspicuous only by her blatant indifference to Tom-Tom and Lily's little melodrama.

Mark bought a newspaper, went to Angela's. Again, she wasn't home. He should have called first. Of course, he hadn't been sure he wanted to see her when he had left his house. He let himself in. He waited. He made himself comfortable. He got bored. He left a note: "Dear Angela, In a display of *chutzpah* unparalleled since the departure of Brother Theodore's four-leggedism from the passing scene, I have eaten your food, drunk your coffee, smoked your pot, and, impatient with waiting, abandoned you for the Appolonian debaucheries of my desk and the lumpen gaucheries of tonight's Warrior-

. . . constructing artificial flowers . . . is work, while climbing the Mont Blanc

76er game. But I am hoping to see you tomorrow, or soon after. The Count of Twelve.''

Leaving Angela's lodge, Mark could not help but hear, from a few docks upriver, the family boarding *The Family Pride*: ''Get into the damn boat, Harry!''

''Phyllis bit me.''

''Leave him alone!''

''Just sit down and shut up.''

''Phyllis bit Michael now!''

''Jesus, Harriet, why don't you grab Phyllis or do something.''

''Don't tell me what to do, just do what I say! Does everybody hear that. I want everybody to shut up and nobody to do anything except exactly as I say. Harry, grab Michael by his throat, so he can't rock the boat.''

Daddy turned the engine over. Michael asked, ''Can I put my hands in the water?''

''No. Just shut up and watch the scenery. That's what we're paying all this money for, isn't it?''

Mark drove to Gumperstown, bought a bar-b-qued chicken to eat down by the riverside. His appetite was curbed in an instant when, leaving the grocery, he spotted Pearl -- with Tug. He felt seasick. Drove home. Lectured himself again that he should not be at all eager to involve himself again with Pearl; she had far too much of the chase-and-be-chased spirit in her to let him have his necessary peace. Chase the work now, he coached himself, and let damned Love find you if it can. Think how jealous you get about women. Be that jealous about your work. Women were not his career. And yet the warmth of the oven and the bed always beckoned.

The sight of the bebearded Saint Barnabas before him was so apt, at that moment, that Mark jammed too hard on his brakes, stopped short and rocked.

As Barnabas got in, he apologized, ''I'm sorry I made your car do that.''

''Think nothing of it,'' Mark replied.

''Where were you?'' Barnabas the Inquisitor.

''I went to see if a particular lady I knew was home.''

Barnabas did not approve. ''I am celibate, of course.

is only amusement.

— *Mark Twain*

Beyond celibacy, actually, for I have not merely transcended the *acts* of desire, but have torn out the very roots. At one time or another, I've tried everything. But only celibacy can harness the sexual energy, which is actually nothing more than a low-level vibration of Pure Spirit manifesting itself grossly on the material-animal level. Can you imagine using all that energy for spiritual growth, all the energy you squander by scattering your seeds to the winds?''

"I tend to scatter them into women more often than winds.''

The Saint raised his hand in a mudra and proclaimed, "The churnings of the profane mind are ceaseless, but the rightous man seeks the stillness within the turbulence, the Christ within the sinner.''

"Let me ask you a religious question,'' Mark replied. "Somebody I was talking to recently was telling me that Jesus actually wasn't the guy who was supposed to be The Man. It was supposed to be his unnatural brother Morrie. But when they told Morrie about it he said, 'Later for that trip, man. I got a nice gig dealing ouija boards to the gypsies. Ask *Jesse* to do it. He's getting burned out on that carpentry trip.' And so Jesse wound up doing it, and getting rubbed out in a grotesque gangland style torture-killing, while Morrie and his ouija board business prospered, and his descendants, to this very day, run a poor but honest frijole concession in El Paso.''

The Saint glared. "Just what is your trip?''

"Games. I'm into play and games. Chess, pin-the-tail-on-the-donkey, monkey-see-monkey-do, jump rope, Politica, that sort of thing.''

"Are you serious?'' Barnabas did a vaudevillian double-take. "You ought to see a shrink.''

Mark burst out laughing.

"Don't be defensive about it. Sometimes a professional like that can help you out of some real trouble. Let me tell you, man, if you don't think a grown man talking about jump rope ain't in real trouble, you're even crazier than I thought.''

"Hey, talk about crazy! Twenty years after Ty Cobb retired,'' Mark said, "an old catcher named Nig Clarke told Cobb his hands were so fast in his prime he could bring them down on a baserunner crossing the plate and trick the umpire

G. K. Chesterton has voiced the . . . opinion that the religion of the future will be

into calling the guy out. He told Cobb he must have done this to him a dozen times. And Cobb got so furious he grabbed Clarke's throat and had to be pulled off by three men, screaming at Clarke for cheating him out of twelve runs he had earned. This is *twenty years* after the man retired!''

"Why are you telling me all this? This is how lower order beings behave.''

"Well, that's not all. Blackburn once threw Steinitz through a *window* after dropping a chessgame. Nimzovitch once congratulated an opponent by jumping up and down on the chess table, screaming, 'Why must I lose to this idiot?!' ''

Barnabas' short fuse ignited a harsh little sermon: "The great Holy Game is not of this world, but beyond winning and losing. The more deeply you are fascinated with the lesser games, the more binding is the web of illusion the unholy demons weave you in. But when you truly understand that the best game is still only a dreary round of winning and losing, then you can cut away the roots of your lust to conquer.'' Thrilled with what had seemed to him to be surpassingly sublime eloquence, Barnabas drew himself up and inhaled the brisk river breeze deeply. "A bit chilly today, isn't it?''

"Chili today, hot tamale,'' Mark replied.

"Yes, I'm beginning to understand you, now, and you are in grave, grave trouble, my friend,'' Barnabas said. "Spiritually and psychologically, I assure you -- God is *deadly serious*.''

"I think heaven is filled with music, laughter, and dancing in the streets.''

"As the blessed St. Chrysostom taught, 'This world is not a theater, in which we can laugh; and we are not assembled together to burst into peals of laughter, but to weep for our sins!' ''

"Was God forced to create the world?'' Mark baited.

"Try not to be worse than merely stupid and trivially blasphemous.''

"Then He created the world freely?''

"God is free,'' Barnabas begrudged him. "All things He does, He does freely.''

"Then making our world, and life, and us -- all that was done *voluntarily*, by God. 'Meaningful but not necessary,' like

based, to a considerable extent, on a more highly developed sense of humor.
— Konrad Lorenz

play. Or like the grace of God -- it's meaningful but not essential, like a game God plays with us.''

"I assure you, my poor deluded man, that God is not playing with us. He is *deadly* serious.''

"He doesn't have to be. It would still be a wonder, don't you think? I mean, the greatest miracle is not how things are, or even why they are, but simply that they are.''

"Do you think it's all a joke?''

"No. No. Calling everything play is old wisdom but a little cheap. Prince Hal soliloquizes that he will play the role of the rogue in imitation of the sun, which permits the dark clouds 'to smother up his beauty from the world/That when he please again to be himself/Being wanted, he may be more wondered at.' Which is to say, to thicken the plot. Which is exactly how Sri Ramakrishna answered the question of why a benevolent deity would create evil -- to thicken the plot.''

Babbling briefly in tongues, Barnabas preached, ''The Lord is not a God of Confusion!''

"All creation is *maya*, make-believe sets and props for the elaborate hide-and-seek game, *lila*, all played by God the Cosmic Puppeteer, eternally losing Himself in the dazzling illusions of His creations, and eternally seeing through the illusions to rediscover His Original Self again. Faith itself is 'pointless but significant.' If you believe because of a reason, that's not faith. Faith believes for its own sake, a kind of holy make-believe.''

"Let me out of the car!'' Barnabas ordered. Without looking at Mark he tapped his Bible and preached, '' 'The foolish have no interest in seeking to understand, but prefer to display their wit.' ''

Mark called after the Saint, ''The whole history of religion is confusion. Did you know that Photius, the ninth century Patriarch of Constantinople, excommunicated the entire Roman Catholic Church?'' No, you don't know, and you don't care, Mark thought, driving on. You've got it together. You *know*. I'm the one who's struggling to make it all add up. My mysticism no longer explains everything. It's an indispensible instrument, but it isn't the whole orchestra.

Home, Mark did not drink coffee and did not try to work. He stared uncomprehendingly at a page of an excellent novel

(Heaven is) a commonwealth in which work is play and play is life.

— *G. B. Shaw*

about money called *JR*, by William Gaddis, but gave up, and closed his eyes. He hadn't caught up on his sleep yet. Take off your shoes and socks, at least, he urged himself, and did, and emptied his pockets and removed his belt before falling face down on the bed. Hide-and-seek, he thought through the darkness, it's the basic warp and woof, like work and women, insofar as anything namable is. Play peek-a-boo with an infant, you see how basic it is to the species. Most widely played children's game in the world. It's also the theme of initiation rituals -- the secret maskings in order to unmask, to intensify the drama of the masquerade, to thicken the plot. Like Roger Callois' category of games of vertigo -- skiing, flying, auto-racing, spinning around until you're dizzy, going to a bar, or a dance, or a fun-house hall of mirrors, or losing yourself in a book. I'm falling asleep, but now the question is am I falling asleep simply to fall asleep or in order to later wake up? Do I wake up in order to go to sleep? Do I have vertigo in order to later be sober, or am I really dizzy, and in danger of falling? Watch out!

Teetering, he finally lost his balance and fell, landing with a thud in the busy intersection in his marketplace of dreams, only barely avoiding a collision with a bewildered duck who was flapping his wings pathetically into the space around him, quacking, "Look at this thing. It ain't got a front and it ain't got a back. Slipperiest dang thing I ever seen."

A string of colored lights curved like space back onto itself, lighting the stage for a dapperly dressed brass band of a man, barking out his pitchman's line. And Mark, the dreamer of the dream, knew, without knowing how, that this was the man to whom he had to speak, and that his name was Bill Beauragard, who frequently posed as a southern gentleman on his way to San Francisco, but was actually a dealer of pentagonal dodecahedrons. Beside him crouched a middle-aged man in a loin-cloth and a large tooth and bone necklance. *Mr. Balungo!* was written in green grease pen across his hairy chest, into which was stuck like a knife, a button reading ANTARCTICA FOR THE ANTARCTICANS.

"But let me take this opportunity," Beauragard pitched, "to remind each of you that the Reverend Doctor Occupant of the Discordian Society has personally blessed a limited

There is no doubt that our body is a molded river.

— Novalis

number of prayer cloths, on sale at the end of the freak show for only $4.98. Each cloth has been exposed to at least four minutes of the Reverend Doctor Occupant's heavy duty biodegradable spiritual light, so each cloth contains within it the power to perform several small miracles, as well as dozens of blessings. Many people also like our Mellow Meditation Candles, made by the Candle Farm people under the super- vision of the Left Reverend Right Austin, K.G. POEE, spiritual slave and disciple of the Living Truth men call the Reverend Doctor Occupant. Only $1.97 a candle, each one good for twenty *deeply* meditative hours. Or you can get a prayer cloth and candle together at the low *low* price of $6.11, all monies going to maintain the inspired ministry of this great and humble servant of the democratically biodegradable."

"Aw, shaddup and let us into the show." It was the primitive, Balungo, shaking a menacing tomahawk at the dapper Beauragard.

"Go on in," drawled the pitchman. "You deserve it."

While the crowd followed Balungo into the show's tent, Beauragard, a golden toothpick dancing across his phosphor- escent teeth, beckoned for Mark to approach.

Angela, looking a bit like Michelle (the way she wore the scarf, perhaps), sat at a small table between the sideshow tent and a trailer, counting ticket stubs. She gestured to Mark to say nothing.

Beauragard leaned across her table and whispered to her, "Something's going on, pass it along, pass it all along, all along, all along the line." Nodding a see-you-in-a-bit goodbye to Angela, he led Mark into the trailer.

The man sat at a desk cluttered with bits of paper, and Mark, the dreamer of the dream, knew at once, again without hope of knowing how, that this was Pepe, the scribe, the mind that manned the vortex, caretaker of the basic grid, Mark's oldest soul. Disengaging his right hand from a coffee cup, Pepe displayed his consummate mastery of dactylology by moving his hand through the sign of the circle while his fingers flashed, in dizzying succession, the *V* for peace, the power-to-the-people fist, the index-finger Zen of Master Dju-dschi, the middle finger street zen, Shiva's fear-not mudra, and a bent pinky salute of inherently obscure

The Tao is that from which nothing deviates. That from which you can deviate

origins, and he intoned, with derision, "Be thou verified and certified as being relatively alive, in the eyes of Abraxis, and of Timshel, and of Complexified Interiorization, for all they're worth."

"Is it possible?" Mark asked.

"Don't be stupid. What could possibly not be possible?" Beauragard asked back.

"Elementary third-stream logic," added Pepe.

Mark, stupified, said, "I feel as though I have been here before, but . . ."

"Who knows where or when?" sang Pearl, appearing out of the shadows, dressed like a well-scrubbed cheerleader. She walked over to a pale young man who had been cowering in the shadows, and hung a sign around his emaciated neck that read, "I died for love," and under that, in smaller letters, "formerly possessed by anima." Mark realized that this was the Poemless Poet, Truly Broody, who no longer had enough life of his own to survive, and he evaporated like a snowflake in the sun.

Pepe, chronicler of the intergalactic conspiracy to invade light's shadow, twirled his mustachio, dotted the *i* in Urbino, and looked up at Mark. "What's Avogadro's number?"

"I don't remember."

"Hahaha!" mocked Balungo. Waving a menacing finger at Mark, Balungo warned, "You would be much better off confessing now. We'll get it out of you, sooner or later."

"Confess what? I don't even know what's going on."

"How quaint," Pepe commented.

"Devilishly clever of Balungo, I'd say," Beauragard admitted.

"This has to be part of the game," mumbled Mark.

"Don't be too sure, kid," Balungo said, "I'm gonna teach you things you thought you knew." And with that he pushed Mark through a door into an alley.

Five leather-jacketed punks emerged from behind the garbage cans and quickly cornered him. The short, crazy one wore razor blades in his shoetips and a thick chain for a belt. But it was the one who stood in the rear who scared Mark the most, and he was the one who spoke, telling Mark, "Now dig it, you bullshit dude -- I know for sure I told

is not the Tao.

— *The Ch'ung-yung*

you last time that if I ever caught you around here again I was going to punish you. Didn't I? Now I can't let my friends here think I'm not a man of my word. You can understand that. Can't you?"

A frightened kitten dashed through the silence that followed, knocking an ashcan cover to the alley floor.

And the main man, the demon with the final enforceable "I told you so" on the block, threw an empty oil drum at Mark's head.

As he sank rapidly into unconsciousness, Mark heard his voice moan, "I've got to get out of here."

MelloJohn strapped him into an electric chair. At the switches, Mr. Balungo, grinning maniacally, asked Mark if he wanted it AC or DC.

He came to, gasping for air and almost mad with profusion, crawling inch by inch to the statue of Our Blessed Lady of the Sarcophogus Mews. There was a lock on the door. "Damn it," he cursed bravely, and passed out.

Mozart stunned him back to a kind of intricate awareness that was, at best, a distant cousin of normalcy. The familiar scent of vegetable soup beckoned to him through a half-open door. "Sanctuary," he hoped, audibly, and staggered through the door, and into a nursery school.

The scale was wrong -- it was either a nursery for the children of giants, or he himself had shrunk to nursery school size, because the room, the toys, the adults, and the other children all seemed immense. Was he a child, then? He couldn't remember.

A green-eyed girl with long red braids was skipping around the fire-hydrant, chanting, "I know him. He's the creep that's got to find out the hard way!"

The hairy grandmother squatting backwards on the rhinocerous laughed so hard at the sight of Mark waddling dumbfoundedly about that she fell off into a fresh heap of rhino dung.

"See what you did?" Grud screamed, and hit Mark up side his head with a shovel.

Brakkle, who used to be his friend, poured Ovaltine in his hair.

"I have to get out of here," Mark repeated.

. . . *the most savage of our maladies is to despise our own being.*
— *Montaigne*

"Don't say we never warned you," taunted the red-headed girl, who grew taller with each passing minute.

Enter Pepe, disguised as a nineteenth century schoolmaster, black wool suit and rimless glasses. The children all ran to join him in the far corner of the room, the kid with the propeller beanie pinching Mark hard, repeating meanly, "Don't *ever* say we didn't warn you."

Pepe announced, "We're going to play Pass It Along. You all know the rules, by now. You just pass it along."

"Pass what along?" Mark asked.

"Pass it all along. All along the line."

"Do we pass that along, too?"

"Pass it *all* along, all along the line."

"Suppose the line itself is crooked?"

"Then say, 'The line itself is crooked.' Pass it along, all along, all along the line. Now let's begin the game itself," Pepe announced, and he leaned over to Mark, on his right, and whispered, "The commutative law of arithmetic holds that *a* plus *b* is equal to *b* plus *a*."

Mark nodded, leaned over to Grud, and whispered, "It doesn't matter if you add numbers forward or backward, the sum comes out the same. One plus three is the same as three plus one."

"What's the exception?"

"I don't think there is one. It's math."

"Listen, you," Grud growled impatiently, "did anybody ever prove that?"

"Yes, I'm sure it's been proved. Maybe not. Maybe it's axiomatic."

Grud smirked triumphantly. "That's how they prove things. By their exceptions. Didn't you ever hear about the exception that proves the rule?"

Mark turned back to Pepe to corroborate this, but Pepe was no longer there. Brakkle was. "Is there always an exception that proves the rule?"

"You're supposed to go that way," Brakkle barked.

"Maybe this is the exception that proves the rule," ventured Mark.

"I *hate* a wise ass," Brakkle snarled. "If there's any one thing I hate more than anything else in the world it's a wise

All men who say "Yes" lie.

— *Herman Melville*

ass. Don't ever say we never warned you!"

"Don't ever say that."

"Enough of this!" Mr. Balungo, Father of Nightmares, stood imperiously atop Pepe's desk and, pointing at Mark, commanded, "Confess! Be serious and confess!"

Before Mark could protest that he was in complete ignorance about everything, and therefore could confess nothing, the dozens of bumps and knots on Beauragard's gold-handled walking-stick transmogrified into piercing eyes. The eyes knew all of him, found everything, forgave nothing.

Mark tried to speak and explain himself, but he found that all he could say was, "I mean I was just I was only I was only I was just I was just only I was only I was only just I was only, you know, I was just, uh, I mean I was only . . ."

"And so although our poor dreamer again finds himself speechless," Pepe's gritty baritone announced, "It is of course an old story, confided to me by another Mark indistinguishable from this one, ages ago, and I have of course set it down ineradicably in blueblack in my book. And so, with your permission, I'll read it out for you in plain prose."

"Shoor, honey," Pearl, in costume as a 1920's floozy, encouraged. "Give it up, Pepe, give it all up."

Pepe read the confession aloud:

> *It is obvious to you, I'm sure, since it is even obvious to me, and I am an idiot, the very idiot in question, in fact, that my alleged quest to be a player of many games or whatever I am calling it these days is a fraud, an imposture that a poor loser of a man like myself finds necessary to cloak himself in. My play-work is nothing but the frivilous doodlings of a tenth-rate talent seeking to enrobe itself in a grandeur it has no hope of claiming.*
>
> *It seems that there is surely a sense in which this all appears very amusing to others, and let me assure you that I am every bit as much one of the others as anybody else, and that I, too, find it hilariously amusing.*

. . . a very modest man but then he has much to be modest about.
— *Winston Churchill*

The games, while not exactly a divine calling, was not a bad plan as bad plans go, since it did afford the hope of providing some expressions and channels for my life's fits of intensity and so forth, all in a way that made sense enough to myself to justify myself to myself. Which is to say that it really wasn't such a bad plan, as bad plans go, although if the present process of my disintegration continues unchecked, I will soon be down to one game. I hope it's an easy one.

To tell you the truth, if I many speak frankly, I was never much to begin with, so it is no surprise to discover that I will end as nothing.

What I mean to say, if I may speak freely, is that this is all posturing, which is plain to anyone who stops to consider, for even a moment, that I couldn't possibly have anything real to confess. Not even, as I have unsuccessfully tried to do here, my essential unreality, since even my unreality is not really felt.

I absolutely refuse, under any circumstances, however, to tell the truth. However, to tell the truth, if I may speak freely . . .

A knocking on a real door roused Mark from his deep dreaming sleep.

It was morning. Mark tried to raise himself up on his hands, fighting to surface, but a powerful undertow of tides native to dreams resisted and strained to return him to the sea, stop his inevitable return to the wake-a-day world. He tried to force his eyes open, but he had no eyes. He had no legs, and even if he did there was nothing beneath him to put them on. He tried to throw off the spell of sleep by shaking his head, but he had no head.

He found a leg, slung it off the bed, and it landed on the cold wood floor. He staggered to the door, and opened it.

No person had knocked. Maybe it was the wind. A breeze blew a bay leaf in, and he shut the door. He fell back on his bed, his mind leaping and stretching to reenter his dream, the intensity he had lost to answer the phantom knock. He couldn't do it, gave up, thought of the day that

What a pity I should have to go now just when I was beginning to show promise.
— Renoir, at 78, on his deathbed

dawning, contemplated caffeine.

* * * * *

He drank coffee. The Tour de France is 2,861 miles long. So what? The world's fast-talking record is held by a sportscaster of greyhound races. So what? The highest dropped baseball ever caught was caught by San Francisco Seal catcher Joe Sprinz, 1,000 feet in 1939 at the cost of four front teeth. So?

In the Japanese novel, *The Master of Go,* both contenders for the world championship get so strung out on tea that the frequency with which they urinate becomes one of the main topics of conversation for all the attendants and officials and reporters. Gin was named after the drink of the same name, and so was rummy, whereas canasta is simply Spanish for basket and refers to the card caddy used in the game. Interesting but so what?

In bridge, if the cards have to be distributed in a certain way for the hand to be made, you have to play the hand as though that's where they were. If they're not, you'll lose anyway; but if they are, you'll win. Conversely, if the contract is impregnable *except* if the cards are distributed one particular way, you plan the best play against *that* lay of the hand. If that's the way they are, you may win; and if not, you're a sure winner anyway. I know that already.

Now this, I like: A bridge partner once told George S. Kaufmann he was going to the bathroom; Kaufmann told him it would be the first time that afternoon he knew what he had in his hand. And there was Kaufmann's *Kibbitzer's Double,* which could be used only once in a *kibbitzer's* life, since he was immediately killed by the players. *Spoof* was originally the name of a Victorian card game. The one-eyed cards are the Jacks of Spades and Hearts, and the King of Diamonds. Diamonds.

King Olaf of Norway and King Olaf of Sweden met in 1020 A.D. to decide the ownership of the district of Hising, and agreed to throw the dice for it. The Swede threw two sixes and so did the Norwegian. Then the Swede threw

No honest poet can ever feel quite sure of the permanent value of what he has written.

another double-six. But on Olaf of Norway's last throw, he tossed one six and the other die split into two, totalling seven, giving him a winning thirteen. Empress Jito outlawed backgammon in seventh century Japan. Richard the Lion-Hearted forbade anyone below the rank of knight from playing the game for money. Bach once lost a wager that he could play correctly any organ work on sight. The score required him to play chords at both ends of the keyboard and a note in the middle. It was explained that the note in the middle was to be played with the nose.

Joe DiMaggio once played a couple of months with a throwing arm so sore that everyone in the league could have gotten away with running on him, had they known about it. Fortunately for the Yankees, DiMaggio had one good throw a day in the arm, and once each pregame warmup he would uncork a bullet from deep center to the plate. Nobody ever ran on him. Walter Hagen and Leo Diegel were once locked in a sudden-death playoff to decide a major golf championship, and Diegel needed to sink a winding, tricky little putt to stay even with Hagen. Diegel studied the green thoroughly, lined up the ball from several angles, studied the grass again, psyched himself up for the putt as much as he could, and when he took his position beside the ball, to make his stroke, Hagen knocked the ball away with his own putter, and said, "I'll give you that one, Leo." Shook up Diegel so bad, he hit his next tee shot into the woods.

Staunton said, of a chess game in the Labourdonnais-McDonnel match, "I cannot see how it is possible for either player to save his game," while Mason is credited with, "Steinitz has invented chess altogether, and Zukertort has invented 1. P-K4."

* * * * *

He woke gagging and gasping for breath, his room filled with smoke. The quilt had fallen off the loft, on to the electric heater, and up in smoke. "In life we are all duffers," said the great Lasker.

It was 4:30 in the morning, but since he was up and feeling far too depressed to go back to sleep, he took some

He may have wasted his time and messed up his life for nothing.

— *T. S. Eliot*

books and papers out to the kitchen table, where the smoke was thinner, and prepared for another session of study. He hated what he was doing -- the mechanisms of strategies in mathematically analyzable games. As the hours passed, and the day dawned and the cars of Lone Buck Bay began their morning duties, the floor surrounding the chair in which he had fixed himself was littered with game trees and charts of Grundy functions, notes on Nim and Kayles and other tedious games of arithmetic. It was mid-afternoon before he came across his old notes on Ovid's Game (so named because of its mention in *The Art of Love,* with a suggestion from the author that women learn the game, so they may be popular with men) which was like tic-tac-toe with movable pieces, or John Scarne's game of Teeko. As with checkers, first move was a disadvantage. Mark liked Ovid's Game, and his little elation at rediscovering a forgotten old favorite made him realize with a start that he had hated what he had been doing since returning from the print shop. It was all facts without truth. It was all mechanical -- the unfree antithesis of play.

He rose and shouted "Emulate Arjuna, conqueror of Sloth!" It did no good. He remembered a large, awkward man who worked a little hole-in-the-wall called The Times Chess club, down the block from Mary Bain's studio, later Larry Evans', who couldn't play chess worth a damn, but who could set up the pieces for the start of a game faster than anyone Mark had ever seen, with a move like a chef might make passing his hands over a salad to distribute the grated cheese.

He passed quickly to something else. Major categories of playspaces -- stadiums, arenas, tracks, courts, greens, courses, alleys, boards, which in turn subdivided into . . .

Yes, yes, you were unquestionably right. None of us was anything special.

*   *   *   *   *

Mark took a walk to clear his head and get his blood going, wondered if it was the weekend. He went down to the beach, sprinted barefoot on the sand. A dog, a big St.

Middle age is when you are sitting home alone on a Saturday night and the telephone

Bernard mix, joined Mark in his dash, the dog's tongue flapping clownishly out of the side of his jowly mouth. What's the game of pet and master, he wondered, panting.

He stopped to catch his breath, leaned over, dropped his head between his knees, rested his hands on his thighs. He was panting furiously, feeling cleansed, when a voice above him asked, "Are you OK?"

Mark looked up. He recognized a friend of Dieter's, but couldn't recall his name. "What day is it?" Mark asked.

"Saturday."

"Anything special going on tonight?"

"Yeah. There's a big benefit at the Lido Grande dance hall."

"I think I'll go to that, citizen. I think this is a night to sublimate the sublimation, and opt to fuck."

From the booth at Crotchky's, he called Angela.

"Hello."

"Hi. Want to go dancing?"

A long silence.

"Angela?"

"Mark -- let me ask you something. The last time you were by here, a week or two ago . . . Did you make it with Pearl, right afterwards?"

He felt it, a cloak as gloomy as his own. Who told her? The tactician in him sensed in her accusatory question a maneuver to trip the dialogue into the kind of heavy heart-to-heart exchange she had been angling for for months. The jujitsu of guilt. An apology would be insincere, and even if he did it ostensibly to be kind, it would not work out that way. It would not be enough for her. Sooner or later, it would come to his negation. Now that she had upped the ante, he decided it was time now to fold the hand he did not need to win. "Yes. It's true."

She said nothing. He was supposed to be the verbal one.

The post-mortems could only be about what went wrong. And nothing actually had. Perhaps he had been implicitly dishonest with her to begin with. Perhaps they both had. "Perhaps I had better say good-bye, Angela."

"Bye."

He went home and moped for an hour; but he was also

rings -- and you hope it isn't for you.

— Ring Lardner

relieved.

What about going out? he remembered. Saturday will pass, unless I do it now. One of the most substantial and least appreciated benefits of living with someone is not having to deal with the weekends, with who to be with when you need to be with someone. Well, get with it, before it's Sunday morning. Nobody does anything on Sunday morning.

Time to cash in my raincheck with Pearl.

You can discover more about a person in an hour of play than in a year of conversation.
                                                        — Plato

The Dancers

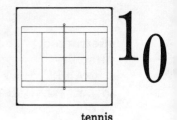

I think reality is for people who can't face drugs.

— Tom Waits

"Joanie called *here*, looking for me?"

"That's right." Pearl turned the back of her smooth bare shoulders to Mark, and said, "Zip me up. She said she tried getting you at Angela's, and Angela said you were probably over here. Did you tell Angela you were taking me to the dance, tonight?"

"No. I wish I were as obvious to myself as I am to everybody else." He brought the phone from between the potted plants on Pearl's windowsill to the kitchen table. "And she said it was urgent?"

"Yes. Do you want me to get you Joanie's number?"

"I know it." Mark dialed.

"You know Joanie's number by heart?"

"Pearl! Hi, Joanie. What's up?"

"We've had an offer from Weel -- $250,000 in thirty days, and we drop the court case."

"Just like that? Out of the blue? What about the gravel and harbor rights?"

"Not mentioned," said Joanie.

"Well, that makes three good reasons for not taking it -- the court will probably award us twice that much money, the court will probably come up with a better arrangement on the gravel and the bay . . ."

"Assuming our lawyers are guessing right," Joanie

121

interrupted. "That's still a chance. Weel's deal is faster and surer."

"And," Mark went on, "Weel hasn't offered us a penny, so far. Why, all of a sudden, is he so interested in making an offer?"

"To make a better deal than the court is expected to order? Or just to feel us out, for future negotiations?"

"Could be," said Mark.

"What do you think?"

"I can't imagine," Mark answered, nodded and mouthed "Thanks," to Pearl for the hot coffee, and told Joanie, "but I remember an old chess story about the great world's champion Emmanuel Lasker, and a game he played with the English master William Winter. Winter gave one particular move a lot of thought, and then moved a knight to where it could be captured by a pawn. But Lasker completely ignored the knight, and steered the game into other channels. After the game, one of the spectators asked Lasker what was wrong with taking the knight, and he said he didn't even think about it, because if a player as good as Winter thinks seriously about a move and then offers you a present, you can assume there's something wrong with taking it."

*   *   *   *   *

In between his long sessions of studying and writing, Mark had been going on bike rides and walks, taking pleasure in wallowing in the simple enjoyments of living in the country. Although he had been a city boy all his life, he had discovered that country living was more like a return to an ancestral home he had left as a child than a move into strange territory. The night before, during a rare California lightning storm, he went for a walk in the rain. The storm's flashes lit the groves of redwoods and ferns, burning gray-green, fading back to black by the time the thunder hit and the afterflash passed from his eyes. He got soaked. He loved it. He laughed. Shivered. Realized that if any official demanded to have an account of what he was doing out at night in a storm like this he'd have no fit reply. He loved

Without music life would be a mistake.

— Nietzsche

that. He laughed and shivered, and, when he began
sneezing, he went home.

* * * * *

Mark and Pearl arrived on time at the dance, which was
of course better than the first band did, and so they waited
in the food room passing the time with the spaghetti and
apple juice and the others who had beat the band there. The
fellow to Mark's right insisted on trying to tell him how his
truck needed a grease job and a new front end, but once
that was done he'd be able to cash in on a big stash of wood
he knew about, once he got his chainsaw fixed. The Lido
Grande plan.

Seating herself across the table and engaging both of
them in a quick exchange of gossip and pleasantries was
Martha -- plump, pretty-faced, earthy, watery, the fry-cook
at the spoon in Gumpers Corners.

From the big hall, the electric scream of an amplified
guitar signalled the band's arrival on stage. Mark's thoughts
drifted back to the last dance he had gone to with Pearl. The
ancient ethic of leaving with the fellow you went in with was
for Pearl, not inviolable, and any claim Mark might have
had upon her for that night's last dance faded before the
sight of her sewing machine repairman coupling with the
knowledge that hers was broken. Also circling her, that
night, was that demented young jock from the junior college
with whom she had gone to the beach, the day before. Not
to mention the band's equipment man, the one she was hot
for. She was in her element, happily at home at the vortex
of a whirl of men in various stages of infatuation and dance.
She actually expected Mark to change, and learn to accept
her as she was. "Pearl, would you like to dance?"

"I'm not feeling well tonight," she declined. Martha,
who had discreetly feigned deafness through this, smiled
pertly and accepted Mark's invitation. They pushed and
picked their way through the crowds in the hall and into the
gym where the country-rock band was beginning. The
band's reputation had preceded them into the area, so they

It is not a move, or even the best move, that you must seek, but a realizable plan.
— Znosko-Borovsky

knew if they impressed the benefit crowd they stood a good chance of winning some jobs on the local circuit. They played a long fast opener that got Mark and Martha loose and sweaty. Mark caught a glimpse of Pearl watching them from the sidelines. The band then tore into an accelerating hoedown, finishing up faster and faster.

All who survived it sought water or a seat. Mark headed for the cafeteria's promise of apple juice, where Pearl's most little-girl-lost voice met him and asked if he would take her home.

"How come?"

"When I'm not feeling good, scenes like this frighten me," she said. "And then you can dance with Martha."

"Oh." He went to get his jacket, but when he returned she was gone. He went outside and around the corner to his car, to see if she was waiting there, but she wasn't. And she wasn't back in the hall and she wasn't back out in the car when he checked again and she wasn't back in the hall. Somebody told him they saw her leave ten minutes ago.

OK? OK. Round Two.

Unhappily for Mark, her first name was Vivian, the grotesque and loquacious, whom he had successfully avoided since the big party at The Farmhouse, and before he could say, "Have you seen what's-her-name?" she stuck eight dollars in his hand to put in his wallet and hold for her, because she had no pockets, and backed him onto the dance floor.

Surrounded by lovelies as young and springlike as the night, he was dancing with Vivian, smiling at him like a coquettish orang-utang. In the middle of the second dance he split on her, headed for the apple juice.

Instead he found Salugi, offering him a small bottle of brandy. Although Mark rarely drank, he took it unhesitatingly. "Wow!" It went down like strong medicine. He grimaced.

"You like that, huh?" Salugi encouraged him, "Have another swig."

Mark took it. The drink burned like hot soup, and he had to open his mouth wide to cool it off. "How do you manage to drink that stuff, all the time?"

Man is the only animal that blushes. Or needs to.

— Mark Twain

"Hey, I wish I could afford to drink this stuff all the time." Salugi lifted his gangster-style hat and scratched his head. "Usually I'm stuck with port or burgundy. This here's a treat." Salugi laughed. "We'll get into the white port later. And beyond that, who knows?"

Mark shook his head. Instead of clearing, as he hoped, it rang like a bell. He stood up, waved to Salugi, and headed back onto the dance floor.

Fate's familiar clammy hand clamped his shoulder, with Vivian's unwelcome face on its tail end. "Are you trying to lose me?" she asked. And Mark cursed himself when he knew he couldn't summon a truthful "yes" to his voice. And so he let himself be led like a captured quarry to the dance floor. He was furious at himself for being unable to brush off Vivian in some way that was acceptable to his sense of compassion for her miserable luck with men, a luck he felt individually powerless to reverse.

Tom-Tom walked by, grumbling, "I ain't gonna listen to this decadent noise. I don't like being shouted at." He was still chasing Lily, and she had just told him in no uncertain terms that she would not dance with him, and that he was the last man in the room she wanted to be with.

Mark split on Vivian again at the end of the dance, heading again for the apple juice, since there really wasn't anyplace else to go, except outside. He found Martha again. Holding her hand, he called Pearl. "Hi. Are you OK?"

"I'm all right," she said. "Just tired, and not feeling much like crowds, tonight. Will you call me tomorrow?"

"Sure," said Mark. "Sleep well." Hands still clasped, Mark and Martha returned to the hall, ready to dance, and were a bit disappointed to discover that the stage was being set up for some kind of nonmusical demonstration or routine. A woman in blue jean overalls invited the audience to a variety show benefit for the Redwood Gay Coalition, featuring Botulistic Mucilage. A slide lit on the wall behind the stage, and it read, "Rock'n'roll Scientists!" The next band's manager carried a table on stage. Then he put a bowl of dry ice on the table. Then he went offstage and came back with a small acetylene hand torch, and then the lights went out, and the audience started to protest. A

If you have nothing to hide, show it; you have nothing to show, hide it.
—Tullah Hanley

direct white spot light blinded the man onstage, and then that went off and several colored spotlights aimed more or less at the stage went on and the man at the mike spun a stupid story about the creation of the Frankenstein monster of rock'n'roll, scrawled pseudoscientific equations on the blackboard behind him. The audience grew impatient, yelled at the stage, cursed the performer, who silenced them all by creating so much smoke with the torch and dry ice that everyone grew too concerned for the safety of the hall to hassle him. And then, over the speakers, came his voice again, "It's working! Here it comes! The Frankenstein monster of rock'n'roll." And, as the smoke cleared, the monster dragged himself like a lunatic to the electric piano and began banging spastically on the keyboard. And then he banged out a tolerably competent boogie, and then the rest of the band joined him, one by one. As a minute routine, it would have entertained the paying customers. But they had played it for six times that long, and had a disgruntled audience on their hands. Martha, Mark could see, was no longer sure she wanted to be with him. Earlier he had told her about Claudette's party, and she'd been interested in going there with him after the dance. Not that he was all that interested in her. He wasn't. But still, he would feel miffed if she left.

And she did, suddenly and swiftly.

Punctured, he also felt as though the letdown was somehow a necessary other-side-of-the-coin. He sat down on a bench. Martha had done no worse to him than he had done to Vivian, and perhaps no worse than he had done to Pearl, although he figured he still owed her a couple of dozen. He began to space out, watching the dancers, the beautiful women, the fond couples, the children running wild and the parents chasing them, the new romances, the old lovers, the atavistic and the reverent dancers, and Mark let up on his self-pitying as he perceived himself not simply as a losing player, but also as an integral element of this vast, generally happy tableau. And in his role as the pensive man, he was comforted by this depersonalized philosophy, and his pain was alleviated by distance and ab-

There are two things a real man likes -- danger and play; and he likes women because

straction. He thought again of the sad lonely lady Pearl was today, recalled Anais Nin's tale of the woman who had set her clothes on fire so she could feel something.

Sensing that he was backing himself into such a moody corner that he would put himself out of commission in real life for the rest of the evening if he continued to indulge himself in it, he turned abruptly to the young woman next to him. A beach bunny dropout if ever he saw one, her dyed blonde hair, now being pushed out by the native black underneath, an abrupt change marking the subcultural switch. Her athletic budding body dripped with sweat and she panted for air out the open window. Mark asked her if she would like to dance. She was very nice, she said no, but nicely, she said she had to stop and try to breathe. "But thanks."

He crossed the floor, realizing that the possibility of winding up the evening alone was far from unlikely now, within the realm of no more than mildly bad luck.

"You look like you could use another drink," Salugi said.

Mark joined him on the sidelines. He drank.

"See, I told you we'd be done with the brandy and into the white port long before the evening's through." Salugi took the bottle immediately, drank deeply, and passed it back to Mark. Salugi's gaunt, pale face glowed grotesquely in the blue light. "White port and lemon juice," he sang. "That's going back a long way. You remember that?"

"I remember, I remember." Old rock'n'roll was an irrational point of honor for Mark, who took another drink.

"You remember who did the original of 'The Mountain of Love'?"

"Johnny Rivers did it."

"He did the rerake," said Salugi, and when Mark shrugged, Salugi told him, "Dorsey Burnett." And then, with an air of bravado, Salugi finished off the remainder of the jug in one great chug-a-lug that left Mark staring at him with some indignation. The indignation melted into a smile when Salugi produced another pint of brandy.

The two of them began to laugh idiotically, and Mark began to suspect that he was drunk, and getting drunker.

she is the most dangerous of playthings.

— *Friedrich Nietzsche*

" 'Mountain of Love' ain't nothing," he said. He shook his head, took a long drink from the brandy that burned his throat, and handed the bottle back to Salugi. "Who did thy . . . see, I don't get drunk, anymore -- my words just get slurry."

Salugi laughed so hard he had to clamp his fingers on his nostrils to prevent the brandy from coming out his nose.

" 'Mountain of Love' ain't nothing," he went on. "Who did 'The Ship of Love,' 'The Treasure of Love,' 'The Book of Love,' 'The Chapel of Love,' and 'The Game of Love'?"

Salugi shook his head. He passed the bottle back to Mark. "I only know one of those. Let me tell you why I remember that one. I was driving down the freeway in my first car, a big old Bonneville with electric everythings, and suddenly this lunatic from the other side of the freeway jumps the divider and turns across my lane, broadside. Bam! I crash into it, going about seventy miles an hour, and my car spins three-quarters over. The other car slams into a pick-up truck that spins into a lamppost. And then, when all the crashing stopped, this incredibly calm voice comes over the car radio, and says, 'That was "The Sea of Love," by Phil Phillips.' But listen, man, I mean I don't want to pry or nothing, but weren't you with Martha, and with Vivian, too? And Pearl? Who are you with tonight?"

"I don't know," Mark mumbled, and took another swig. "Vivian, yeah, she was telling me about what she really wanted, and at the moment she wasn't even really, and if she had to do it all over again, and no matter what anybody says, and she did the only thing she could possibly have done under the circumstances, such as they were. You get the drift?"

"Hey man, I know, I know," said Salugi. "I know Vivian from a long time ago, I see through her completely, an old whore in a new dress."

Mark could no longer ignore the fact that he was drunk beyond immediate recall. The band started to experiment with painfully high decibel levels, and he began to black out, closing his eyes and fists. He sunk, he spun, he settled, and when he opened his eyes and fingers he found himself at the rites of a voodoo rock cult, drugged and drunken hippies

She wears her clothes as if they were thrown on her with a pitchfork.
                                                    — Jonathan Swift

worshipping their bizarre multi-colored gods. Revolution and fornication in the streets, now that there are no horses left to frighten. Salugi had vanished. "All alonely and drunk," he said. "But this is a Home Square," he reassured himself. "See!" he pointed to nothing, "It says, 'Safe.' "

Here came Vivian.

"Wrong again, turkey!" he cursed himself. Through the liquid prisms of the alcohol, she looked even worse than before.

"Where did you go?" Vivian demanded.

It took him a minute to make sense of her words. When he did, he felt seasick. The music stung him, personally, and whistled away. The bench was tipping over, or he was.

"Are you drunk?" she asked.

An opening! one of Mark's instinctive game-playing selves realized. A chance to be declared temporarily out of the game. Her game, anyway. I need a role, a character even more drunker than I am, far too drunk to be held accountable. "Whirtemurp?"

"What?"

Mark raised his head, just a bit, and slurred, "No soap, radio. And you know what else, when they took the gold screw out of his belly-button his ass fell off and he said, 'No, she's not dead, my good man, she's British.' "

Vivian looked critically at him, and commented, "You get really kinky when you get drunk." She leaned back, to try to see him from a deeper persepective. "Drink some coffee. You look awful," she said, and left.

"Thank God," said Mark.

"Want some more brandy?"

"Salugi! Where were you?"

"Hiding, until I saw whether or not you were going to be able to ditch the witch. You look a little weird. Are you all right?"

"I'm not in a physician to say." Mark thought that was extremely funny, himself, and went into a paroxysm of his own private laughter.

Salugi was so drunk he was dribbling saliva all over himself. He was able to remain seated, without falling over, only by weaving back and forth. Overcoming great obstacles,

He said, "Dig Infinity!" And they dug It!

— Lord Buckley

he succeeded in passing the bottle to Mark.

"No more, Salugi. I'm still hoping to pick up some nice lady, tonight."

Salugi gave no sign that he had heard.

Mark continued, "You see, getting drunk, it's like spinning around to get dizzy like a little kid. Right? Or a whirling dervish." Mark did a small dervish whirl, to demonstrate. "You know what I'm talking about?" Salugi stared with red and vacant eyes into a dim apparition in the middle distance, and Mark went on, "Like a test, just to see if we can do it. You know what I mean? Or is this just my own weirdness?" Mark worried to himself for a few minutes. "What do you think? Is the joy of getting drunk in the challenge of executing? Or would you say that the state of being smashed is in itself the end of getting drunk? You know, like a kind of quasi-mystical experience. Huh?"

"What?"

"What do you think?"

"I think you need another drink."

Mark stood, did three fast knee-bends. He almost blacked out. "Whoah! We're going to have to *ease* back into functional consciousness."

"One more for the road?" Salugi offered.

"The third from the last one was my one more," said Mark. "Maybe in my old age I'll take up serious drinking. 'If die I must, let me die drinking in an inn.' Walter Map, you know, the twelfth century author of the classic *De Nugis Curialium.*"

"See!" said Salugi, vindicated by obscurity.

Mark swam through the dark air, quickly discovered he was still too drunk to hazard the dance floor. Another sideline bench. There's one. Made it. He took some deep breaths. Blonde hair to his left. She turned. Very cute. Very young, too -- high school, or college freshman. So? She's noticed me. She's getting up! She's dancing, right over there. Maybe she wants me to join her.

OK, Jack, Mark called to himself, get in gear and see if you can make this act work. He followed her, trying to ignore the sensations of the liquor, of the weights on his back, his dislocated thigh, the buzzing in his ears which may

What is immobile must suffer violence.

— Lasker

or may not have actually been coming through the amplifiers, and the feeling that his face was twisted into a Quasimodo-like grimace. She stopped dancing and smiled at him. Mark smiled dumbly back. She joined a group of four other girls, her friends. Mark wished he weren't as drunk as he was. He walked over to the group of girls.

And one of them seemed to light up, when he looked at her, and he was unable to take his eyes off her. The blonde he had followed was forgotten, and Mark was drunk and enchanted with this dark, black-haired nymph. She knew he was staring at her, avoided his eyes. Hers were black diamonds. She was the sun. The song ended, and when the next began he asked this goddess to dance with him. And she did, praise God, he thought, Who is above us all, and a strict neutral in all these proceedings. It was a good tune that went both fast and slow, so they danced apart and then together. He pressed her to him. She tensed and then surprised him by relaxing against him. He thought she was the most beautiful woman there. It no longer mattered much that he was drunk. If anything, it helped make his dancing freer. He began to enjoy all the liquor in him.

What am I doing here? Am I crazy? I'm chasing high-school girls. I'm thirty years old. Of course, I never did near enough of it then. Hey, you don't do that much of it now, chump. Carry on.

But there was Martha, again, smiling and waving. Martha had realized that this was the last set and the evening was now even older than they were. He nodded to the beauty at the song's end, consoling himself with the thought that she was no goddess but just another local piece of silliness.

Martha gigled a girlish ''hello'' to his approach.

''You have one of three choices,'' he put it to her. ''You go to Claudette's party and I stay here, or I go and you stay, or we go there together now and I take you home afterwards.''

''Let's do that one,'' she agreed. ''You smell like a distillery. I have to get my shoes. They're on the other side of the hall.''

He started to follow, then turned to the beauty he was

He was a fiddler, and consequently a rogue.

— *Jonathan Swift*

132

leaving for this round fry-cook. What a face! And look how she holds herself. "Thanks a lot for the dance, ma'am. I enjoyed it very much." She looked puzzled, not so quick to understand that he was saying good-night, and probably good-bye.

He told himself that if he saw her, ever again, he would speak to her, and find out if this was, as he suspected, in spite of his intoxication, only a pretty idiot. Maybe he was the idiot.

Mark and Martha drove to Claudette's chatting more like old friends than lovers-to-be, for they had been and would be friends longer, and they arrived at Claudette's charged enough to recharge the whole party. There were still a dozen or so guests left, along with a like number of emptied wine bottles, many more cigarette butts, and a few scattered record jackets. The very pretty Jane was there, and Mark was sorry at once that he had brought Martha. He and Jane talked, her companion too drunk to join in. And what about Claudette's new roommate Sandy, a roman candle of a short, well-stacked Jewish girl from the Bronx?

Joanie's wuzband, Mitch, posed a puzzle: "Three sailors and a prostitute have only two condoms among the four of them. How can all three sailors fuck the prostitute prophylactically?"

"Come on," jeered Sandy, a priestess of parties, scolding an heretical interloper.

Mark winked at her. "Everybody likes what they're good at."

"What's a crandum?" Jane's escort asked as he sank into Phase IV drunkeness.

"Here: You put crandum #1 inside crandum #2 and give it to sailor A to fuck prostitute P," Mark began. "Remove #1 and let B fuck P with #2. And then turn #1 inside-out and put it back inside #2 for C and P. Right?"

"Absolutely," Mitch said.

"Back up a bit," mumbled Jane's friend. "I came in a little late. What's a crandum?"

"Windowsill carpeting," explained Mark. "Eightpence to the nautical mile." He whispered to Martha, "Who's he?"

compu   forgiuve   me   anbd   bless   this   umble   galley

"Don't ask me," she answered. "My family don't go back that far."

Dieter showed up unexpectedly, called Tom, Dorothy, and Mark into an urgent huddle. "Listen carefully -- a small-time punk from San Francisco has been picked up on a murder-two charge in San Diego, and he's turned state's evidence in the Lone Buck Bay arson case."

"Incredible. What did he say?"

"There's a warrant out on Johnny Carmody."

"Can they get Weel, too?"

"Probably not. Unless Carmody fingers him."

"Weel must have gotten wind of this before, and that's what motivated his offer," said Mark, fighting the alcoholic feeling that his mouth was stuffed with cotton and alum. "What was decided on that?"

"You mean Weel's deal this morning?" said Tom. "We all turned it down. First unanimous vote we've had on something important in months."

"Where's Carmody?"

"Nobody knows."

"They haven't caught him?" Mark asked.

"No. We figure he's been given a fast car and a bankroll," said Dieter. "I'm going to try and find Joanie and Charlie," he went on, "but listen, I don't think we should be too free in spreading this around."

"That ought to prove conclusive in the civil case, if it wasn't already won," said Tom. "Hey, what's with you and Martha? Is that going anywhere?"

"Not really. But I'm not looking for anything heavy, right now. Something lightweight and part-time would suit me better. I wasn't thinking of Martha, though. Maybe Barbara."

"Barbara who? Space-Barbara?"

"Yeah."

"Shit."

"Don't give me none of your lip, man. First of all, space-Barbara is a foxy lady, even if. And secondly, I don't get on your case about you and Dorothy, and that's supposed to be for real."

"Well, tonight's the night."

The light at the end of the tunnel might be a train.
— Arkansas football coach Lou Holtz

"Yeah? Can I watch?"

"You can play me a game of chess before I make the big move. You look so totally bloodshot tonight I might have a chance."

Back in the midst of the party, they set up the chess-game. Tom told Mark how he intended to handle the Courier's editorial stance regarding the O'Brien brothers who had the burl shop. The brothers had recently been arrested on a pot bust. They were set up for it by a woman from one of the free advertising tabloids. She began by selling them an ad subscription and ended setting up a sale for her alleged old man. He turned out to be one of the county narcs. "These guys don't normally deal. But she pestered them so much they got her a couple of pounds, to get her off their backs. And why did they zero in on the O'Briens? They're making a go of a legitimate business, here. You'd think the DA would at least recommend probation, but no, he wants *years* out of them for this bullshit."

A half-dozen moves into a Boleslavsky variation of the Sicilian Defense, Tom was in deep trouble, and getting deeper.

Dorothy floated by.

"It's your move. You have a bishop under attack."

Tom mechanically retreated the bishop. Then, "I resign."

"Just like that?"

"Just like that," and Tom put on his jacket and followed Dorothy through the far door.

They overlooked the river. A bullfrog belched his bloated song. A moth shone, like mother-of-pearl, in the streetlamp, and fluttered low over the trillium and oxalis. The winds whooed and the redwoods groaned and crackled, while mosaics of milk white moonlight spread on the grove's graygreen carpet, blinking and rearranging the cool spots and splashes that freckled the forest's floor. And this time, for the first time, they found the ways to say what they had both been trying for so long to say.

"Someday we will be old lovers, and know each other inside out. Can you see that far into it?" Dorothy whispered.

There are two classes of men; those who are content to yield to circumstances, and

Someone downtown yelled, "Two o'clock! Two o'clock and all's well."

"This ain't bad," Tom said.

They were both crying, glad and relieved. The streetlamps lit bright beads on the dark river's face, and they warped and broke when whirlpools spun through them on their way west, to the sea. "Can you imagine knowing the world itself like an old lover?"

From a porch on a hill above them, Mrs. Mimi Wemmenlime watched the whole town of Lido Grande spread out below her like a map of the last ten years of her life, and each house, cabin, downstairs apartment, the people who passed through them and their stories were all a part of her. And it seemed that her life had been shared with so many people over so many years that she herself was no longer contained just within her own flesh, but was by now woven into the world's body, and it seemed to her that this expanded mortality was the closest she could come to immortality. Her lover, who was fifteen years younger than she was, said he wished they were both young again for just one night, drinking and laughing in that rowdy bar they could see from the porch, "One more taste of Springtime in Babylon." But Mrs. Wemmenlime thought to herself that she had had taverns and drunken laughter enough, in her time, whereas this autumnal ripeness the winter's fogs had brought was brand new, deeper and dearer. She said nothing to him, for he was not like her, and would not understand. She hugged him when he said, again, "Just one night to be young together with you, nervous and silly and drunk in that bar down there."

"Two o'clock!" came the voice from the street. "Two o'clock and all's well."

Inside the bar sat a boy and a girl, all drunk and silly and nervous, excited and horny. He made faces at her and she laughed hysterically. She threw her arms around him and giggled. "Teddy bear." And she kissed him continuously until he had to push her away and cry, "Woman, you'll suffocate me like that!"

Outside, a voice cried, "Two o'clock! Two o'clock and all's well."

who play whist; those who aim to control circumstances, and who play chess.
— Mortimer Collins

The lassie curled up next to the laddie, and he rubbed her back with his caring hands, and held her high firm breasts, and he said, "Sure wish I had my truck here."

"Why?"

"Because it has my bed in it. It's at my mechanic's, though."

"We can go to my house."

Neither of them knew that at that very moment his mechanic and his mechanic's wife were in that very bed in that very truck. She had come out of the house to see how late he'd be working, and what with the moods of the night and one thing and another, they decided that the truck's owner would unquestionably extend the hospitalities of his bed to them if he were asked. The spontaneity of the occasion helped make the usually good sex between the well-wed couple even better. But afterwards, as they lay quietly together, the mechanic became uncharacteristically self-conscious about his garage's smells of oil and gas, and the omnipresent dirt and grime, and he told his wife he wished they were away from all the cars, somewhere clean, sitting on some hill overlooking the town. "I like it just fine, here, with you," she told him. "Somewhere out in the fresh wind," he said.

Across the bend in the river and hundreds of feet above it, Grool and Amy Greco looked down at a Saturday night town from a moonlit meadow on a hilltop. The wind was brisk on the hillside and Amy's long hair blew all over them. Grool peeled the strands from her face. "Think what it must be like to be the wind," said Grool. "To be able to blow all over the world like that." She laughed and laid her head in his lap. Seeing the town sideways from above, she said, "Look at that!" Grool looked, rightside up, and tonight he was as alert to its details as Mrs. Wemmenlime. He saw the couple watching the river from a rock on its shore, although he couldn't make out who they were; he saw the people leaving the noisy bar, now closing; he saw two shadows on an orange-lit porch on the hill across the river; and he saw a couple strutting like royalty down Main Street, and heard one of them call into the night, his voice echoing up and down the river's valley, "Two o'clock! Two o'clock and all's

We do feel, in our most valued musical experiences, that we are making contact

well." Grool drank it all in like a liquor, and told his lover, "Oh, Amy -- think what it must be like to be a *person*."

"Go on," she laughed. "We *are* persons."

"Two o'clock! Two o'clock and all's well," yelled EZ Beazly into the small town's streets.

Folva Thoolman rammed a sobering elbow into his bebrandied belly and ordered, "Keep your damn voice down, you idiot. Don't you realize it's two o'clock?"

with a great spirit, and not simply with a prodigious musical faculty.
— J. W. N. Sullivan

Never So Again As Much In Love

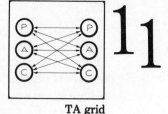

TA grid

11

Mark returned to work with enthusiasm. He reread Freud's essay, "Creative Writers and Daydreaming," which likens the creative writer to the daydreaming child in the sense that both imaginatively rearrange their worlds to create a make-believe one which is better tailored to their ego than the real world. The writer, however, modifies his fantasies with enough formal aesthetic elements to prevent them from sounding too self-centered and presumptuous. His old notes on Freud directed him to Freud on the playfulness of free association, which allows repressed material to surface. And play as the repetition of pleasurable experiences. And Freud's very interesting writings on repetitious play as a method of stabilizing disturbing situations. All this led Mark to Erik Erikson, and his ideas on play as the child's way of mastering skills without being penalized while he learns. Erikson generalized that idea to include the concept of play as the medium by which the child uses his limited mastery over some things to *imagine* he is master of his world -- the way I *play* chess. Through play, the child recovers the sense that he is able to do something, to act effectively. Other notes on Erikson made Mark realize he had lost one of his source books. He called Larry, to see if he had it. Larry told him he had not untied his psychology books, but would look for it.

Mark reread George Herbert Meade's *Mind, Self, and Society,* in which Meade makes the important distinction between playing play and playing games. Playing games, for Meade, serves the socializing function that 'imitation' has for Jean Piaget. That led Mark back into Piaget and his delight at rediscovering that for Piaget play is the opposite of imitation -- through imitation, the child learns to conform to society, but through play he affirms his own experience, what Buhler calls the child's pleasure in "being a cause."

Mark wrote and studied all week, and into the next. He reviewed Goffman's social-psychology of life-as-drama -- we are the performers enacting the characters we have created. To Goffman, we spend our lifetimes "training for a part." This led Mark into digressions on the ideas of will and intentionality, the question of how man makes real what he at first only imagines.

Mark read and wrote until he was too weary to think, and then he typed his longhand notes. His files of typed notes were his artificial memory banks, his extrasomatic storage units for information too important to be trusted to mere memory.

Two weeks into his happy, monastic retreat, Mark put his phone back on its cradle, and called Peterson.

"Where the hell have you been?" his employer yelled. "I'm swamped here. And I've already farmed out all the quick and dirty work. Get the hell down here!"

* * * * *

The work was routine. His fingers did it, along with his eyes. His manual adroitness at the press reminded him of his grandmother's facility with bingo cards -- she could play two dozen at once. As a child, Mark had accompanied her, a few times, to the big games at Rockaway. Like all great athletes or games players, his grandmother would permit no distractions during the contest itself -- any intruding words from Mark were dismissed with a no-nonsense "Shah!" The caller would announce, "B7," and his grandmother's fingers (like his own, now, putting on blank sheets and taking

The only reason we have a culture is that some men have retired from the world

printed ones from the guides on the packing of the moving press) would scan the columns, and drop her red plastic discs on the appropriate squares.

Peterson's estimation that he had loads of work had been exaggerated by his mild sense of panic at the rush of jobs. After three twelve-hour days, Mark had caught up.

Without thinking too much about it beforehand, Mark drove to Pearl's, but abruptly changed his mind, at the last minute, and drove past her house with a cry of "Emulate Arjuna, the Unsleeping and Indefatigable Conqueror of Sloth!" He drove home, spent a week with Eric Berne's games of transactional analysis. For Berne, "Every game is basically dishonest . . . " because there is a concealed angling for the payoff. The personal goal becomes the state of gamelessness, which is arrived at by mastering the no-game game. Some of the games themselves were interesting, to Mark, and he felt that the Parent-Adult-Child matrix was definitely worth looking into further. He delved into Jay Haley's writings on psychoanalysis as a game of one-upsmanship.

Gregory Bateson's ideas on play held special interest for Mark. Bateson perceives play as activity whose significance is modified by a conceptual frame that alters the nature of the activity it contains. To Bateson, schizophrenia is the breakdown of the metacommunicative frames, the distinctions between symbolic and concrete, play and reality. Bateson therefore talks about psychotherapy as the play activity that plays with the rules of play, the rules governing the contextual frames. And then on to the writings of Thomas Szasz. In a particular chess game, or dance contest, or tennis match -- will you play, first of all, to win, or to appear to be a gentleman? How do you decide? By meta-games, Szasz says. But then, how do you decide how you will decide, and so forth? Yes, well, we'll leave that problem to Reb.

Mark called Peterson, and asked for work. He went in the next day, and worked for four more. He enjoyed it. He felt clear, unburdened, and at peace with himself.

Home again, Mark found, on his kitchen table, a book by Erik Erikson with a note from Larry reminding him of his

of action to play games with ideas, to set them in motion and see where they go.
— Douglas Stewart

weeks-old request. Next to the book was a white shoebox fastened with a brilliant blue ribbon tied onto an even more brilliantly fanciful bow; and a note on a torn half of an envelope (Larry had retrieved it from the paper-to-burn bag, and opened it along one glued seam and one folded crease into a scalene trapezoid) which read: "Dear Mark -- two unordinarily pretty women brought this box, and the taller and even more uncommonly of them said to please tell you that she, Pearl, brought this for you. I said I would, and told them that you were working at Peterson's today. So then the taller one again reminded me to tell you that Pearl brought it by, because she had hoped to see you and didn't put a note in the box. Larry. PS -- Pearl said to tell you, please, that it was she who brought the box by, and I assured her I would."

"Yea, swore it on Agamotto's mother's last good eye," Mark muttered. Pearl's box's bow yielded to his first tug, beneath which snuggled chicken prepared his favorite way, albeit cold, a miniature of brandy, a mustardy but nonetheless smashing little cup of potato salad, and one little cherry tart.

He called, assuring himself, as he dialed, that the progress of his work was strong enough to weather any tempest Pearl might stir up.

"Hello."

"Hi."

"Mark!"

"Yeah. Want to go to the movies tonight?"

"I'd love to."

"Great. I'll pick you up at six."

*   *   *   *   *

" . . . so, see, it's gotten so bad I'm afraid to go into the bathroom with a cigarette by now, because I have to fight so hard with myself not to burn a hole in my cock. I wonder what it would smell like, burning?"

Pearl covered her ears. "Reb! I don't want to hear any more of this."

If White plays differently, he merely loses differently.

— *Weaver Adams*

"It's getting so bad that the last time I decided not to light one so I wouldn't be tempted, and I couldn't even get my zipper unzipped, I couldn't believe it, I couldn't get my zipper undone and I knew the only way I could do it was to light up a cigarette, and then after I lit one and took it out, you know, I touched the match to my cock, as a kind of a penalty."

"I'm not going to listen any more."

"It didn't burn that much, because it had cooled down while I was doing all those other things, but . . . who's that?"

"It's probably Mark. You have to get out of here."

Reb abruptly stood up, headed for Pearl's bedroom,then turned and headed for the front door. He opened it and passed Mark without looking at him.

"Hi. Bye. What is this? You and Reb have a regular thing going?"

"He has to stop coming over here. He has problems you wouldn't believe. I'm really sorry for him, but he has to stop telling them to me. I can't handle it." She reached for a soft, silken fabric, silver and blue diamonds, and wrapped it snugly around her bosom and her hips, like a sari. "Isn't this fine?"

Mark heard little, his attention on Pearl's face and form.

She wore a clinging green blouse that flaunted what she had no reason to hide, and a big, bulky country-style skirt, of yellow and the same green as her blouse. Why was he seeing her again? Was it just to undo her rejection? All ego, and no love in it at all? He felt his loins fill with what Joyce called *love*. That was not ego. Lust, at least. And what was that? What's this genital power by which she literally has me by the balls? The smells of this woman's house, not to mention her body, make my blood race.

Smooth as satin, her blouse clung to her breasts and he caressed them. "This blouse is nice and cuddly."

"Shall I take it off and leave the two of you alone?"

"Naw, it wouldn't be the same without you."

She spun away with a giggle, while she told of a friend of a friend who was a milliner who knew a milliner who had

In life we are all duffers.

— Emanuel Lasker

a customer complain about the price tag on a ribbon hat, "It's only a piece of ribbon," so the friend of the friend of the friend unravelled the hat and held out the ribbon to the customer saying, "The ribbon is only ten cents."

He couldn't take his eyes off her.

"Why did you stop coming around?"

"Because it seemed senseless."

"Does everything have to make sense?"

"And because I cared, and didn't want to have to deal with seeing you with somebody else."

"Oh. And now you don't care as much?"

"I haven't thought about it much."

"You always . . . " She stopped. "You still haven't said why you came by this time."

"It's different now. Let's just go."

"Where?"

"Out."

She wrapped a green and brown shawl around her, locked the door behind her. "What's that?" she yelled indignantly. "Get off my arm, rosebush!" She wrenched it off, and smiled pertly as she got into the car. "Where are we going? See the way I trust you, I don't even know where you're taking me."

"A French movie, 'And Now My Love.' A beautiful story of love at first sight, traced back three generations."

Pearl took it all personally, and blushed.

"The lovers don't meet until the very end." Mark added.

After the movie they drove to an all night place for coffee and pastry nobody should have bothered to bake, sell or eat. They shared the newspaper, as was their custom. He had always been a newspaper reader, out of an arrogant sense that if people like him did not keep up, who would and what would become of us all. Well, what has? She, on the other hand, had been converted during the Watergate scandal, which had the soap opera appeal of illicit and tawdry details revealed, step by step, in serials. Someone once described Watergate as heroin, and when it was finished we were all hooked on the methadone of gossip.

"Oh, this is wild." she cried. "This dude in Argentina flipped out because his father-in-law served him a lamb

To become mature is to recover that sense of seriousness which one had as a child at

dinner, and then told him, after he had eaten it, that it wasn't lamb, it was *dog*, so the guy strangles forty chickens, kills nine mules and three cows, breaks 1200 eggs, and then burns down the farmhouse.''

"What did they do to him?''

"Let's see . . . they haven't found him yet.''

"Did you see the one a few days ago where this Japanese guy killed a woman and then killed himself by biting off his own tongue.''

"Ooh.'' Pearl put her hand to her mouth, as though the thought of that had somehow wounded her tongue. "I don't believe this world. It doesn't believe in me either, so we're even. I definitely don't believe this place. Look at it.''

Mark scanned it, then whispered to her, "What we got to get is some of that plastic-eating bacteria, and let it loose on these restaurants all over the state. What would be left?''

"If they ate all the plastic? The paper packages of sugar,'' she demonstrated, holding one aloft like an insect she loathed. "And the phony milk, the glass salt and pepper shakers, a couple of the waitresses.''

"Not ours, ours would go with the plastic. You know what? I still like just being with you.'' They were words repeated from a year ago, last spring.

She remembered, said softly, "You still do?''

"Yeah.''

"I still do, too.''

* * * * *

He left early in the morning, before they started a new spring day together. This was Mark's season as a Puritan -- although he was working on play, he could not work by playing. He took time enough to listen to the splashing of the hillside stream that slid past Pearl's house, given a little life by the rains of yesterday and refreshed by the early-morning shower. Puddles of all sizes and shapes mottled the road, and tiny rivulets meandered through the trees and weeds to meet the stream, and the stream ran to a pipe that took it under the road, into the river, to the river's mouth at Jenner, to the Pacific.

play.   *— Nietzsche*

Mark stopped to pick up a turkey and swiss sandwich and some yogurt, both of which he stuck in the refrigerator, back home, and he went to his desk to work. Instead he fell into a long and pleasant reverie about Pearl, his cockles warmed in a way he had missed too long. Do one thing, he ordered himself. To prove you can concentrate if you want to. Reactivate something from the old notes, update the cross references, understand it again, send some fresh current through the old cells, see if anything new lights up.

What's this? An exchange of articles, this'll do, an article and a reply, actually, from the mid-forties, as I am. Article in *American Naturalist #785*, by F. A. Beach. His premise is that you can analyze play behavior just as you can mating or any other specific behavior. He mentions Schiller's theory that play is a release of surplus emotional or mental energies, but concludes that this theory presupposes the existence of energies we know so little about it is useless to base even more elaborate theories on their unknown natures.

Beach disputes the widely used definition of play as *non-utilitarian behavior* by pointing out that labeling an activity as 'purposeless' is often no more than an admission that its purpose is not understood. He mentions the fish that seemed to play by leaping out of the water, until it was discovered that they were brushing parasitical insects off their backs as they scraped against floating twigs, on their way back down. Cute example, thought Mark, checking back through his old notes for reference to the rebuttal to Beach.

In *Psychology Review #54*, Harold Schlossberg makes a quick dismissal of Beach. He says play is not a speciific stimulus/response behavior, and can not be analyzed that way. Play, he says, cuts across *all* categories of behavior, and cannot be approached by Beach's kind of rationalistic, Aristotelian naming ceremony. He has no alternate theories to propound; except a kind of anti-theory, which writes off playful activity as a category so broad it is of no practical use to psychology.

Are my studies done now, Master? May I call my sweetheart?

Yes, you may.

Chess is "an art appearing in the form of a game."

—*The Great Soviet Encyclopedia*

"Hello."

"Guess who?"

"I was just thinking about you." That wasn't true.

"I haven't stopped thinking of you." Neither was that.
"What's up?"

"Sewing. Then I have to go to Sebastopol to get a pollution control certificate."

"Can I come too?"

"OK. I'm going in about two hours."

"Bye." said Mark. In the sky, through his windows, he watched two turkey vultures skate smooth spirals, then break for the shelter of the trees when two intruding jets scratched their tracks across the sky.

*   *   *   *   *

"Don't be so naive. Lily's just mad about Tom-Tom," Pearl explained. "The higher the fuss factor, in a relationship, the more the woman being fussed over loves it. And with Tom-Tom treating her as though his life depended on her loving him, they've got the fuss factor pumped up so high they won't be down until next winter, if they start dropping now."

They left in her car. "Listen to this, Pearl. Joanie was telling me she had heard a lecturer last week -- somebody on the same bill with one of her jugglers, or something, I think -- and the lecture was about love as a struggle. And different people need different kinds of love struggles. Like the woman who repeatedly loves men whose love has to be squeezed out of them, drop by drop, which is often a re-enactment of her relationship with her father. A woman like that would put aside an 'easy' and 'loving' relationship because it doesn't fit her feeling of what love involves. Isn't that an interesting idea? What do you think?"

"Joanie gets as complicated as you do. I don't think about feelings that way." She opened the paper. "Listen to this -- there's a language in Alaska that's only spoken by two old sisters, when they meet. All the others are dead. And there are some languages with only one person left who speaks it, and when they go, that's it."

Chess is a matter of vanity.

— A. A. Alekhine

Mark shook his head, "That's what I was saying about that lecturer -- a solid proof by diverging irrelevancies and infinite repetition."

"I take what I said about Joanie back. Nobody makes things as complicated as you do."

Her flirtatiousness with the mechanic at the smog-control certification shop annoyed Mark, even though he knew by now that she considered such behavior no more than sound business practices. On the way back, they picked up a hitchhiker, a student of linguistics, and Mark talked to him about the theory that poetry was primarily characterized by linguistic compression. Pearl felt left out. She knew it would take no more than the merest gesture to turn this scholar's complicated head away from all that to Herself. And she did. And he did.

It was just mischief to her. She knew Mark would be upset by it. He wanted to ask her why, if she liked him as much as she said she did, she kept carrying on. But he knew she could not answer that question any better than he could. After the hitchhiker got out she interrupted his brooding by asking him how his playwork was going. "I've never been entirely sure if you were actually accomplishing something, or just making lists."

He, too, was grateful for a change of mood. "I'm probably trying to do too much, but if I'm lucky I'll get some few things done in spite of that. Tolstoi has a character who is told he can keep as much land as he can run around, but if he is not back at the starting point by sunset he gets nothing. Well, I am now just turning the first corner, and I'm a little frightened to see how far out I've gone; and, from here, how much further I have to go."

They stopped for dinner on the way back, later watched her idiot-box from her bed. She had an easier time staying interested in the television than he did. He watched her watching the screen, and wondered at his being there. How beautiful she is, even in television light.

Mark stayed with Pearl all the next day and the next night. The morning after that he said he needed to go home to do some work, and he'd see her the evening after that.

I work out my own moves, all by myself, and let my opponent think about

He worked, all that day, on words -- on the roots and uses of *ludics, ludicrous, ludible, ludibrous, ludificate,* and *ludify.* And that sterner face of play called *agon,* the competitive element in our natures that played such a large role in the ceremonies of ancient Greece, and in the theories of Huizinga. From *agon* came *agony* and *agonize* and their branch of the family. Mark cross referenced it to his board game notes on a French court game called *Agon* -- played, in the eighteenth century, with finely crafted silver pieces; now made of plastic, and called *Hi-Q,* or some other gimmicky name.

In the afternoon, he listened to the news and ate three steak sandwiches. In the evening he turned to the word *fun,* to which Huizinga attached such unique importance, and on into other words basic to his studies.

He slept well, and headed for Connie's in Lido Grande, to grab a breakfast, and begin to think about and plan the day's work. He did a little skip step when he saw Pearl's car parked in front of the restaurant, but fell seven stories when, through the window, he saw her trading fingers with Tug Henry across a shared breakfast. "The first fucking night I leave her alone."

His desk was as he left it, but he was not. The papers were spread out, grouped, requiring only his participation, but he was not there. His mind was busy raging at Pearl, and she was not there either. He condemned himself. What a pathetic thing I am, to be knocked so senseless by her fickleness. Couldn't have come as a surprise. No matter, it's laid me out just the same. Affected my damn brain, too, immobilized the intellect that might otherwise have found the remedy. But now the funk was too thick to think his way out. One thing was for sure -- he wouldn't call the bitch . . .

She called. "Hi." Bright as a schoolgirl. "I thought you were coming by."

"I don't want to."

"How come?"

"Because you're a whore!"

She hung up.

A half-hour later, she called back. "What's wrong?"

"I just happened to pass by Connie's this morning."

his own moves.

— *Alekhine*

"So? What? You saw me? So? I wasn't doing anything."

"You were with Tug."

"Oh. We ran into each other at the post office," she said. "And he asked me for breakfast. That's all. Don't make more out of it than it really is. Why don't you come by? We'll talk about it, at least. We owe it that much, don't we?"

She let him think, gave him time to talk himself into it, and he finally agreed. "OK. Not tonight. I've been furious at you all day. I'll see you tomorrow, for lunch."

"Good. 'Night, love."

Mark read, interrupted by an unexpected visit from EZ Beazly, "I've got some lids you might like. Come by. What's that?"

"What?"

"The record."

"A Beethoven symphony. The moment in music when romanticism emerged from its classical upbringing. In chess it was the other way around -- classicism followed romanticism, and tamed it."

EZ looked around Mark's house with amused disbelief. "You live as crazy as anyone I know. The house looks like rodents live here -- all those little pieces of paper. You're weird, man."

"Have they found Carmody yet?"

"Not that I've heard."

"EZ -- what do you think of Pearl?"

"Hey, come on, man. I barely know the woman. She's pretty."

"Yeah, a real natural beauty. Actually she has fat legs. I guess I'm really asking if she was the kind of woman you would get involved with?"

"I wouldn't get involved with *anyone*. I'm a goddamn outlaw. I got to travel as light as I can."

* * * * *

Pearl had poured him a cup of coffee, but Mark was too angry to sit and drink it. Pacing up and down her kitchen, he snarled, "You were seeing Tug recently, just before you and I started up again. How do you expect me to believe

In the long run, we are all dead.

— *John M. Keynes*

that you just happened to run into him at Connie's? You?''

"Don't give me that *you*, like you know me so well. You don't, and you don't know what happened, either. Nothing can be innocent, with you. You're so paranoid and possessive, everybody's out to run a number on you. Right? Why the hell are so insecure?'' Her voice and eyes softened, and she added, ''Why do you find it so hard to believe I'm really into you, that you're the one I want?''

"Because of what happened last time around,'' he said, finally sitting down for coffee.

"We both learned from that,'' she told him. She put her hands on his shoulders. Very lightly, at first, until she was sure he wouldn't shrug her off. And then firmly, and fondly, ''You learned some things about me, and I learned about you. This time we can make it work better.''

The backbone of his anger was broken.

"Your coffee'll get cold,'' she said.

By evening, the last of Mark's rage had dissolved in her arms.

Next morning, they drove to Lone Buck Bay, took the unusual step of bringing with them Mark's typewriter and several folders and books back to Pearl's house.

*　　*　　*　　*　　*

Pearl flounced into her bedroom with a newspaper and an an ebullient, ''Look at this. Here's a story about a woman coming up to Adlai Stevenson after a campaign speech, to assure him he'd got the votes of every thinking American, and Stevenson told her, 'That's not enough -- I need a majority.' ''

Like Queen Victoria, Mark was not amused. He had been rereading and revising his notes on the extraordinary quality of our make-believe symbols -- that their logical con-sequences are the symbols of the natural consequences of the objects themselves -- $1 plus $1 = $2. It was this train of thought that Pearl derailed, and he snapped at her, ''Yes, I know! Would you please not barge in on me like that, when I'm working.'' Her face hid nothing. Seeing that she was hurt and indignant, he added, "I'm sorry. I was engrossed in this," waving nebulously at the books and papers behind which he had ensconced himself. "You startled me."

"It's all right," she said, in a way that made plain it wasn't, and left the room.

He thought about following her, pumping up the fuss factor. She'd love it. Naturally. Vaihinger and Cassirer won.

Pearl sat sulking on the back porch. Had she been shooed away (from her own bedroom) when Mark was making it with another woman, she would have known how to respond. But this bothered her.

Hours later, at dinner, he spoke to her about it. "I'm sorry I snapped at you like that. When I get very engrossed in something, it's my instinct to push everything else away." She ignored him. He continued, "Reminds me of the story they tell about the great bridge player Waldemar von Zedwitz. A waiter accidentally spilled a pitcher of ice water on him. Without looking up from his hand, Waldie shook the ice cubes off his shoulders and said, 'Don't do that again. I don't like it. Four diamonds.' " Mark laughed. Pearl did not even smile. "Pearl, I'm sorry. Look, would you like to go someplace tonight? I still have some money left over from last week's work for Peterson. We could do us as much as three or four dollars worth of high living."

"I have my own money."

"Are you still pissed at me because I barked at you before?" She said nothing. He went on, "I get like that because I take my work so seriously. Maybe because nobody else takes it seriously, I take it too seriously."

"I know you're very serious." She ran her hands through her hair. "And I'm sure the time will come when whatever you're doing will be recognized. Every dog has his day."

They finished the meal in silence.

After dinner she put on a t-shirt and jeans, and a cape.

"Going for a walk?"

"Something like that."

After an hour, he could no longer concentrate on his work. By ten, he was smoking cigarettes and mumbling. At midnight, he was staring out the window into the black

What chess has in common with fine art and science is its utter uselessness.
— Ernst Cassirer

night. By two, the blackness had penetrated all through him.

At two-fifteen, she returned -- alone and slightly blurry and slurry from drink. "Ooh, do you look mean." She looked again. "Well, let me get a little coffee in me and we'll get into it."

She spun her cape off her with a graceful sweep, less perfect but more endearing for dropping it on the floor when she missed the chair. Pausing in the midst of the domestic warming of the coffee, "I didn't *fuck* anybody tonight. You don't have to keep looking at me like that. Whatever you're trying to accuse me of, I didn't do it."

"Why didn't you at least call, and tell me you were OK?"

"Did you worry?" She was still giggly. "You probably would have given me a lot of shit, if I did. Let's go to bed and talk about it in the morning."

*   *   *   *   *

In the morning, they drove north on the freeway, just to drive, to talk.

Suddenly very sure of herself, Pearl told Mark, "I'm not used to being accountable to anybody for my daily decisions." She looked like she had bitten into something bitter. "And I can't live with that. I've lived most of my mature life alone, and I know that whenever . . . Mark, what you're trying to do to me feels like a very tight pair of shoes -- you can't wait to take them off. Why isn't it enough for you to know that you can always stay at my place?"

"Although there's no guarantee that you'll be there? I couldn't live like that, Pearl. I'd always be losing --you're so much prettier than I am."

"It's not a competition."

"That's easier for you to say than me," he said.

"It's not."

"Right. So, even if it is my hangup, it's not worth all the energy it would take to overcome it." Mark shrugged. "Yeah, my hangup."

"I wish you believed that. I might open you up to discovering some new things about yourself."

I want what I want when I want it.

— *Henry Blossom*

"No doubt you would," he said. "There are just a few things I'd like to discover before I see how many women I can fuck in how many ways."

"Oh, you're really foul-minded. You always try to cast the worst possible light on everything you can't control. I'm not talking about fucking."

"Could have fooled me," he said.

"I'm talking about letting yourself, and the people you love, be open and free, responsible to themselves for what they do."

"Short of fucking around?"

"*Free.* Why are you making so much out of that one act?"

"Pearl, I sympathize with your problems."

"What problems? What are you talking about?"

"The ones I can't help you with."

She sighed. "Maybe we both have to give in a little."

He turned off the freeway at Healdsburg, came back toward the coast by Westside Road, winding through mile after mile of lush vineyards, small private wineries, families that have lived in the same white haciendas for forty-thousand years. "Neither of us has given an inch, so far. We scratch and claw over everything. Jacking up the fuss factor to the crisis point. I think that's a victory for you."

"You think I want us to fight, like this?" She was getting angry. "I don't want us to fight. And, listen, I don't want to lose you, and I don't want to be your property. Can you understand that?"

"Yes, I can. But I'm not signing up for the program."

"Do you know who lives in that house?" she asked.

"Yes. I always liked him best as a son-of-a-bitch. Like in *The Apartment* and *The Caine Mutiny.*"

She said, "Try to see it from my point of view. I've been through monogamy, and I know that for me it would be a step backwards to return to it. What makes you think monogamy is the best set of rules for you, if you haven't given other ways a good try? Why don't you consider changing. Instead of putting me on the spot, every time, why don't you deal with not doing that?"

Most of the vineyards were still rough from the winter,

I wish he would explain his explanation.

— *Lord Byron*

but here and there was a vineyard that had been disced and pruned. Mark, too, felt half cultivated, half wild. Should he risk what she was asking? It would be as demanding, in its way, as the town. He prepared to go through it all again, stopping himself with the reminder of how many times he had been over it before, how futile further analysis would be. "Let me ask you, Pearl -- if I went home now, and put in three solid days of writing and studying, would you promise not to get it on with Tug or anybody else?"

"Here we go again."

"They're different things. I have my studies and you have your studs -- is that what you want? Look how completely Tom-Tom was taken out of his activism by Lily. He didn't do anything except pine away, for all those weeks."

"Tom-Tom is a little boy. Are you? Don't you have more continuity to your life than that? Maybe if you took what you're supposed to be involved with more seriously you'd think less about my activities."

To have heard that from her. "Of course, Tom-Tom is younger and less solid than I am. But then again, so's Lily. She's by no means a coquette of your caliber."

"Stop the car."

"Why?"

"I'll hitch back." Which she did.

*   *   *   *   *

Talking to himself furiously, he was beyond caring that other drivers noticed. "Every dog has his day!" she tells me. Not only have I not yet succeeded, but she will deprive me in advance of the value of my victory if I ever should win it. To hell with her. Why the ongoing fascination? Is it just her displayability? Or her eyes? Am I that shallow? Look what I've been reduced to. I've done nothing for the better part of a week except deal with my feelings about this bitch."

"Salugi," Mark noticed and stopped the car, ready to talk to anybody.

"Hey, my man, what's shaking?" Salugi was sunning

See everything, overlook a lot, correct a little.

— *Pope John XXIII*

himself on a rock overlooking the river, taking some of the bite out of the heat with a shaded jug of white wine.

"Oh, some woman's running some numbers on me."

Offering Mark the bottle, Salugi advised, "The key to the trip is this: Don't take no shit from no bitch, and if the slit gives you too much lip, it's hip to split. Who you talking about anyway? Pearl? You want to know what I think of her? I think she's a cunt. That's right. You asked me so I got to tell you."

Barnyard wisdom -- piggish, and macho enough to survive. Mark got back in his car, drove to EZ's.

Beazly had an angry blues song on the stereo. "Dude sounds like he's got a serious complaint."

EZ sat enthroned like a rebel chieftain in his big mahogany and purple plush chair, next to the desk with the gram scale, the hooded bright gooseneck lamp, and the telephone, and reached over to the shelves next to the desk and lowered the volume. "What's up?"

"Just burned out."

"Pearl again?"

"Yeah."

"Now the last time you asked me what I thought of you and her, I didn't say anything, because I don't think you can say for another guy, but in this case I think you just need a little support in thinking the relationship's lousy, so that I can give you. First of all, I think that if this was meant to happen between you two it would have been easier, it would have started to break your way by now. I think if she really cared for you she would've made the whole thing easier for you. And, just on a very subjective level, I could never really see the overall Jones of your relationship with her. You know what I mean?"

"Not exactly."

"You don't have to understand *exactly*, chump. Close counts too, just like in horseshoes, as long as you get the drift."

Mark did, and in fact he found himself so much in accord with that drift that the more they talked about it the more adamant Mark became in his resolve to end it now, get back to his work, and put this whole bittersweet episode behind

When I die I want them to play "The Black and Crazy Blues." I want to be cremated, put

him before it became too bitter. By the time crazy Reb and his older brother Teddy arrived, Mark had settled it -- he was through with her.

Teddy's slow southeastern drawling, "Hi, y'all," sounded overtly out of state, even amidst California's catholicity of accents. Teddy was Sam Francisco's partner in dealing, and he and EZ were working on a deal.

Reb took his beer can to an oversized pillow on the floor, talking earnestly into it. When Mark gave him a look of friendly concern, Reb asked him, "Are you hip to the zombie state, man? The state where you attain oneness with zombie consciousness."

"Hmm. Other than that, how have you been feeling?" Mark, the incorrigible big brother.

"Feeling?" Reb was upset by the question. "I wasn't feeling anything. I was just reading this book." He had no book. "You can't fault me for that, can you?"

"No. Of course not. What's the name of the book?"

Reb held up the hallucinated book, and turned it over on its spine, reading, "I Seem To Be Alive -- a guide for the incomplete."

Teddy had pulled a chair up to EZ's desk, and they spoke quietly about their business. Then EZ packed an attache case, and wrapped his balance scale in a cloth and put it in its box.

A knocking at the door. It was Wally, trying to trade a refrigerator for a lid. "I can't do it, Wally. What the hell am I going to do with another refrigerator?" EZ challenged.

"Sell it."

"I'm not looking to expand into the refrigerator-dealing business. Besides, Wally, how the hell you gonna live without a refrigerator?"

"I'm moving out of my cabin tonight."

"I see."

"You gotta do it, EZ!"

"No I don't, Wally. Hey, Teddy -- would you and Sam trade a lid for a refrigerator?"

"No, but I got a cousin in Nashville in the major appliance business, if you all are ever out that way."

"Why don't you bring it over to old what's-his-face, in

in a bag of pot and I want beautiful people to smoke me and I hope they get something out

Gumpers Corners?'' EZ suggested. ''See if you can get something a little more readily negotiable than a refrigerator. Like money, for instance.''

Wally flapped his arms and complained, ''Your house is always so fucking cold, EZ. How come you live in a house that's so cold?''

''To discourage freeloaders.''

''Ah, you're starting to get hemorrhoids on your crown,'' Wally said as he left.

EZ passed a small meerschaum pipe. ''Try some of this, kid -- first puff's free. This is the kind of hash smoked only by very holy Tibetan monks who swear they don't smoke hash. Anybody seen my roachclip? What is it with roachclips? I swear, somewhere, somewhere remote, eastern Montana, maybe, somewhere there is one all-powerful fetishistic rip-off artist with sixty million roachclips.''

''I find it rather astonishing that you're ever able to find anything, in this place,'' Teddy drawled.''All this antique type stuff.''

''You think this is a weird pad? This ain't weird. This is kind of straight,'' EZ said. ''Talk about freaky, now the all-time freakiest pad I ever saw belonged to these three peyote dealers I knew in New York. A tri-racial threesome. They had this studio apartment, in a nice building, and they filled the whole fucking place with *sand.* A foot-and-a-half of sand. Don't ask me how they got all that sand in there. I don't know and to this day neither do the cops. And they opened the valve on their radiator, so their apartment was like a sauna, and they planted peyote all over the place. Put in some decorative cactii, too, and a few snakes and lizards. And they had sun lamps all around, for the peyote, so they wore goggles all the time. What a scene! This incredibly foxy black chick, and this Italian and Chicano dude, in this desert scene, in New York. Landlord finally blew their trip when he realized something was very screwy with his hot water situation, so he finally gets into this place, with this threesome sitting around with the lizards in the dunes, wearing nothing but their goggles, and of course goes absolutely bananas. But by the time the cops got there, the three of them and their peyote were gone. Cops couldn't

of it.

—Rhassan Roland Kirk

believe, couldn't ever figure out how they got all that sand in there without being seen.''

Teddy answered the insistent knocking at the door. It was Wally returning with the money for his ounce of pot. Wally and EZ negotiated the lid in unfriendly silence. When Wally pocketed his pot, he sarcastically said, ''Thank you oh so much oh wise and humble master.''

''Don't mention it, oh stupid and arrogant slave.''

Wally no sooner left than the phone rang. ''Speaking.'' EZ handed the phone to Teddy.

''Yeah. Sure.'' Teddy nodded to EZ, and they got their jackets on, took the attache case and the scale, and left. Mark left, too, astonished to see that they left Reb alone with EZ's drugs and telephone.

* * * * *

He was washing dishes when the phone rang, three times, then stopped. She'll call back in the morning, he prophesied. He felt as though much of what he was going through with her had been the consequences of his sentimental fondness, during adolescence, for torchy songs of unrequited love. More bitter and a good deal less beautiful than I remembered from the lyrics, he thought.

The pleasures of pain? There was Hannah Arendt's piece on Lessing, he recalled -- the Greek idea of tragic pleasures, pain and anger being positive emotions because they plunge us more deeply into life, while hope and fear are negative because they overleap or shrink from reality. Who was it -- La Rouchefoucauld? -- who said that people would never fall in love if they hadn't read about it first in some book? The trouble, of course, is that the Pearl I'm in love with isn't really Pearl; just a Pearl reshaped to suit me better, with nothing visibly altered.

Right. I'm going to change her life around. It's all so selfish. What does she want? Look at it from her point of view. She is asking me for permission to let her pursue her happiness the way she sees fit. She's telling me I should be glad to see her gladdened, instead of being resentful that

Be not angry that you cannot make others as you wish them to be, since you cannot

somebody besides myself could make her happy. That's a good point. There is a kind of greed in that jealousy, the lover's desire that the beloved be incomplete and incapable of true happiness without the lover.

She also needs the sewing machine repairman, the muffler man, the hitchhiker, Tug . . . there's never any end to them! She's playing a game I can barely imagine; and she's moving me around in it, like a minor piece in a chess game.

Accepting the fact that I might never understand what her whole erotic dance is about, can I learn to accept that and continue to be very involved with her and still have enough peace of mind to do my research and my writing? I don't think so. It would take years. I don't think I have enough personal mass to do all those things. He smiled to recall Goneril's, "Am I not worth the whistle?" She must despise the men she can manipulate with her sashaying and eye-batting and all that. Maybe that's the real reason she does it. Do such things have real reasons?

The whole affair is such a distraction. Break it off tomorrow. Or, at the most, give it one small shot more, on condition that it all fall into place effortlessly, and be ready to walk away from it in a moment without a backward glance.

She called back first thing in the morning. "Did you eat breakfast yet?"

"No."

She waited for more. When no more came she invited him over for eggs Benedict and cinnamon toast.

"What's the use? Let's just put back on the shelf."

"I don't want to write you off."

"Neither of us wants to. But it's just not in the cards, Pearl. We have to face up to that."

"We can work it out, if we want to badly enough. Come over and talk about it here. I don't want to talk about this on the phone. I want to see you."

Yes, and even more, be seen by me, he knew. "I can't believe it's worth the trouble. There are too many heavies to work out between us. Let's put it off until some indefinite future, when it doesn't involve such a long and tortuous

make yourself as you wish to be.

— Thomas a Kempis

struggle.''

She sighed a despondent, "OK," counted six silently, and said sadly, "Maybe we're all just dealt a certain number of unrequited loves.''

"Maybe.''

She thought she heard it in his voice. "Angela's nothing like me, is she?''

"No, not much.'' The question startled Mark into the realization that he had barely thought of Angela, since the day he called her to go to the dance in Lido Grande. That was over a month ago. He had never really missed her. "She was a change of pace from you, as you are from her.''

Complimented, though that was not exactly how Mark meant it, Pearl remembered, "That's good show business: Never follow a banjo act with another banjo act.''

He laughed at that. She smiled, realizing that they were back to talking boys-girls, which was her game, and she knew that without even trying she had won him back almost as easily as she had always been able to do before, like shooting fish in a barrel. They made a date for that afternoon, and another for that night, and began discussing the day after.

*　*　*　*　*

The afternoon event was a country music concert and fair in a Sebastopol apple orchard, and nobody was more surprised to run into them together than EZ Beazly.

"Well shut my dumb ole mouth. Here's Pearl and Mark out promenading together again. What a surprise.''

"Hi, EZ.'' Her soft, throaty voice gave 'EZ' 4½ syllables.

"You know what the Good Book says," Mark offered.

"What the hell does the Good Book say, you dumb fucking salami?''

"The Good Book says there are many things that passeth the understanding of man.''

"Just passeth your fucking understanding like it wasn't even there.''

Mark bid a laughing, "See you later," to EZ and motioned for Pearl to join him at the balloon-busting booth.

"Bye-bye, EZ Beazly," tootled Pearl.

What men call gallantry, and gods adultery,/Is much more common where

Mark went to Peterson's, to help with a rush-rush job, while Pearl had an appointment in Gumperstown, to measure a customer for a dress and a bonnet. She said she would meet Mark at a chamber music concert in Santa Rosa, that evening.

He called at eight-ten. "What happened to you?"

"Oh, uh, something came up beyond my control." A man laughed behind her.

"What?" Mark was furious.

"My car. I had car troubles. It steamed up. Wouldn't go. It was the radiator hose."

"Why didn't you call?"

"I tried, but I couldn't find the number."

"You couldn't have tried very hard. The ticket office is in the book."

She said nothing.

"I'll drive over then, if your car's not working. We'll catch the last half."

"No."

"Why not?"

"I'm not going to be here."

"Why not?"

"This guy that helped me with my car asked me over for dinner, and he was so helpful, I mean I was almost hysterical, I didn't know what was happening with the car. It was steaming up all over."

"It is impossible to deal with you. You make me sick. You do this every fucking time. I hate it!"

"I needed help. This guy went out of his way to help me. What am I supposed to do, say thanks for the help and the dinner invite, but my boyfriend is so uptight and insecure I have to split? Look, it's no big deal. If I hadn't promised the guy, I'd say, sure, come on over and watch television, or something."

Watch television? What am I doing talking to this idiot? he screamed to himself, furious for not having ended it the day before. Maybe it was better this way. Had he ended it then, he might have been stuck with second-guessing himself for who knew how long, whereas this way he could walk away from her with few regrets. "Listen, I left a couple

the climate's sultry.

— *Lord Byron*

of books on your ironing-board. Do me a favor and bring them with you to the Sebastopol Library at eleven tomorrow morning, and we'll see if there's anything left to say to each other.''

"OK. Mark, you're not thinking, just because of this, that you don't want to see me again, are you?'' She permitted herself just a trace of her usual condescension toward what she had always tried to make him feel was his adolescent possessiveness.

"We'll see tomorrow," he concluded, and hung up.

He lit a cigarette, idly watched the smoke from the match ascend in swirls from the ashtray. That was it. He was sure of it. "Something came up beyond my control." The bitch. He was through, now, he was through because . . . did he need reasons? This whole relationship had been lived so far outside the realm of reason, the reasons could only be excuses or afterthoughts, at best. There's just nothing more to say, is there?

Well, let's see. I shouldn't have a completely closed mind, even though it is certainly over. She'd have to show me a complete change of heart. Oh, Christ, to hell with both of us.

Too keyed up to sleep and too distracted to work, he went for a drive. Finding himself driving from Lido Grande to Gumperstown, he drove the old road, instead of the highway, knowing the old road went past her house. Just for a change, not to spy on her, he lied to himself so transparently even he could see it.

Tug's car was parked there.

He cursed her, "Bitch," and "Whore," all the way to Santa Rosa and back to the coast again.

*　　*　　*　　*　　*

Instead of meeting her in the library the next morning, Mark bought a newspaper and sat in the morning sun in the library's little mall.

She joined him on the bench. She looked upset, and a little sheepish, and waited for him to say something. When

. . . a man that studies revenge keeps his own wounds green, which otherwise

he didn't, she prodded, gently, "You have something to say?"

"Why don't you say your piece first."

"Look, Mark," she stopped for a minute, then went on. "I *have* to lie to you. I get some things from other men that you can't give me, like you get from your friends and your work. And somehow you still can't understand that."

"You could have called . . . " He got up, went into the library, slammed the door as loud as he could behind him. It was childish, but since it was the child in him she had been abusing for so long, he let the child take revenge.

would heal, and do well.

— *Francis Bacon*

Almost Everybody

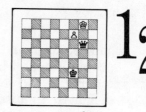

*"I have devised seven separate explanations,
each of them which would cover the facts as
far as we know them."*
— *Sherlock Holmes*

The next morning, Mark set to work with a vengeance --
to forget her and carry on. To hell with her. He would work
through the depression. He would recover the great, un-
shakable confidence he 'had achieved, before the box lunch
appeared.

He tried to work, couldn't concentrate. The phone rang,
stopped. He read, the words fogged. He breathed to clear
his mind, it clouded. He started to call Angela, stopped. He
called Peterson to see if there was work, got no answer.
What went wrong? He got no answer. He started to call
Pearl, stopped. He tried to clarify his notes on growth and
models, they clouded. He listened to a ball game, it ended.
The phone did not ring. He thought, maybe I should play
poker. Maybe all this is the other side of some fantastic
winning streak in cards I'm not cashing in on.

After a week and a half of unproductive depression, it
seemed clear that everything -- his life -- was a huge mistake.
It was pieces of clockwork, not a timepiece. He theorized
like a child, syncretistically -- the fire-engine goes fast
because it's bright red and has a siren. He was the appointed torturer of his own fraudulent dreams -- Time would
be their executioner. He realized how disheveled he must
look when grocery clerks began unpacking cartons or taking
inventory near him, to check him out for shoplifting. He took
to practicing complicated varieties of cat's cradle string

167

games, without string, in public places, loved the way people watched him and sadly shook their heads. He took to mumbling to himself, and walking in grotesque ways, was delighted to discover that people were leaving him alone more. Since that was what he sought, he kept up the act, dancing behind the mask.

He worked for Peterson. It was just as well. He could still do presswork, cut paper, and score book covers. Peterson complimented him on his particularly good work. Little do you know, Mark did not tell him, that I have been awake so long, Peterson, that you look like an oversized potato bug.

He went home. It was the same. The phone did not ring. Nothing got better, nor would it. There was always *est*, the little fat kid, the Rosicrucians . . . Face it, Lerner -- it's all downhill from here.

He read, wrote, thought, nothing mattered one way or the other. Nothing seemed good, so he could not tell if what he did was.

I should call Pearl. After all, after all is said and done, and overdone, she is a woman I love, who will see me.

Pearl -- a shield, isn't it. Something to wall off the irritant, protecting the mollusk from its pains.

He stood in place, shouted, "Emulate Arjuna, Conqueror of Sloth!" It no longer worked. He embarassed himself, sat down.

The enormity of his resignation from the public life of Lone Buck Bay hit him, it seemed, for the first time. The quest for a model town had been real. Its problems were down to earth. Progress was tangible. Colleagues were human, and near. But this, this ludics . . .

He couldn't look at his work any more. He couldn't look at his house any more. He had to get out. He had to do something else. He paced, decided he wanted to prove something, decided to push through with it, carry on, stay put to do his work, not make too much of a loneliness that was, after all, only a mood which would pass. As he would, too, and all of us. Maybe ludics was a survivor. Who knew? Hell, maybe we were too, some way. Who knew? Back to work.

Make the most of yourself, for that is all there is of you.

— *Emerson*

He couldn't concentrate. He kept thinking of women -- of Pearl, of Lily, of the girl with the diamond-black eyes at the Lido Grande dance. He tried to persuade himself he was celibate, but couldn't, knowing there was a real difference between practicing celibacy and not getting laid. He hadn't tried, of course. Not even a turtle gets anything without sticking its neck out. He didn't want to. It was useless. He knew that if he went out now to seek companionship, he would only find another lonely, horny person. How could two lonely people help each other? On the other hand . . . He decided to call Martha, the fry-cook.

*   *   *   *   *

Mark and Martha talked until three, and had only been asleep for a few minutes when the phone rang.

"Jesus. Can you get that?" Martha asked. "I'm still asleep."

Mark did. "Hello."

Joanie's voice, "Mark? Is that you?"

"Yes."

"You are at Martha's then?"

"That's right. That's two-in-a-row. Now you have a shot at our special early-bird three-in-a-row bonus. What day is it?"

"It's the morning after. Now it's your turn to play. Which store has had all its goods rearranged into one big pile in the middle, along with all the glass from the windows that got kicked in?"

"The Farmhouse got trashed?"

"That's right. And who do you think the prime suspect is?"

"Weel?"

"Two in a row! And the question of the moment is, what are we going to do about it?"

"Are you putting a meeting together?"

"We all are. Some of them are at The Farmhouse now. Why don't you pick me up and drive me out."

"OK."

The dodo never had a chance. He seems to have been invented for the sole purpose

"And don't dawdle. Dorothy says there's a lot of loose talk about repaying Weel in his own coinage tonight. She and Tom are trying to keep a lid on that, but Charlie and Tom-Tom and Vivian and Amy and some of the others are itching to do something. So don't take too long saying goodbye."

* * * * *

Even from the parking lot, Mark and Joanie could both see that it was worse than they thought. Several of the bugs, vans, and old pick-ups in the lot were slumped over their slashed tires. Two of the garage's trucks, parked in front of The Farmhouse, had their windshields smashed. All the shop's windows had been broken, most by having boxes of produce thrown through them. The ground surrounding the store's side of The Farmhouse was littered with bits of broken glass, figs and dates, slats from fruit boxes, nectarines and plums and other signs of chaos. Through the broken windows, they could hear shouting and crying, and the sound of a gavel banging ineffectively for order. Dozens of mimeographed notices, Coastal Couriers, and magazines were pinned by the wind against the nearby shrubbery. "It wouldn't look this bad, if it weren't for the full moon," said Joanie.

Tom and EZ came out of The Farmhouse, and herded Mark and Joanie onto the porch. "Something new," Tom told them. "The sheriff just called, to see if we knew anything about Weel's office getting trashed."

"Jesus," Mark said.

"I think it's a cover," EZ theorized, "to take the suspicion off him and Carmody."

"It's not," Tom assured them. "According to the sheriff, Weel's place got hit much more professionally, and a lot more damage was done. They had to be good to get into his plant in the first place."

"Who?" asked EZ.

Tom shook his head. "Don't know."

"Maybe it has nothing to do with the town," suggested

of becoming extinct, and that was all he was good for.

— *Will Cuppy*

Joanie. "Weel's been cutting across some powerful orbits, lately. Maybe one of his new found friends wants to send him a message."

"Come on!" EZ wasn't buying it. "And this unknown party just happens to hit him a few hours after we get hit? How do they know that?"

Joanie shrugged, then smiled and said, "It's refreshing to see you taking such interest in community affairs, EZ."

"Oh, come on inside," EZ ushered them. "You won't feel so damned refreshed, after you've taken a look around."

The entire spice and herb section lay smashed and shattered, and Dieter bitterly examined each shard of the two dozen spice jars he had designed and made in his pottery shop for The Farmhouse's spice shop. All the windows were broken, and Katrina was crying her eyes out. She had worked for almost a year to make the magnificent stained-glass mandala-window on the west wall, that had always made the shop feel like a chapel, at sunset. And Will Deal, the carver, cursing to himself at the mutilated reliefs he had worked so lovingly on; and the four regular cash-register operators, talking conspiratorially to each other at their demolished work-station; and the dozens of crying and screaming children, all of them aware that something awful had happened, but none of them able to understand just what, and what its limits were. Wince and Willoughby had fallen back to sleep, even with all the noise. And Tom-Tom and Vivian were demanding revenge, calling on the people to rise up then and there and spill Weel's blood for this.

This was the best turnout for a town meeting in a long time, maybe since the firestorm the town was founded on. Takes a disaster to make them all pay attention at once, Mark thought. And why not? Who says people have to be so involved and attentive to their governments? Or is that the price people have to pay for good government? Yes, and where and when was there ever a good government?

"Danger!" Reb, standing on a chair, again cried, "Danger! Do not underestimate the severity of the situation. There is very grave danger here."

Government is not reason, is not eloquence -- it is force.

— George Washington

"What the hell is your trip?" Charlie pounded the gavel for order. "Sit down."

"Do you know who I am?" Reb demanded.

"No, I don't," said Charlie, pointing an authoritarian finger at Reb, who stood undaunted, "and if you don't know either, sit over there in the corner and we'll put your problem on the agenda."

"You shut your insolent mouth," Reb shot back. "Know your place! Bring me the files. Got it? I want the files, the guns, and the money. There is grave danger here."

"See Amy?" EZ whispered to Mark.

Mark looked. "No."

"You know," EZ began, in a lowered voice, "There is one person from Lone Buck Bay, more or less, who does have the money as well as the motive to hire some experienced people to do a job on Weel."

"Does he have the connections?"

"Through Amy he does. Salugi knows people who will do that sort of thing. So does my man in Santa Rosa."

"Salugi's in South City."

"Guess again," said EZ. "Salugi's in Santa Rosa. Salugi was expecting to see Joanie, tonight, but she broke it off at the last minute. Amy and I went to Santa Rosa together, this afternoon, to cop. And she said she was going to the cave, after that. You get the picture? I think I do."

"We might be smart to end this discussion here."

"Personally, I think it works out well this way."

Mark was unconvinced.

"It's good to know we're covered," EZ continued. "So that when things go beyond the point where the town can deal with them, somebody's there to back us up. Like a goalie, or a catcher. You can understand that."

Mark looked grim. "Sure. Like when Casey Stengel drafted Hoby Landrith first, for the Mets, he explained, 'You have to have a catcher, because if you don't have a catcher, you're likely to have a lot of passed balls.' "

"Close enough," EZ decided, and then remembered, "Spahn and Sain and pray for rain."

Charlie banged the gavel. "We have a motion on the floor."

Chess is as much a mystery as women.

— *Purdy*

"What's the motion?" Mark asked, realizing regretfully that it would have been his turn to chair the meeting, had he remained on the council.

Tom, looking confident, his hand locked in Dorothy's, told Mark, "Charlie wants to pass a motion supporting whoever staged the raid on Weel's."

"You misrepresented that," Charlie countered.

"Point of order. You're chairing the meeting. You can't speak to the issues," Joanie said.

Charlie passed the gavel to Dieter, the evening's vice-chairman.

"Look at that back and forth bit," Reb shouted. "I don't stand for that sort of stuff!"

"You're out of order," Mark said quietly.

"You watch yourself. You're only Number Two," Reb warned him.

Putting aside the almost irresistable temptation to ask who numbers one and three were, Mark asked that Charlie please explain his motion.

"All right. Tom-Tom and I were thinking that . . . "

"You didn't talk to me about anything," Tom-Tom exploded. "Don't go putting words in my mouth. I may agree with you, but you ain't my ventriloquist."

Lily had been trying in vain to catch Tom-Tom's attention, and immediately after he spoke she came behind him and pressed her breasts against his back.

Tom-Tom turned to her angrily, "Fuck off, bitch," he snapped. "I've been crawling after you like a fool, and you ain't even given me the right time of day. Well, this is real!" and he crossed to the other side of the room.

She followed right behind, whispering disbelievingly, "Don't you like me anymore?"

"I was starting to explain," Charlie continued, "that I'd like to see this council pass a statement denying involvement in the raid on Weel's; deploring the raid on us and demanding swift police action on it; and saying that while we regret the violence done to both sides, our frustration at the numerous unredressed injustices inflicted on us over the years compel us to feel in sympathy with those who have taken this drastic but understandable step against Weel."

You know there has been murder and larceny in every generation but that hasn't made

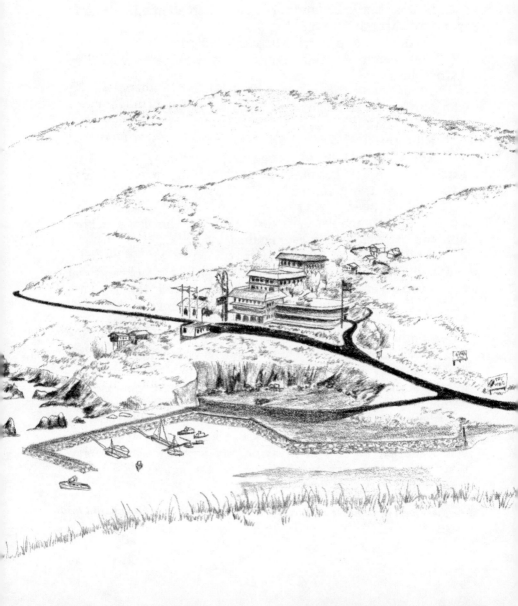

"The Lord reserves vengeance for Himself alone," proselytized an impassioned baritone.

Mark nodded greetings to Saint Barnabas.

Charlie took the gavel back from Dieter, and recognized Joanie.

"I think Charlie's motion is the most out-of-line and undesirable proposal I've ever heard," she began. "We know nothing about this raid, we know nothing about who did it, and we ought to have no connection with this action, including any endorsement of it. It's illegal, and we shouldn't identify ourselves with it."

"It'a *extra*-legal," Charlie rebutted.

"Bullshit. It's criminal. And you're out of order, again," Joanie snapped. "The motion is also contrary to the ideals on which this town was built."

Reb, standing on a chairtop, shouted to them all, "I assure you, gentlemen, that this situation is much more dangerous than any of you can begin to suspect. *I* know, but *only* I know, which is the way it must be, but I can tell you this much -- I can tell you nothing."

Charlie banged the gavel, but too many people ignored him. The meeting was getting out of hand. It was zero o'clock in the middle of the night and everybody was tired and bummed out and in no mood to watch Lone Buck Bay's elected representatives engage in debate and decision-making according to Robert's Rules of Order. The kids were still crying. Nobody wanted to watch a meeting. The people in the gallery talked about going home, and hoped all this could wait until morning. Sensing this was the finale for much of his audience, Charlie leaped on top of a table, and shouted, "What the hell am I doing here? I'm surrounded by grotesques -- these chickenshit liberals, adolescents with puppy crushes, a paranoid going through a full-blown psychotic episode, a dope-dealer drugged into insensibility . . . "

EZ raised his head and said, "Listening to you, I wish I was."

Joanie shouted over the crowd, "Can I have your attention for just one moment. There is no reason for everybody to be here, and I want to ask everyone who

murder meritorious or larceny legal.

— Senator Sam Ervin

doesn't have something to contribute to this meeting, or who has other responsibilites that ought to be taken care of, to please leave."

"I object!" Charlie was enraged. "Everyone should be here. We're all in this. We don't want this decision to come from an elite. Everyone should be involved. This situation may require mass action, instead of just a council vote."

"Right on," yelled Vivian.

"What do you have in mind?" asked Joanie.

"Well, I'm just throwing the idea out, for discussion," Charlie hedged. "I'm still in favor of the resolution I introduced. I think we should go on record as being in sympathy with the people who hit Weel's. I think they expressed a valid rage in this town."

"We don't even know they're from this town!" Tom shouted.

"And it'll screw up our chances in the court case," said Joanie. "Think how the judges are going to view an endorsement of violence, like that."

"I agree," said Tom. "We can't go on record as supporting vandalism."

As the business of the meeting reclaimed center stage, many of those present left, and the crowd noise dimmed. Many in the town stayed, though, and most of those who did were interested, and attentive.

Joanie said that since there was obviously an active debate on Charlie's motion, Charlie ought to relinquish the chair until the motion was disposed of.

Charlie agreed to that, and passed the gavel to Dieter.

Reb leaped to his feet, "There's that back and forth jazz again. I told you *not*, repeat *not*, repeat *not* to do that again. Gentlemen, we must not underestimate, one, two, three, four, repeat *not*, repeat *not* . . ." He clutched his throat.

"Chain yourself to the bed, my son. The moon is full tonight," Joanie advised.

"Danger!" gasped Reb, sinking to the floor.

Joanie rose to a point of personal privilege and asked that the Council designate an acting sergeant-at-arms to remove Reb, at least until the business end of the meeting was concluded.

In Japanese chess, pieces are promoted when they enter enemy territory. In

EZ volunteered. "I'll take him. I don't think I can take much more of this anyway. Come on, clown."

"Number Four! Follow me!" Reb's voice had the confident crispness of authority. And EZ followed him out, grinning, delighted that Reb seemed to consider the whole thing his own idea.

Barnabas stood up. Dieter reluctantly recognized him. "Barnabas, do you have something to say to this august body?" Here it comes, thought Mark.

Rising to his feet, Barnabas spoke in a slow, scriptural tone, "Now the sainted genius wakes, butterflies chase leopards, hawks circle crickets, thunder booms through a clear blue sky, snakes sprout fins and swim, marauders pick the cities clean, the oceans fill with blood and oil while the trumpets of destruction blare in the heavens, tomorrow, next week, next year, fifty-thousand years from now, and we will weep when we remember all the fallen multitudes, and we shall glory, and we shall raise our voices in this glory, singing to the Heavens, 'Glory, glory, hallelujah!' "

"Well, pat my ass," sassed Lily, winning Tom-Tom's smile again.

Having said what the Universe compelled, Saint Barnabas quietly sat down.

At last successful in passing the gavel to Joanie, Mark told the others, "I think we should take no action tonight. I think we should wait. Like a *zwischenzug* in chess, an in-between move. It's a checkers maxim that whoever disturbs the position least disturbs his opponent most. I think we're in a situation like that. So I'm going to ask Joanie to introduce a motion to adjourn."

"Motion to adjourn," Joanie called.

"Do nothing?" Charlie shouted.

"What bullshit," Vivian out-shouted.

"We have to do something," Dieter said.

"We can wait," Mark said. "Waiting is a move, too. There are no good confrontation moves. So we make a waiting move. Let's give the cops a little time to find Carmody, and get some more information on the situation, and the episode at Weel's. Let's be a little cautious. Playing it bold here will lose for us. The court case is still the most

Burmese chess, pawns promote when they reach the long diagonals.

important consideration, hundreds of thousands of dollars are at stake, so let's be sure we don't jeopardize that. Weel would like nothing better than to be able to show the judges that our town council passed a resolution supporting the criminal vandalism against his manufacturing plant. I know it's almost unnatural not to act, in an emotionally charged time like this; but if you think realistically about the options, waiting is our best play.''

Charlie roared, "That is the most chicken-shit cop-out I've ever heard. And exactly what we've come to expect from you, Lerner.''

"It's not debatable,'' Mark prompted.

"Motion to adjourn has been called,'' ruled Dieter. "Those in favor?''

"Roll call vote,'' Charlie demanded. "I want it to go into the official record, who voted to go home on a night like this.''

"Roll call vote,'' acknowledged Dieter. "On a motion to adjourn. Joanie?''

"For.''

"Tom?''

"Yes.''

"Charlie?''

"No.''

"Dorothy?''

"Yes.''

"Motion to adjourn carries. This meeting is over.''

"Where's Reb?'' Mark asked.

"I think EZ took him to the old tack room,'' Joanie told him.

"Tell them Vivian called the psycho-squad to take him away,'' Charlie said.

"Vivian?'' They all looked at her, to see if it was true. "Did you really?'' Dorothy asked her.

"Yeah,'' Vivian admitted. "He was flipping out. And I had had it up to here with him and Weel and all you bullshit do-nothings who run this town. And you,'' pointing to Mark, "still owe me that eight dollars I gave you to hold for me at that dance, you son-of-a-bitch. Just look at this place. It's ruined!'' she cried. "I can't even stand to look at it any

History -- an account, mostly false, of events mostly unimportant, which are brought

more. I've got to get out of here," and she did.

* * * * *

EZ had taken Reb to the old tack room, which now served as a combination office and pantry for The Pleasant Peasant Restaurant, on the north side of the Farmhouse. "Danger!" Reb announced, wheeling toward the door Mark opened, to enter. "Ah, it's you, Number Two." Reb greeted Mark with obvious relief. "Four! Danger. Gentlemen, you must not underestimate, repeat not, but I must have, that's all I need. Did you bring the files?"

"What files?"

"What files? You're expected to know which files. Isn't that why you're Number Two?"

"Oh, *those* files. I know what you mean. Tomorrow."

"I think you underestimate the severity of the situation, Number Two. There is no time to waste. There is grave danger here. So now, let us begin. First of all . . . " He pointed to himself, touched his chest, raised his index finger, and with the softness of secure and confident power, proclaimed, "One." He pointed a fast index finger to Mark and decreed, "Two." He jerked a thumb over his shoulder and commanded, "Three."

"Who?"

"Greco's mural in the restaurant," EZ explained for Mark. "Reb is sure it was done by Salvador Dali, who is masquerading in this town as Grool."

"You *see*," Reb gloated to Mark. "I *know*."

"I see."

The loud bang of Reb's boot hit the floor as he ordered, "Ssh!" Waving a loose, disparaging hand to EZ, he said, more like a concession than an honor, "Number Four." Reb looked at Mark. "Now we have something solid to go on. That's all I need. How much does the President make?"

"I think the chump's on straight commission," said EZ.

"Where are those files? Kissinger? Helms? Africa? I need that. I want that now! Do not underestimate the severity, gentlemen, repeat, repeat, repeat!"

about by rulers mostly knaves, and soldiers mostly fools.

—Ambrose Bierce

"I'll get the files for you in a minute, man," Mark assured him.

"I want the minuteman files too," Reb ordered. "And the pyramid files. And the pyramids. All of them -- the Egyptian ones and the Mexican ones and the Transamerica pyramid and Pyramid Lake and the pyramids under the north and south poles."

"Vivian called the crisis clinic on Reb," Mark told EZ. "They're sending out a counselor and a *gendarme.*"

"What the hell did she call the cops for?" Understandably, all police, regardless of their assignments, made EZ apprehensive.

"Might not be that bad an idea," said Mark. "He's been getting further and further out."

EZ shook his head. "You know, there are some basic things about life that you just don't understand."

"Like what?"

"Like Reb's whole trip is bogus."

Mark was shocked. "What? No, my friend. This dude is really going through some difficult changes. I can't believe you're that insensitive to him."

"All right, have it your way," EZ agreed, with the salesman's instinct for being agreeable.

Reb pointed a menacing finger at EZ, then swung it abruptly to Mark. "Number Two!" They nodded esoterically, confirming some shared, secret knowledge, and laughed. Then Reb stomped his foot and shouted, "Nixon, Brezhnev, Hughes -- I want those folders here tonight, with the guns and the money!"

The door opened. Charlie, weary and disapproving, looked around, groaned, and not finding anyone there he wanted to talk to, announced to nobody in particular, "The shrink and the cop are here. Let's make it simple for everyone."

"The cops!" Reb rose mechanically. His face froze. His suspicion that they had come for him took ten seconds to congeal into a chilling certainty. His palms out-turned, hexes and whammies flew from him like sparks in all directions, defending himself against the advance of the invisible hordes. "Danger!" His voice faded into invisibility, too, and

Any member introducing a dog into the Society's premises shall be liable to a fine of

he mouthed, Danger!

"I don't believe in insanity," EZ bitterly rebuked Charlie. "I try to take people at face value. I mean if some monkey tells me he can fly, or he's the greatest painter since Picasso, who am I to say fuck you to this man? Maybe he is. And even if he's not, if he's given it a good shot, he'll probably have something to show for it. Two jokes and a funny face. Something."

"Well, that's nice to say," said Charlie, "but look at this boy. This kid is *out* there."

"*You're* out there! Reb shouted at Charlie. Suddenly smiling, to EZ and Mark, Reb urged them, "Let's give them Charlie. They'll never know."

That cracked Mark up, and he roared so robustly with laughter that the gigantic policeman who came through the door just then was sure he was the nut, and grabbed Mark firmly in a huge bear hug. The psychiatric crisis counselor followed. "Not me!" Mark cried out. "I'm only Number Two. Reb -- tell them who Number One is! Aren't you Number One?"

Charlie shook his head and pointed, so the policeman released his hold on Mark and looked at Reb.

"Two answers come to mind to that question, gentlemen," Reb, the picture of composure under pressure, told them, "Yes and no."

The cop grabbed Reb, and the shrink ordered, "Put him on 72-hour hold."

Reb fell limply in the policeman's grip. "I'm dead."

"Don't hurt him," Mark asked. "He won't give you any trouble."

The gigantic cop turned to face Mark, swelled and said, exuding contempt, "Nobody gives me trouble, kid."

Mark returned his tough look, but secretly he smiled. It had been a long time since anyone had called him "kid."

The Least Worst

poker

"Tactics is knowing what to do when there is something to do: strategy is knowing what to do when there is nothing to do."
— *Grandmaster Savielly Tartakower*

Peterson had a rush of jobs, so Mark had to put in six straight and long days at the shop. The latest exchange of hostilities weighed heavily on his mind. His depression made it seem as though his decision to withdraw from the town's politics in order to reinvest himself in play and game theory had been a blunder. The town was real. It was important. How could he walk away from it?

He had been through all this before, of course, and he recognized that. It was just a mood. He was not indispensible to the town. He was indispensible to his work. The latest round of melodramatics with Pearl made everything look worse than it actually was. He washed the cobalt blue off the Heidelberg, and inked it with the dark green.

* * * * *

Home, at last, he fell into bed at once, taking with him his alarm clock, which he set for one hour later, and his transistor radio. He wanted to catch the basketball game.

He fell asleep at once, and when the alarm went off it was as if it had been an instant. Feeling thoroughly exhausted, Mark nevertheless turned the radio on, just in time to catch Forrest Pritchard's conclusion to his beloved militaristic third verse of our ill-chosen national anthem. And the game got underway: "E.C. hits the free-throw. 1-0 Warriors, biggest lead by either club."

Before the first quarter had ended, Mark had fallen off to sleep, with Bill King's eloquent rapid-fire play-by-play booming into his left ear from the little radio on the pillow. He dreamed he was in the Oakland Coliseum, with the play-by-play being piped in over the loudspeakers.

Mark spotted Professor Ross near the front row, center court. Ross spotted him, and pointed him out to two graduate assistants, dispatching them to fetch Mark. Not eager for the inquisition he feared was in the the the offing, Mark left his seat.

He went up to the last row in the balcony, lay down against the wall, and fell asleep on the bench. He dreamed he was with Pearl, by the edge of a pond in a beautiful wild meadow. The two of them leaned over, to look at themselves, but their reflections were broken to bits when Pearl threw a handful of dirt at them, and left. When the dirt sank, the water stilled, again, and Mark could see himself more clearly.

He woke, a little stiff for having slept on the board bench. Suddenly everyone turned to the loudspeakers, something had happened in the game. "What's up?" someone yelled. "Barry just got thrown out of the game on back-to-back technicals," someone yelled back. "Warriors cut a Phoenix lead of twenty down to four. Two minutes left."

"Holy Toledo!" the broadcaster shouted. "Dudley on a steal and breakaway. Warriors cut the lead to two. Westphal tatoos the dribble up the floor, Smith hounding him. If the Warriors lose this one, you can chalk it up to that grandiloquent egomaniac Richie Powers!"

Mark realized the game was in fact coming from a little plastic radio, next to his head, on the pillow, in his own warm bed. And he was glad of that, because he was very tired. He fell asleep at the final buzzer, curiously ambivalent about Mahalich's noncall on the foul on Parrish's buzzer shot, which probably would have sent the game into overtime.

Pitching great Cy Young claimed all the Youngs could throw -- his grandfather

Mark woke to a dark morning, feeling rested. He didn't know if it was twelve or five. He turned on the light. It was three-twenty. He made coffee, cleared his desk.

Out of the brooding of the previous week, and its depressing sense of obligation to the town, a clear question for the student of ludics was emerging. Mark's involvement with the town had crystallized into a commitment the night of the meeting he debated a radical professor. That night, Mark had equated utopian community experiments with models and prototypes, that would be of practical value later. But he was wrong. What went wrong? And could he express his error ludically?

He poured the coffee, put on Bartok's fifth quartet.

It wasn't so much that his idea was wrong, as that it was incomplete. It had left human villainy out of the equation. The model situation was invaded by a conflict situation. That's it! The town was *not simply a model, but also a competitor* in a very complicated lifegame with various adversaries.

Far from being free of the conflicts of the greater society, we found ourselves victimized by them. We lost the unique freedom our little territory was supposed to have had.

Well then, what kinds of games *are* the town?

It's a theatrical game. The town's a stage, upon which our little histories and dramas are played. Our characters are the performances of the myths that possess us, and by playing them out we may finish with the parts, and move beyond them, into the world of the new myths.

The town's also a model reality, or strives to be. Which is to say that its idealism is still alive.

And the town's a player in a prolonged conflict game with Weel. What kind of conflict game? A war game -- complete with physical and emotional violence, mixed and complex strategies on both sides, incomplete information (more like cards than chess), and masks of disguise and inconsistency. Just like war and poker.

He turned to the branch of mathematics called game theory, which was developed by John von Neumann, from watching poker players at work. Game theory deals with the

once killed a flying turkey buzzard with a rock.

calculation and selection of optimum strategies against opponents who also have a choice of strategies and includes in its equations their conflicting desires and actions, the need for uncertainty, bluffing, inconsistency, and so forth. Mark's favorite primer on the subject was the one by the Rand Corporation, which was filled with examples from military applications of game theory, such as the calculation of how best to deploy the available offensive and counter-defensive weaponry against an enemy who has such and such options of how to deploy his available defensive arsenal, how many bombs, how many anti-missile-missiles, how to mix them up, and so forth.

Before going on, Mark reviewed the basics of another play-related branch of mathematics. Probability theory was discovered by Blaise Pascal to help a gambler friend answer questions like, "What are the odds of throwing three sixes in a row with a pair of dice?" or, "What are the odds of improving a pair of sevens with a king kicker in a seven-man, five-card stud game?"

And then back to game theory, the nuts and bolts of it -- fragmentary knowledge, randomization and the mask of inconsistency, saddle points, mini-maxes (simply: the least worst outcomes), mixed and pure strategies, oddments, zero-sum games, signals (as between bridge partners, or secret agents) and bluffs (as between poker players) and interfering with them, and so forth.

"Mark! Mark!" followed by a loud clubbing at his front door commanded Mark's attention. "Are you in there?"

Mark opened the door to find, "Grool!"

He never comes to town, Mark realized. Why is he here, now? He looks very worried. Something's wrong.

Oblivious to the amenities of social relationships, Grool pushed his way past Mark and seated himself in the most comfortable chair in the house. "Sit down," he ordered Mark. "I have terrible news."

Mark walked to his desk, turned his work chair around, and sat facing the agitated recluse.

"Listen, you," Grool began, in a foul mood, and far too out of practice to care about clothing it. "Do you swear to keep what I tell you confidential?"

In tournaments it is not enough to be a connoisseur of chess; one must also play well.
— Sigbert Tarrasch

"Short of illegality, yes," answered Mark.

"And long of illegality?" asked the troll.

"Depends how long, and why."

Grool smiled. "To tell you the truth, I don't have too many options, so I'll take my chances with you. Listen: who do you think trashed Weel's place?"

"To tell you the truth, as you say, I thought you were behind that."

Grool nodded, wondering how many others suspected him. "Me and who else?"

"Salugi. Amy. And an experienced hand, or two."

"Do many people think this way?" Grool asked.

"No."

Grool relaxed a bit, went on with his story. "Listen: Salugi got busted a couple of days ago, for selling a couple of ounces of cocaine to the wrong man. And I have heard, through let us say mutual friends, that Salugi is sorely tempted to cop a plea on the coke bust and turn state's evidence in the vandalism case, implicating me and Amy." Grool's elvish, angular body moved from one ungainly posture to another, in Mark's well-stuffed chair.

"That could ruin the whole court case." Mark now realized the reason for Grool's unprecedented appearance. "Could ruin the whole town's future."

"Yes. Listen: there is something I've never told anyone before," said Grool, "but I'm all out of plans now, and I need help, so why should I hold back? Listen: the day before the studio was burned down, Johnny Carmody paid me a visit. He told me if I didn't leave town for good, Weel would see that everyone else in Lone Buck Bay left, one way or another. I thought he was just trying to scare me, but that night they killed my wife and my best friend in the fire. I had to take him seriously after that. That's why I left the town, and haven't been back. Until tonight."

Mark took a deep breath. "Why haven't you told anybody?"

"Well, as I say, at first I thought it wasn't worth taking seriously, and I ordered Carmody out of the studio."

"You were in the studio when he threatened you?"

"Yeah. I was taking gamelan lessons from this dude

One real world is enough.

— Santayana

from Jakarta, who was staying with Vivian, for awhile.''

"I remember him.''

"And that night,'' Grool began, but could not finish this thought in words. There was a long silence. "Our town is filled with cowards. Nobody's done anything!''

"Grool, the age of blood feuds is past. Look how much trouble your recent adventure in revenge has been.''

"We'll see,'' said Grool. "To tell you the truth, it was very satisfying to me.''

Mark did not like that tack, returned to an earlier one. "You were explaining why you never told anyone about Weel's threat.''

"Yeah. Well, I couldn't think straight right after they murdered my wife, and I was in no condition to deal with other people getting killed, because of me, so I figured the best thing to do was leave right away, and try to sort it all out later. By the time I began to realize that maybe I should have told somebody else about the threat, it was months later, and I would have had the additional problem of explaining why I hadn't said anything until then. Why would anybody have believed I was telling the truth? You see, I had no proof. It would have been my word against theirs. It still is.''

"What about the guy from Jakarta?''

"Brilliant musician,'' said Grool.

"Where is he? Did he hear anything?''

Grool shrugged. "I think he went back to Jakarta. He wouldn't have been any help. Carmody talked to me quietly, and anyway the Indonesian dude only knew about two words of English. 'Hash' and 'fuck,' I think they were.''

"But he saw Carmody, that day?''

"So what? Carmody used to come by a couple times a week, in those days, to bring messages, and take a look around. It was no big deal for Carmody to be visiting the studio.''

"Was anybody else around?''

"I don't think so.''

"Was there a tape going?''

Grool laughed. "Wouldn't that be handy. To tell you the truth, there was a cassette recorder there, but we weren't

. . . I could see in a minute (Tom's plan) was worth fifteen of mine, for style, and

using it.''

Mark reared back on his chair's hind legs, and rocked. ''Time is very critical, in this matter. The more time we spend doing nothing, the greater the chance Salugi will talk. And if you're indicted in a criminal case, especially for vandalism against Weel, that might ruin your contract case against him. And if that goes, there go all the town's plans for the future again. Not to mention probable prison sentences for you and Amy.''

''Wow! Can I listen to that?''

''*What?*''

Grool skidded over to Mark's pile of records on the floor. ''Ceceil Taylor's 'Indent.' You don't care if I put this on, do you?''

''Go ahead,'' Mark invited him, half in horror that Grool could be so indifferent to the impending tragedy, and half in envy that he could so easily immerse himself in his world-apart of music. As Grool put on the unique piano piece, Mark recognized, beneath the howling urgencies of the immediate disaster, his own regret at having been reclaimed by the town, and diverted from his gamework. But he couldn't consider walking away from this. Grool had come out of his retreat. The crisis was pressing. Nonetheless, he felt sorry he had been sidetracked.

From what? Oh, yes, he recalled, game theory, and why my model theory of Lone Buck Bay was insufficient. Ain't that the truth? Yes, game theory, poker, masks of inconsistency, yes . . .

And by the time Grool had finished listening to all three layers of ''Indent'' Mark had thought things through enough to say, ''I have an idea, Grool. You know, there's an old poker adage that you can only bluff the stronger players, because the weak ones call everything. Would you guess Weel was a good poker player?''

''I can tell you from experience, he's an excellent one,'' Grool said.

Mark permitted himself the tiniest of smiles. ''That's what I thought.''

* * * * *

''Look, I will do what I must do, Joanie. I must tell you

would make Jim just as free a man as mine would, and maybe get us all killed besides.
— Mark Twain

everything Grool told me, and I have,'' said Mark. ''And I have a plan. But I know how one move leads to another, and this is a season for limiting my participation in the game of Lone-Buck-Bay-must-win. I am not your problem, here, Joanie -- Salugi is. And Weel.''

''Your plan sounds very iffy,'' Joanie said.

''It's not foolproof, and it will take the performance of your life to bring it off. But it's a good plan. Weel's smart move is to take it. And you'll be sensational! What great theater. The theater of life, with hundreds of thousands of dollars at stake! How can you resist?''

''How can you?''

''You're so much better at selling and acting than I am.''

''Flattery won't be enough. You'll have to convince me this wild plan will work.'' She explored Mark's chaotic kitchen. ''Can I heat his up?''

''Yes. But no, I don't have to convince you this'll work. All I'm saying is it might work. I have to convince you that doing something is better than doing nothing, now, and that this is the best we have to go with. Remember how I argued for a waiting move, after the vandalism. Time was on our side, then. And there weren't any good plans open to us. But now we have to act. The longer Salugi stays in jail, the likelier he'll be to talk. We're compelled to make a move.''

''It might make things worse,'' said Joanie.

''What do we have to lose, if the bluff doesn't work?'' Mark asked. ''I don't see that there's too much risk attached to this. Weel can't use it against us. The one thing we know that Weel doesn't is how vulnerable our court case suddenly is with Salugi threatening to sing. It's the right move, Joanie. I can feel it. We have to bluff the ace in the hole, and hope he doesn't call us on it.''

''What's that? Poker?''

''Yeah. And the name of that game probably comes from the Germanic word *pochen,* to bluff, or brag. Look, Joanie, none of our options, at this point, are sure things. The bluff isn't. There's a real chance he won't go for it. But it's a lot better than nothing. And it might very well work. He can't be sure we don't have an ace-in-the hole. I think Weel will go for it. In his position, it's the mini-max, the least worst

The art of being wise is the art of knowing what to overlook.
                                                    — William James

course. It's the way Petrosian plays chess. It's the prudent course. Weel doesn't know about Salugi yet. So he's probably counting on the court ordering him to fork over $300,000 -- $500,000. All we're asking is an additional $250,000 or so, whereas we're threatening to wipe him out completely. We're claiming we have evidence linking Weel to two deaths committed in the course of a felony. That's heavy. Unless he's very sure we're bluffing, he has to go with the out-of-court settlement. That's the mini-max, the least worst outcome.

"You think Weel knows about your mini-maxes?"

"I'll bet he can pick them out of the stack, time after time. Intuitively," Mark assured her. "His success in business depends on it, and he knows that, even if he doesn't know the theoretical basis of it all."

"Grool's problems aren't helped by this, are they?" Joanie said.

"No." Mark conceded the objection, and that it was a hard one to accept. "No. All this action would give us is funding to carry on with building the town. But, we should also get Weel to sign an agreement not to mine Goat Hill or dredge Pebble Creek or Lone Buck Bay. That ought to take away his last set of options in the town."

"Maybe we can tie Grool's troubles into this deal," Joanie suggested. "Make Weel promise not to push the case against Grool, or we'll release the tape."

"He doesn't know he has a case against Grool, and we don't want to tell him," said Mark.

"Might not be so bad a plan," Joanie said, in a new tone. "I just thought of something. As long as Grool is willing to swear the tape is genuine, or as long as Weel *thinks* Grool's willing, it doesn't matter much whether or not Weel thinks the tape is legitimate. Carmody won't be around to back him up. What did you have in mind for the dummy tape? Who'll do Carmody's voice?"

"Nobody. I don't think we should even try to make a tape. The fewer people who know about this, the better. We don't need a tape. We're not offering him the one and only copy of our evidence. You're not walking alone into his plant with the one thing that can sink him. You're claiming that

Whatever women do they must do twice as well as men to be thought of half as good.

someone -- Grool -- has the tape hidden somewhere, and another copy with the lawyers, let's say, and if he doesn't go along with our program, we're going to turn over the lawyers' copy to the right Assistant DA. He doesn't even get to hear the copy. He's in no position to set conditions for us. We're the ones in the position of strength. We can't make a half-hearted bluff. We either have the whip hand, or we don't. That's why we have to ask for more money than the court will award us, and total control over the creek and the bay. Otherwise he'll wonder why we didn't. To carry off the bluff we have to deal with Weel, at all times, as though his only choices were to pay the penalty in cash, to us, or in years of his life, to the state."

"OK. So I treat him with a bit of sadistic relish," said Joanie, "because I know I've got him, because I've listened to an old cassette that Grool had. And the tape is filled with gamelan improvisations . . . "

"Do you know what a gamelan sounds like?"

Joanie raised her nose, and viewed Mark along its length. "Of course. Then there's a break in the music, and Carmody comes in."

"Grool says he spoke first," said Mark, "and accused Carmody of having an informant, who was spying on the town, and keeping Carmody and Weel posted on all the news. Carmody just laughed in his face, and asked what the hell he was going to do about it."

"Who was the informant? Priscilla?"

"That's right. I don't even remember her. Who the hell was this Priscilla?"

"Remember the Wingates?" Joanie asked. "The family that had the gas station and garage, before Charlie took it over? Priscilla was their daughter."

"Grool said she was having an affair with Carmody."

"They deserve each other. I always wondered what was behind her sudden interest in our town. I like that, about Priscilla and Carmody. That will lend some more authenticity to the bluff, if I drop that in. Well, since it looks like this is the only plan we have, let's rehearse. You play the bad guy."

"We need to contact the lawyers, too." Mark wrote a

Luckily, this is not difficult.

— *Charlotte Whitton*

note as he said, "The papers for the out-of-court settlement have to be all ready for Weel to sign. And yes, let's rehearse. Rehearsals are a great idea. A role simulation game, to explore the situation and sharpen strategies. Very important new play field. A friend of a friend of mine worked for a government funded think tank that specialized in very serious role-simulation games. He worked on a game called *Politica,* which was designed to study the options and strategies necessary to overthrow a supposedly fictional Latin American country. They tested the most effective ways to manipulate and coordinate the military, street agitators, police, media, how to time things, recognize the crucial situations, and so forth. And according to my friend's friend, the game-tested conclusions were later used by the CIA in their successful orchestration of the coup that overthrew the Allende regime in Chile. The winning strategies were all worked out in the playroom, during rehearsal time."

"We want to work on my delivery, too. As well as the lines," said Joanie.

"Definitely. In the last analysis, whether or not Weel goes for the bluff may depend on how persuasive your performance is."

A distant mood descended over Joanie, and she appealed to Mark, "You may have to get more involved again."

"I'm not moving away. I'll be around." Mark gave her a hug. "Do you think you'll have any difficulty getting in to see Weel. Time's crucial."

"He'll see me right away. Weel's A & R man tells me their company's very eager to produce the 'I'm The Rear View Mirror On Yo' Pickup Truck of Life' album."

"Can't you talk plainer than that?"

Joanie laughed. "You've been out of touch. 'Rear View Mirror' is the hit single of my hot new country-punk band, 'Botulistic Mucilage.' "

"They sound very wholesome," said Mark. Then, really seriously, "You're not actually thinking of signing with Weel, are you?"

"Make believe you're Weel," directed Joanie. "If your grand illusion works, we'll soon have our own fine studio, and the question won't even come up."

You can never be too thin or too rich.

— The Duchess of Windsor

Sam Francisco's City

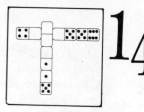

dominoes

14

> *"It's an odd thing, but anyone who disappears is said to be seen in San Francisco. It must be a delightful city and possess all the attractions of the next world.*
> *— Oscar Wilde*

"EZ Beazly, here -- antique merchant extraordinaire!" came the voice through the telephone.

"Hi. It's Mark. I'm going to San Francisco, so I thought I'd call, to see if you were heading down, and I could catch a ride with you."

"Doesn't your car work?"

"Yeah."

"Yeah? Say, are you going to be down there for a week or so, by any chance? You are? Great. Listen, the fact is I am going to San Francisco in a couple of days, but in a rented car filled with you-don't-want-to-know and you definitely don't want to be in it. However, I will be coming back just about the time you're planning to return, so if you want to trade me a ride for a share of the gas, give me a call at Sam Francisco's in a week."

"OK," Mark agreed. He left a note on his door: "Gone to San Francisco. Back in a week or so. Can be reached through the Shakespeare people, phone number at the Courier."

* * * * *

Mark parked his car downtown, near the San Francisco Civic Center, and walked around. A grave-eyed pamphleteer mutely urged his fiery words on a bureaucrat rusing to the notary's with forms in quadruplicate. Nearer Market Street, a pair of Jehovah's witnesses hawked their magazines, and their childlike vision of life hereafter in God State Park, feeding the squirrels forever, time without end.

The wind sped around the buildings with a faint wail, like a dying witch. In his little booth, now buttoning his overcoat's top button, the newsvendor scowled at the chilling wind; selling news, one old and weary change-making vendor.

Mark turned toward Union Square, noting that it was not that San Francisco women were necessarily prettier, but that they looked like they had flesh under their clothing, unlike women of other cities.

He evaded a sign-carrying leafleteer, committed to publically asking, "WHERE WOULD I BE IF MY MOM ABORTED ME?" Better as a koan than a political statement, Mark judged.

"Hare Krishna."

"Hare Krishna to you too, brother," replied Mark, "but not a cent." He turned up the block, into the Tenderloin.

"Any coins for some wine?"

"Tap city, friend." He had to smile at the foxy, vampy prostitute across the street -- blonde wig and chocolate skin, black and blue eye paints, heels up to here and a pink micromini even smaller than her sheer panties. City supposedly starting a big new anti-hooker campaign recently. Reason totters. Whole fucking economy's a whore that makes whores of us all.

"Buy a pie. Change the world!"

Who was *he* with? The Moonies? Aside from the guy in the gorilla suit playing a tuba, the clothes were starting to look better.

"Do you want to be tested? For free. A psychological profile."

"It's all right," Mark assured her. "I'm *clear*."

*   *   *   *   *

...wit turned fool: folly, in wisdom hatch'd,/Hath wisdom's warrant and the help

Joyce was Mark's true love between Michelle and Pearl, his ex-old-and-still-something, the only one of the three with whom he could work out a happy post-relationship relationship. Joyce made her living, then as now, doing bookkeeping out of her home, and teaching *go*. She played the great oriental game at *sho-dan* strength, acquired primarily during her year-long exchange of *go* lessons for English lessons with a Japanese engineer. His original English tutor had thought it a grand joke to mislead him on some of the fine points of colloquial American speech, and by the time Joyce inherited him, he had taken to answering the telephone with a breezy, "Hey, motherfucker, what's happening?" and addressing the Dean of Students as "Grandprofessor Shithead."

When they first met, Mark and Joyce vowed they would have to be dragged kicking and screaming into their next serious relationship. But the sweet play of the courting game itself provoked them beyond good sense into love, and with little ado they agreed to chance it all (or so it seemed) and throw in their lives and lots with each other. Unfortunately, they both talked so much the rooms of their house were crowded even when they were alone. Neither of them being the type to stand upon the order of their going, one day he went.

He rang the doorbell. A child in a very long yellow gown, with a big string of oversized white beads, opened the door with one hand and held a wiggling snake in the other. She was the daughter of the witch and the magician who shared the flat with Joyce. "Remember me? Joyce's friend, Mark?" She let him in. "Is she here?"

Joyce was in her room, giving a *go* lesson to a small woman with two-inch wide eyes and round black eyeglasses as big as her head. "Winning?" he asked.

"Ha! A typical greeting from this *schmuck*." Her face said she was very glad to see him. It had been a while. She joked to the fish, "I don't see this guy for four months, five days, and ten hours, and the very first word out of his mouth is 'winning.'"

The fish gaped with awe at her *go* teacher's mastery of memory.

of school/And wit's own grace to grace a learned fool.
— *William Shakespeare*

"You have a mind like a sieve," Mark could not resist. "It's been five months, a week and a day, almost to the hour." To the odd life that lived behind the big eyes behind the big glass bubbles, he teased, "Did Joyce ever tell you about her debut at the San Francisco *go* club?" Fearful that her eyes would burst, spattering all over the walls, unless he finished soon, Mark hastened to tell her, "They told her it was customary for a beginner to demonstrate that he or she could at least beat the worst player in the club, before playing anyone else. So they set her in front of this not too bright, degenerate looking, old Japanese dude. And Joyce lost eight games in a row!"

"Give me a break! The son-of-a-bitch was cheating." Joyce to Joyce's rescue, just like in the days of yore. "He used to move stones around, screw up the eyes on my groups, fix connections, all this sneaky shit. That's why they make you play him -- so you can learn to spot all that coffeehouse bullshit." Joyce laughed.

The fish out of water laughed too. More because she was flipping out than because she saw the humor in it. "Do you want to end the game?" She reached for her handbag, hoping Joyce would say yes.

"No." Dear Joyce.

"Do you have a cigarette?" Mark asked, making the obligatory fumbles about his pockets, although he had not bought a pack in weeks.

"I stopped. You made me do that. Before I lived with you, I used to smoke and keep a journal. You grubbed my cigarettes and spied into my journal, so now I don't smoke cigarettes and I don't keep a journal." She propped her head upon her cupped palm, reentering the world of stones and space.

The *go* student smiled shyly, shook her head to show that she had no cigarettes, either. Mark now noticed how cute she was.

Joyce told her pupil, "What I'm considering is playing here, which threatens to secure this connection between this little group and all this stuff, which would kill this black group in the process; and it threatens to cut you here, on the next move, which would kill off all this and have a good

Imagine Joe Louis at his prime in a country where his most dangerous opponent

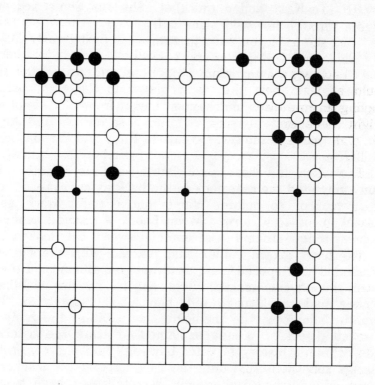

chance of eating away most of this side, before you can contain me. So I do that, and you now, as black, will absolutely have to play where? That's right. To defend against this devastating cut, which would cost you many more points than you'll lose by allowing me to make this connection here, which I will do, saving this and killing this, in the process."

"Does this group of mine have a chance of coming back to life?"

"I wouldn't count on it, honey."

was five-foot-six and weighed 150 lbs.

— Reuben Fine, on Paul Morphy's chess career

Mark excused himself, to wash his face and drink some water. He met the *go* student in the hall outside Joyce's room. "Leaving?"

"Hi. Yeah. It ended quickly." She ran some nervous fingers through her wild black hair.

"Did she give you stuff to study, for next time?"

"*Sekis* and *ko-threats*, and a *joseki*."

"Well, stay away from thickness and watch for the snapbacks."

Inside, Joyce was undressing.

"Very subtle."

"I'm taking a shower. Go talk to Rudy and Wanda, for a while."

The witch and the wizard. One always met Wanda first. Rudy inhabited the rear nook in the back room.

A year or so before, Wanda had brought Mark, as a special guest, to a Horned Moon Esbat, a witches' sabbath, to bless a new athame (a ceremonial sword) that looked like it had been grown rather than carved with the Order's Winterhilt (the special knife used to carve athames). He had sat in the sky-clad (naked) circle, and felt the way of Wicca. Wanda had revealed to him her special search for The Grand Catholicon, the medicine that enables the body to cure all diseases. Wanda explained to Mark the witches' side of man's history of witch-burning. And she confirmed Mark's suspicions that only the lesser secrets of witchcraft were hidden, since the greater secrets never have to be. Unlike magicians, who were natural solitaries, witches were *people*-people who shared a deep need for social ritual, pagaentry and group-worship.

Best of all, Mark loved the witches' light touch with ritual, the way they called their holiest incantations' 'sacred bullshit.' His playwork had taught him that this was precisely the way primitive people understand their rituals, scoffing while they threw themselves into them, understanding that the mood and not the logic of it was the important thing. Religion deals with our sense of evil, not evil itself, according to Erikson.

Mark recalled Huizinga: "In the sphere of sacred play, the child and the poet are at home with the savage." A ritual is

There is a sacral secret at the root and in the flowering of all play: it is man's hope

not to be won, but to lose oneself in, in order to rediscover life anew. Vicarious participations in divine processes: funerals, feasts, communions, oaths.

Mark and Wanda shared a beer, gossiping incessantly. Witches in general were superior gossips, being not merely people-oriented, earthy, sexy, and talkative, but free of guilt about it. "Come see Rudy," she invited, "if only for a minute. Before Ms. Stein returns from the machine shop."

Rudy worked alone. The magician's way. He forged his magic from his will alone, his magic providing the dramatic framework for the performance of his intense life. With Wanda stationed at the gate to rebuff most potential invasions, he was able to inhabit a secluded reality in which his will ruled unchallenged.

He was the man the doorbell listed as *Malaclypse the Major, The Count of Seven, Der Meisterschemer of the Bavarian Illuminati (World's Oldest and Most Successful Conspiracy)*, and *Special Correspondent to Sirius*.

"Mark!" Happy Rudy the Ready. "The question is, were the gnostics essentially correct in interpreting Eve's snake as serving the same function as Prometheus? Which would of course make Jehovah no more than old Nobodaddy, one fully deluded step removed from the first god, The Alien. Do you see what I'm getting at?" All of Rudy's questions were rhetorical. You didn't get to see him unless you knew that. "Ontology regurgitates philanthropy, The Seven Deadly Virtues, and all that. Or as my Indian friend is fond of saying, 'Truth is what you find out for yourself.' "

"I heard you had a gig? A government endowed research project?"

"What?" Rudy seemed more stunned by the news than Mark. "You mean the *I Ching* pinball machine? No, I know. You mean that bullshit, that paper for that large midwestern testing laboratory on the relationship between Planck's Constant and the distribution of gerunds in 'Playtime for Bonzo.' Fascinating, the joys of gerunds, Steeth-Thompson Tale-Type Index and all that dandruff. Yes, that's led me to the study of an obscure small classic -- believed to have been written by none other than William Fuld, the inventor of the ouija board -- called 'The Footprints of the Master

for another life taking visible form in gesture.

— Fr. Hugo Rahner

and His Dog,' the central chapter of which deals with the
inexplicable Grant Street Find, popularly known as The
Elaborate Sentence of Felix Fandreaux -- popularly, and
certainly inaccurately, since Fandreaux was illiterate. He came
to San Francisco in 1850 in search of gold. Two years after,
he was spurned by a Sausalito fishmonger named Molly
Balew, and he hit bottom, drinking and wandering the
streets of San Francisco's Chinatown, babbling endlessly in
Canuck. The authorities found the Elaborate Sentence in
1903, when they took his body out of the gorilla cage. The
sentence and all the rest of Fandreaux' personal effects were
extensively soiled by pigeon droppings. In 1923, a dis-
reputable group of quasi neodadaists called the Jo-Jos
published Fandreaux' sentence as a party hat, and then it
promptly fell back into the obscurity that everyone believed
it deserved. But in 1951, a team of biologists working for a
prominent cosmetic firm synthesized a living frog, using the
sentence to program the specifics of the genetic code. And
three years later, a Pentagon cryptographer -- code name:
Deeto Sleet -- uncovered the . . .''

Mercifully, Rudy's bottomless monologue was plugged
by Wanda, Joyce, and Wanda's friend Inana, entering
talking, all three of them at once. Inana, the angular, all
black lace, feathers, and cameos. Mark was as eager to
leave with Joyce as she was with him. He tried to remember
how many fingers he had, before Rudy started talking.

Joyce. Joyce's bed. She is in a bra and panties, saying
she needs sympathy; she just broke up with Lance, the guy
she'd been seeing almost every day and night for the past two
months.

"Among your many virtues, Joyce, you have two of the
world's best tits. They're a beauty and a wonder. Who was
this guy? Buck the Duck, from the bowling alley?"

"Fuck a duck. Lance McArdle, from the comic book
company."

"Oh, yeah. I know who you mean."

"He's a five-way schizophrenic. Damnedest thing I've
ever seen." She tried to joke, but could not come close
to laughing about it yet. "Five ways. Two of them I really love.
One of them I could put up with, if I had to. The fourth one

If Jesus were to come today, people would not even crucify him. They would ask him to

is so vegetative it doesn't enter into the calculation, one way or another. But this fifth one that just showed up last week, him I can't take at all."

They talked. It was good being with her, he thought. They held each other, and touched each other. Taking off her panties, she said, "I'm feeling really lucky that I have one dear old lover, like you, to help patch me up, when I need that."

"You really are lucky. I wish I had somebody like that," Mark confessed. He saw in an instant that she did not like that at all, so he added, "Only kidding."

She shook her head. He had hurt her before with his brand of joking. She pulled up her panties, got out of bed, put on her bathrobe. "I gotta pee."

She came back dressed. In the days when they lived together, his remark and her response would have been big deals, but now even the major emotions between them were channeled into something like courtesy. "I have a *go* lesson in an hour."

"Yeah. It's getting to be time for me to go to Oakland. Basketball game. Can I come back here later? I'd like to."

"Actually, I was thinking of getting into it with my advanced student, later tonight." She waited. They both waited to see if he would say anything, and listened to hear, in his voice, how much he wanted her. He knew he could not risk speaking unless he was ready to gamble Life Together with her again. Certain he did not want to do that, he kept his quiet. Love and the best intentions had not made a happy couple out of them, last time, and wouldn't this time. After she waited an unmistakably generous length of time, she added, "so it might be best if you didn't call on me again, this visit."

*   *   *   *   *

Basketball is a team game, and if you know how to listen you can hear the sound of it, 'Good *D*, pick up the guards early, get position under the boards, move the ball, move without the ball, get it downcourt fast, give it to the man with the hot hand, give it to the open man, take the good

dinner, and hear what he had to say, and make fun of it.
                                                    — *Thomas Carlyle*

shot when you have it, get back fast on *D'* -- the basics that drove it and the glue that bound it. Ancient Aztec game of *Ollamalitzli* a lot like basketball. Wonder if anybody knows how much team strategy and coaching the Aztecs brought to the game? A sport of putting a solid rubber ball through a stone ring mounted on a wall. As an incentive, they would chop off the head of the losing team's captain.

Warriors favored tonight, having won four in a row. The smart bet is the percentages, not the probabilities -- if a team is on a winning streak, bet them to win rather than figure they're due to lose one.

Smith had a good first half. Barry made a breakaway pass to Parker that went seventy feet in half a second and was right on the money. And doesn't this kid Cox look good?

See how, at their best, the indidvidual players become selfless, and the Team-mind and Team-body come to life -- Smith makes the big man come out on him, passes off to Barry, who gets a pick from Ray, fake by Barry, Ray rolls to the hoop, pass from Barry, slam-dunk Ray, two points! A perfect model of the kind of creative cooperation that Lone Buck Bay had hoped to achieve.

In the second half, Gervin was uncanny with his jumper. Kenon and the quaintly named Colby Dietrick looked good, too. But Barry and Smith started hitting from outside, which set up Ray for ten, count 'em, ten slam dunks, and the Warriors won by eight.

Not having been invited back to Joyce's, Mark called the Shakespeare troupe, knowing that even if he showed up at midnight, many of them would be beginning their day.

The only parking spot he could find was on a main thoroughfare. He would have to get up at six, and move it. Sidewalks to the right of him, sidewalks in front of him, sidewalks behind him. Play a little box ball? A little king-queen, with a spaldeen?

An old man in a shabby overcoat beckoned from a doorway, his dribble hanging like icicles from his face. He reached into a pocket, removed a dead pigeon. Mark's feeling of revulsion was swept away by sudden recognition. "Are you . . . Felix Fandreaux?"

One right we never had in this country -- we never had the right to fail.
— Bill Russell

The creased face of a ruined undertaker returned the pigeon to its death pouch. "No, I'm not."

Ray Ravelli, Mark's oldest and best friend in the troupe, answered the door. "Well, what brings you to Calcutta?"

"I wanted to see what the public and college libraries have, down here."

"You can use my couch and my window nook, for a week, if you want."

"Thanks. I'll take you up on that."

Like cats and owls, they were all awake at midnight. One new beauty stood out among them. A broad-featured Mediterranean face, her lucky figure displayed just right in her pretty bourgeois polka-dot dress. She talked to Prentice. Mark worried that she was his girl. Could be. This scene was always confusing, in those ways, at its simplest.

"Talk about costuming, though," said Del, "I read where the police arrested a seven-foot woman in the world's longest lamé evening gown, breaking into a jewelry shop at four in the morning. Turned out to be a six-foot-four transvestite on platform shoes.

"Reminds me of Grasshopper's old claim," he continued, "that the weirder you dressed, the greater number of people who would refuse to believe they had seen you. So if you could create a completely unbelievable costume, you would effectively be invisible. Then you could go everywhere, secretly, see and hear everything, take over the world."

The polka dot fox had vanished. A black actor introduced himself to Mark, said he had joined the troupe the day after he had come out from Nebraska.

"Nebraska? Is that right?" Mark had not thought there were any blacks in Nebraska.

"Yup.　There's about a million-and-a-half of us, out there."

Mark's mouth dropped.

"Mostly cows, in Nebraska."

"I see."

Del came to Mark, "I'm sure Joanie knows, but tell her we'd love to have her back with us."

"I'll tell her. But don't count on it. Everybody up there wants her to sell for them. She can pick and choose. She likes it."

"The troupe can use that kind of promotion too."

"She was into *acting*, with you, not selling."

"She can do both."

"She probably can't. Joanie does almost everything very well, but if she has to deal with one person in two different Joanie-roles, she gets confused and all tangled up."

Mark felt very tired.　"I'll be by your place in the morning, Ray. I'm going to crash." He got an alarm clock, a mattress, and floor space in the laundry room with instructions from Del on resetting the clock and which room to put it in, after he got up.

*　*　*　*　*

The wires that held Mark to the Web of Associations all connected, eventually, at Pepe's desk. Mark had to find that desk. He had to talk to Pepe.

Man cannot live without God, but God cannot live without man, either. Without man,

A match lit the face of a riverboat gambler. He blew out the light with a bit of a flourish. "Beauragard's the name. I play all the games. A southern gentleman, you might say, on his way to San Francisco."

"I thought we were *in* San Francisco."

"Just goes to show you." Beauragard laughed.

The lights went on. Mark was in a games club. Beauragard had vanished. The others gawked, then went back to their games. Four were at Scrabble (a copyrighted game), two at chess (public domain), three played mumblety-peg (of French origin, actually), and one in a corner played Russian Roulette (Hades).

The maniac with the gun pointed it at Mark and commanded, "Pick a number between one and seven thousand. You get two guesses."

"What?"

"Don't be so dramatic," the mumblety pegsman scolded the gunman. "The monks don't like that."

"They're not here."

"Here they come."

Five indistinguishable monks in yellow Buddhist robes entered the room and seated themselves along a short wall. The second oldest monk rose and spoke to the group:

"If you were to say 'I doubt it' would you mean that you were certain that you doubted it or that you doubted that you were certain of it? And so in summation, any of you who may be interested in learning more about this simple biological means of contacting the Non Don Va Don within yourself, and making it work for you in everyday life, in your business affairs, your sex life, I invite you to come and speak with us after we adjourn and we will talk to you about our Home Study Program . . . "

The alarm rang. He woke drowsily. The car wouldn't start. The third night in a row the battery had gone dead. Something would have to be done. He rolled the car to a legal parking space, half a block and around the corner. He carried the battery two blocks to a gas station, had a paper cup of bad coffee and an atrocious apple turnover while he waited for the battery to get charged, carried the battery back to his car, and drove to the auto-electric place the

God wouldn't know he existed.

— Meister Eckhardt

garage suggested. Not there, they told him, they rebuilt generators and alternators, but a guy who used to work there had a shop across the street, and he could fix a short.

Sure enough, this place actually worked on cars. The busy boss was finishing up a shiny Mustang, told the Thunderbird owner he'd have to leave it all day, and spent what he thought was too much time helping his two assistants remove a Fleetwood's engine that had slipped into an awkward position. He then came to Mark's funky wreck armed with a four-foot-high meter on wheels. He hooked some clips to the battery and to something mounted in the back, walked to the rear of the shop and emerged with a little box. He took out a small part, replaced the old one, and nodded.

"That's it?"

"I could spend a couple of more hours on it and charge you another $50, if you want."

"How did you know what to look at, right away?"

"After you work on this model about 150 times, unless you're incredibly stupid, you begin to catch on to the fact that the stoplight switch tends to short out before anything else." A pro at the game. He handed Mark his change. "Here, this is yours. Try to take care of it."

*　　*　　*　　*　　*

"My sex life runs the gamut from nothing to not enough," Raymond said. "My job's a step up, though."

"The last time I saw you you were patrolling the aisles of a porno movie house, enforcing the 'No-Jerking-Off' regulation. Be hard to make any move at all, from that position, without stepping up. You're teaching, now? That right?"

"I like it. It's not kids. I teach the history of philosophy to professionals who've been out of school for a while. They do a lot of brain work in their specialties, but haven't thought philosophically for years. Mostly engineers and computer types. All bright, mentally alert, and out of practice in thinking systematically about life. The companies they work for pay for it, through USF extension, probably for some depressingly pragmatic reason, tax break, maybe."

As soon as a man apprehends himself as free and wishes to use his freedom . . .

Mark saw in Ray an independent scholar like himself, who believed the world ought to take him far more seriously than it did.

"Been getting any writing done?"

"A little. Yesterday I made a 'W.' "

"Planning on getting your PhD?"

"Maybe. Eventually. My bent is for classical philosophy -- truth and beauty, splitting the inexplicable and tickling the inarticulate. Most of the modern philosophy they want me to take is about the nature of the dots within the dots. As though abstraction was philosophy -- an end in itself instead of a tool. I tried to explain all this to my assigned thesis advisor, and he says, 'I'm not tracking you.' Like a fucking radar blip! 'I'm not tracking you.' You thinking of school, again?"

"It would be a step backwards. The academies are all into first-generation justifications of play as a legitamite field of scholarly inquiry. I think that's already been proved. It's like research into psychic phenomena -- the first-generation thinkers are concerned with documenting its existence, its claim to be taken seriously; the second-generation thinkers in the field assume its reality, and proceed from there, to examine its specific elements and dynamics."

"Maybe there is no unified science of play. Maybe you're dealing with several unconnected fields, related only by certain family resemblances," said Ray.

"The field is there," said Mark. "It's the study of freedom and autonomy. Play is never required. It's free from the physical necessities of survival, or the moral compulsions of a belief system. Therefore, it's not explainable by the laws that govern inevitable processes. Play strives to be self-contained and closed. Pick-and-roll plays and arpeggios have no meaning outside the context of their play worlds."

"Well," said Ray, "that's, in fact, how Bergson defines individuality -- as a closed and isolated system. And he says that this is what life is always struggling to create."

"Far out. The autonomous life of a self-contained system. The editor of *Chess Life and Review*, Burt Hochburg, described chess as a 'surrogate life, lived in a clearly defined area where the operative forces are known, predictable and analyzable, and where chance plays no

then his activity is play.

— *Sartre*

part.' Do you see, Raymond? There's a kind of perfection in that, and I think that element in play is the basis of all art and science.''

Raymond looked ill. "You think play is what makes science possible?''

"Exactly! Science, which is abstract, makes possible the practicalities of technology and engineering; and mathematics, which is even more abstract, makes science possible; thought is what makes mathematics possible, and play is what makes thought possible.''

"Well said, but how?''

"The process of making believe is a form of play, and make-believe, as Cassirer and Vaihinger both point out, is the basis of making symbols and abstraction.''

"To tell you the truth, it sounds pretty off-the-wall to me, although no more so than a lot of other jive that passes for legitimate studies.''

"Reminds me of a story about the Zen Master D. T. Suzuki,'' Mark replied. "After a dinner-party, a woman asked Suzuki how it was that although they spent all evening interrogating him about the nature of the universe, nothing, finally, had been decided. And Dr. Suzuki replied, 'That's why I love philosophy: no one wins.' ''

"Speaking of winning, last time we didn't get to play a single game of chess. I wanted to try out my new defense against you.''

"Well, set it up,'' agreed Mark.

Raymond fetched his set and board, asked Mark, "How would you classify chess? A game? An art?''

"Yes. The Great Soviet Encyclopedia calls chess an art whose medium is a game. Also, it's an improvisatory art, like jazz and some kinds of theater, because the creative composition and their performance go together, within an alloted playtime.''

Raymond set up the board with himself as black, and after playing 1. P-K4 P-K4 2. N-KB3, Raymond paused and nodded to Mark, with obvious pride, as he played his new defense: P-KB3.

"This is your move? Are you kidding?'' Mark shook his head. "This is Damiano's Defense.''

It is the remarkable -- and seductive -- genius of chess to evoke, in the context of play,

Raymond looked crushed. "You mean it's in the books already?"

"For a few hundred years. This opening is so bad it's named for the guy who said *not* to play it." Mark took the pawn. Raymond looked around and then took the knight. Mark gave the queen check and it was all downhill for Raymond after that.

*   *   *   *   *

Mark called Peterson, arranged to take the bus up in four days, and put in a concentrated twenty-five to thirty hours at the shop. He also agreed to take the pages of a small book back to the city with him, to bring back fully collated, the following week.

He spent the days at the library, mostly cursing or brooding about Pearl. Nothing hung together. He felt as though he had been condemned to dig his way through granite with a blunt ballpoint pen. By the third morning, he gave up trying, and yielded to an awful moodiness. He walked the street in the spring rains, listening to the soft wet rain sounds, the passing cars, the slanting rains strumming on the windows of the shops and apartments, the puddles exploding -- the whole rainscape diffracted through the mosaics of his inturned eye. He thought about the way he was so crazy for Pearl, in spite of everything, and San Francisco, San Francisco, how we came to you, diving for the lost continent of the deep and the better, and Golden Gate Park, and the view from Twin Peaks, and the way the fog oozed coolly through its cleft, tumbling down in big billowing bundles into Noe Valley, and the rains, the silences, and the sounds of the soft spring rains on the streets of the City of Saint Francis.

It was night. He headed for a coffee house, the one on Twenty-fourth, where he knew he'd find a game of chess, at least. Well, go on, go in, try to act normal.

*   *   *   *   *

Coffee machines as tall as he was, small tables, close

feelings normally generated only by the rare crises of life when safety and self-esteem are

walls (crammed with nature photos) drawn closer by junk constructions (prices on request), carrot cake and coconut pudding on the waitresses' small trays, and, all the way in the back, behind even the *go* players and the symbolic logic student with his textbooks filled with dots and squiggles, were the chessplayers -- an oversized and unbearable obnoxious man with an over-wide tie that gave Mark a headache at first sight, who was kibbitzing a game between two could-be attractive young women, both hunched over the game.

Nothing could be better. Except me, he qualified, and headed for the bathroom. In an eleventh hour bid for normalcy, Mark splashed cold water on his face, consoled himself with the graffiti -- "If God had intended us to have pay toilets, he would have made us with exact change."

Watching candles drift by him like landing-strip lights, he eventually arrived at the chess-players in the back. Both women were good-looking. Mark's cock went thump, thump. The woman on the verge of losing a lopsided rook-and-pawns ending was fidgety and flirtatious, dressed store-bought well, and Mark could not imagine what a woman who looked like that was doing here, playing chess. Not the type at all. Made him wonder who was hiding inside her costume.

The other, yes, it was she who was like the woman Mark never found and was always seeking in coffeehouses.

The fat man with the obnoxious tie looked even more so and croaked, "They say a girl who plays chess too well shows the the signs of an ill-spent youth."

The shopgirl giggled, and resigned her game. The other turned and asked Mark dryly, "Is that truly what they say?"

"Only of boys and billiards." Mark flushed when their eyes met. He begged, as to the Pope, for a blessing. She smiled, and he knew she liked him at least well enough. Mark's head felt ready to explode, and he wanted to talk to her, but he couldn't remember his name, much less Earnest Jones' theory that the drive to win at chess was not merely competitive pugnacity, but the far grimmer motive of father-murder. Why do you want to talk to her about that, right off the bat? You better keep your mouth shut, for now, he

desperately at stake.

—Robertson Sillars

coached himself.

He took his place at the chessboard. His opponent pushed a center-pawn and Mark played a Pirc defense. By the time the opening moved into the middle-game, Mark felt renewed. He was putting himself together while he was putting his position in the game together. At the critical juncture, he chose the subtler, more strategic path. It was also the more immediately risky. He winked at the woman, swapping two knights for a bishop, two pawns and some counterplay on the queen side. A gambit, at this point. But unless the obnoxious opponent was able to capitalize on his advantages in material and mobility before the board cleared and they entered the endgame, the rival was in trouble. Mark's two bishops and extra pawns would get stronger the longer the game lasted. Mark's queen was better placed, and his rooks were more mobile -- he wasn't worried. He looked at his first pick and she smiled, too.

*   *   *   *   *

She played piano for him. She played Brahms and Schubert and Bartok. He was happy to see that they both liked each other, and confused to see that she was not altogether glad about that. He tried to get close to her, to make arrangements for future meetings. But it did no good.

"No."

"Why?"

"Oh, Mark, you hardly know me at all. Talk to me. Tell me more about your theories about prodigies."

"They're not mine. Do you have an old man stashed somewhere? Are you gay? Or what's wrong with me?"

"Oh, I do like you. I do. Call me, later. Next fall. I know it sounds crazy, but do. Call me next fall." She talked faster and faster. "You barely know me. I need . . . a rest. I need to learn emotional self-sufficiency."

It went far beyond balling her, Mark knew, knowing he could have got wrapped up in this one. Looks like the all-things-considered prettiest girl in class, plays piano like an angel and chess not that much worse, and warm and real.

Arthur Schnabel explained that he has limited his piano repertoire to Beethoven, Bach,

He supposed he could hassle with her and try to make her change her mind, but if he did, of course, then they'd always have that between them.

The dull ones bored him and the bright ones were all bananas. His vestigial sentimentality had been scarred often in recent years and would soon become so deadened its intermittent tyrannies would end. Next fall? He felt he had to ask, "What was your last love like, that you put yourself on this restriction?"

"Oh, it wasn't him. He was nothing. Really. The final straw, perhaps. It was a tragedy that I could be reduced to caring about a nothing like him. He was the old man of my friend down the block. We used to talk about how we wanted to spend the rest of our lives together with each other. He used to tell me she meant nothing to him and he used to tell her that I meant nothing to him. He was telling both of us the truth. One day he left. We heard rumors he's in Portland. But it wasn't him. It used to be so easy to trust people." She shook her head and shoulders to clear herself. "Look, I like you, I do, so I'll say it again -- I can't see you or anybody for a while. I've assigned myself to a full year of celibacy, sexually and emotionally, and so far I've only done seven months. It's what I have to do. Try to understand. If you do call, after I'm through with my commitment, and we get to know each other better, then you get to hear my life story, and you'll see what led to this."

"What led you to your insanity? You must be at least half-mad, to be doing what you're doing. You may spend your life fact gathering and theorizing about nothing. Don't you wonder whether or not what you're doing is going to add up to something worth the effort?" When Mark was quiet for awhile, she said, "Well, anyway, on the way here, you were telling me about prodigies. Will you tell me more?"

Mark was quiet another minute while he reconciled himself to her decision. "OK. Prodigies generally are found in music, mathematics, and chess, which are all classical playspaces; that is, self-contained worlds. What goes on within them has nothing to do with the real world. One can still be a

Mozart, Brahms, and Schubert because "I only play works that are better than they can

little kid, and yet be master of these otherworldly fields. There's reason to believe that almost all prodigies have a childlike style, and prefer simplicity and clarity to complexity and ambiguity. Think of Capablanca and Fischer, in chess, and Mozart and Medelssohn, in music.''

"Have there been any prodigies of both chess and music?''

"I don't think so. Very few grown men have been outstanding at both -- Philidor, Prokofiev, Taimanov. Can't think of any prodigies, though.'' He was still a bit glum.

"Tell me more,'' she said. And he did.

* * * * *

He slept on her couch, felt dejected because they would not take off and soar into something new and wonderful, the way he knew they could, but gladdened to feel that he was still alive, inside, still able to feel again.

He awoke abruptly, but with his eyes still shut. He tried to think where he was before he opened them. Remembered. Opened just a peep. Saw her standing in the hallway, watching him, silently. She stood there half an hour.

He left for Peterson's at dawn.

* * * * *

Mark put in forty hours at Peterson's in three days, with nothing to revivify him but a few rags of sleep on Peterson's office couch, and the morning Chronicle with a hearty breakfast in the spoon down the block. He finished at dawn the fourth day, waking with a start at 4:45 a.m., realizing he must have fallen asleep at around midnight, trying to finish up the saddle stitching on the church booklets. Came close, too, before he conceded he was getting as likely to put a staple through his fingers as through the booklets, so he'd better not waste himself or the man's little books. He finished at six, slept in Peterson's den from seven till noon, and then headed back to San Francisco to watch a bridge partner of his compete in the Fifteenth Annual World Domino Championship.

be performed.''

The domino tournament was held in the Commercial Club's game rooms in the Bank of London building in the rich white heart of San Francisco's financial district, and sponsored by Hearst's Examiner. The tournament's proceeds went to a poor black neighborhood's boys' club. Western Airlines contributed not only the flights to Acapulco or Honolulu for the champions, but also a half-dozen stewardesses.

Mark stared in astonishment when he saw the man who raced to join him in The Commercial Club's elegant elevator. "Hello, Weel." He had not seen him in years, not since the days of the planning meetings in San Francisco. "Are you here for the tournament, too?"

"The tournament?" Weel now recognized Mark, more with revulsion than surprise.

"Dominoes?" Mark suggested, sensing that Weel's apparent calm was more the studied evenness of a poker player than the trouble-free ease of the serene.

Weel looked at Mark as though Mark were taunting him; as though Mark knew what he was, in fact, only fishing for. "Actually, I'm here to play Monopoly," Weel told him with hostility. "You know how that works -- you have to mortgage something on one side of the board to pay off your big out-of-court settlements on the other."

"I see," said Mark, fighting the smile.

"I'll bet you see," Weel answered. The elevator doors opened on one of the Commercial Club's luxurious lobbies, and as they closed again Mark watched Weel turn down a red carpeted corridor.

"We won!" Mark shouted, very quietly. The goddamn bluff worked. Lone Buck Bay is three-quarters of a million dollars richer, and a quarter-million better than we would have got out of the best court decision. What a change for all of us. The crazy bluff worked. That son-of-a-bitch bought it. Of course it *was* Weel's smart play. Face it, Lerner, you worked up a good plan. Yeah, they always look great after they work.

He skipped out of the elevator and into a bar, which Mark passed through and into the big gaming hall. Thanks to Weel, Mark smiled as he saw the hundreds of bridge tables,

People of the same trade seldom meet together for merriment and diversion but

the long wall lined with scores and pairing assignments, the dominoes in all stages of play, the computer people in the corner behind the scorer's table, the old San Francisco finery of the great hall itself, and the whole splendid ceremony of it all. And yet more like a bridge tournament than anything else, thought Mark -- two pairs at a table, the east-west pairs travel while the north-south duos remain statinary. But this game was five-up dominoes, a supspecies of dice and dominoes which sprung up in San Francisco around the turn of the century, and by now had grown to be the most popular domino game in the west.

Mark's competing friend was a Car Barn Domino Club regular. A domino hustler, some might say, since that seemed to be Manny Jackson's sole means of support. He was a crotchety old top sergeant type, and Mark's regular San Francisco bridge partner, on those now rare occasions when Mark went south to play for cash or master points. Scribbling on the back of an envelope, Manny made an unpleasant face at his partner, another Car Barn old-timer, named Woody LaRusso. "We're going to have to have a very big last round, to be in there for the finals. If we lose even one game, that might keep us out."

They creamed the rookies, racked up the fourth highest score of the round, qualified nineteenth out of the thirty-two pairs to make the knockout rounds of the finals. Woody was elated, but Manny only leaned over to Mark, knuckling his three middle fingers together and extending his thumb and pinky. "If you ever see a guy holding his dominoes like this, that's a tip-off the guy learned the game in jail. No good tables there, see? So they play it on the floor, and hold the dominoes in their hands."

"We have a pair who came here all the way from New Jersey," announced the speaker.

"They didn't come here to play dominoes," derided Manny, "they just came to get the hell out of New Jersey. Did you catch the opening? Of the tournament. See these chandeliers?" Mark looked up.

Expensive, the elegance of old money, nothing unbecoming either the San Francisco Commercial Club or The Bank of London. "When Mayor Alioto threw out the first

the conversation ends in a conspiracy against the public or in some contrivance

domino he smashed one of those deals to smithereens. Mayor Moscone looked OK today.'' Manny mugged throwing out the first domino. "He was an all-city high school guard, basketball. I still wouldn't vote for him. Or against him. I don't vote anymore. Fuck 'em all. Ain't none of them looking out for my interest, because I know who's looking out for my interest, and it sure as shit ain't any of them.''

"They seem to run these a lot looser than they run bridge tournaments,'' Mark said. "Partnership communication, I mean.''

"Goddamn right. Catch you doing some of this coffeehouse bullshit at a respectable duplicate game, they'll throw you out on your ass. Can you imagine slamming down a card in a bridge tournament, when you want it to be a signal, the way they slam down these dominoes? Run you out of the League. Thing is, though, this ain't nearly as much of a game as bridge is. There's much more luck in dominoes.''

"Luck evens out.''

"Your girlfriend's chest evens out. Luck is what you get or you don't get, when you need it. That's what luck is. It doesn't even out. It's *yours*. Like your name, or your face -- you got your *luck*.''

"Well, mathematically,'' Mark pleaded for reason, "they say it all evens out.''

"Mathematically, they're saying something like, 'If you added up all the good luck and all the bad luck in the world, it would come out even.' Even if that's true, who cares? Who cares whether or not the universe comes out even with itself if it plays poker with itself? Of course it does! But so what? What does that have to do with *your* luck? Or more importantly, with *mine*? Mathematics doesn't tell you that!''

"What tells you that?''

Manny couldn't believe the question. His face's round and aging rings seemed ready to spring, like a jack-in-the-box, out of its setting. "You're asking *me*? How the fuck am I supposed to know? You're asking *me* about getting good luck? Are you crazy?''

Mark thought it opportune to change the subject, and

to raise prices.   — *Adam Smith* brought up the Brooklyn Dodgers. "Do you remember Jake Pitler and Andy Pafko?"

"Yeah. Do you remember Billy Loes and Happy Felton?"

"Remember Jackie Robinson?"

"Ah."

"What do you mean, 'Ah'!"

"To tell you the truth, that goddamn nigger got away with so much bullshit you wouldn't believe it."

"I think he was the greatest Dodger of them all, on and off the field," said Mark.

The hostesses were packing up the dominoes in their boxes. A dozen tables still clicked with casual games. And Manny and Woody and the rest of finalists settled themselves, their drink, their food, their scoresheets, and their cigarettes into the sixteen tables roped off for the first round of match play.

Behind Mark, a man's voice, "Why don't you come by sometime?"

A woman's: "Because my husband needs you as a friend, and because I need you as his friend more than I need you as a lover."

"And Heather?"

"Yes, it's a problem. He still sees her. I don't exactly know what to do about it, but I do know that competition's not the answer."

Pearl, Mark thought, positioning his chair.

Manny and Woody's first pair in the finals looked like they meant business -- one sat up straight and drank straight double bourbons, and one slouched and smoked Toscanelli cigars. No turkeys left to play. This was the finals. All these players know a few things about this game. The talk quiets. The play grows slower, sounder, less flamboyant. The Toscanelli and the double bourbon take the first game 62-59.

The game got rough. Partners communicated increasingly now through an atavistic language of glares and leers that expressed a whole spectrum of loathsome emotions.

Woody starts to set in game Two, hesitates. The double bourbon calls, "Balk." Woody looks like indigestion. Manny looks ready to start smashing furniture. Instead, they

Up to this point, White has been following a well-known analysis, but now he makes

collaborate on some savvy dominoes and clobber the Toscanelli and the double-bourbon in the next two games.

Next round they faced a team from the Bakersfield Petroleum Club, one of the strongest outside the Bay area. At a nearby table, a team of elderly Bakersfield Petroleum veterans were matched against what appeared to be a team of domino hustlers pretending to be very drunk. The supposedly drunker of the two bellowed at one of his opponents, "Water? You told the waiter you want water? Fish fuck in water! You know what I don't want, waiter -- I don't want water! I want a double scotch. Yes and also a double bourbon. And you'd better give me a double martini to wash all that down."

After five hands, Manny and Woody and the Bakersfield pair were all even up. But in the decisive third game, Manny's bad luck popped up and hit him with a knockout shot. Not only could he not match the opening domino, he had to pick up every stick in the boneyard before his turn was over. They dropped the game 61-57, the match 2-1, and this year's shot at the title.

The victorious Bakersfield team rolled over the next pair in two straight, and then had to wait until the senior Bakersfield team complete their match with the pair of imitation drunks.

Upon closer examination, the drunks revealed themselves as the real thing. The one keeping score was, perhaps of necessity, merely quasi-drunk; but his partner was completely drunk.

Mark recalled that some of the greatest chess champions were blasted out of their minds during their prize brilliancies. Blackburn customarily drained a bottle of whiskey before sitting down to a big game. The immortal world's champion Alexander Alexandrovich Alekhine once found himself so drunk, at an exhibition, he decided that rather than hazard all the obstacles of a trip to the distant bathroom, he'd simply relieve himself on the floor beside a playing table. The drunker opponent addressed the older of the Bakersfield ancients -- a tall, frail, pale man, who carried a cane and a hearing aid, "Hey, Pops -- what are you doing after this is over? Come by our hotel, we got a couple of

a fatal error -- he begins to use his own head.

— Sigbert Tarrasch

broads coming by that'll short out your hearing aid.''

The drunk's partner began laughing, and kept laughing.

The old man, without looking up at either of them, "No I think I'm just going to turn in, when we're through here.''

The lesser drunk laughed. "See? These guys mean business. Coffee up. Coffee up.''

"I just had a cup of coffee. Before.''

"That was ages ago. Now you got new drinks. You got to have a new cup of coffee. Well, the waiter is waiting.''

"That's what they do.''

"How do you want your coffee? Black?''

"Blue.''

When he got it, black, he poured the greater part into an ashtray, until it overflowed onto half the table, tasted a drop, spit it out on the floor, laughed to his partner, "This shit's awful! Needs a little something to cut the taste,'' poured most of the rest of it on the Commercial Club's red carpet and replaced it with the liquor in one of his two new drinks.

"What was that?''

"I forgot what I ordered. Looks like gin or vodka. He tasted, smacked his lips. "*Much* better.''

*   *   *   *   *

Mark fell asleep on Ray's couch immediately, slept long, was wakened around eleven by an old and ex-friend, Grool's original sound engineer, Paul Kenner.

"Nice to be able to sleep so late,'' Kenner remarked.

It had taken time for Mark to realize that Paul and his entire squadron of friends had been treating him patronizingly. Years. Like the King in the story of *The King and the Corpse,* thousands of details added to the pattern, but the pattern remained unseen, until a single detail revealed its nature, and through it revealed the lengthy pattern of events that had preceded it.

"Did they give you the Nobel yet for your research into Chinese checkers?''

Now they no longer even held to the forms of respect for each other.

Mr. Bell, after careful consideration of your invention, while it is a very interesting

"Don't you feel stupid saying the same thing every time you see me?"

"No. I just want to be real sure I don't miss it when it happens."

Mark felt like an idiot beside this man who was actually succeeding in making lots of money. After the arson and deaths and Grool's retirement into seclusion, when Paul and his colleagues were packing for their return to the prosperous normalcy of San Francisco, Mark and Charlie had made a last minute appeal to Paul to stay to give Grool more time. Mark realized he should never have expected that from Paul. There were basic differences in their natures, different things mattered to them, and he had no right to hold a grudge about it.

"Did you ever get Salvador Dali to do the cover for that album you were doing?"

"Couldn't afford him. You know what he said? '$10,000, I keep the painting, and I don't have to listen to any music.' How's Grool the Great?"

"Grool is always fine." A stylized reply, intended to mean: This answer is no more sincere than your question.

"Is he still into masterminding his own career? If the terms are applicable, in his case."

Clever boy that Paul, Mark remembered. Pricky, but clever. "Sure. Why? What's on your little mind this morning? What can you offer him that's better?"

"Records. Television. Whatever he wanted."

"He doesn't want any of those things. He's not into media. Why only the other day I asked him if he wanted cablevision installed in the cave. But he doesn't have electricity, anymore."

"I've had offers, specific offers . . ."

"You're wasting your time, and mine. He's not interested in anything you have to offer."

"Tell me where he lives, at least."

"I'm not supposed to."

"Tell him to call me."

"He won't."

"Well, then tell him he's way off base about media. Media's not only where it's at now, but it's going to be

novelty, we have come to the conclusion that it has no commercial possibilities.
— J. P. Morgan, about the telephone

more so. I have friends who are working on multisensory recordings of experience." Paul lit a cigarette, "That's right, experiences which can be plugged into the brain directly, for playback. Within ten years your average businessman's lunch will include a two-dollar dessert of a neurologically simulated experience of Moses getting The Word from The Boss Above, while Helen of Troy sucks him off below."

"I'm sure the prospect of taking part in a world like that will be too much for Grool to resist." The phone rang. "Morning. Paul? Hold on." He handed Paul the phone. "You taking messages here?"

"I just left the number this morning, in case. Yeah? What! The trunk's stuck? What trunk? Why the hell didn't you put it in the *truck*? Fucking idiot. All right, listen, find the nearest hardware store and get yourself a hacksaw. Lift out the back seat and saw your way through the assembly. You ought to be able to get them out that way. And listen, when you see Junior, tell him to tell Frank to make sure Reeva gets back to the office right after the mixing session, so we can shop for that new mike. All right?" He hung up. To Mark, "Maybe it's just as well. Grool's probably been away too long." Paul looked around him. "This is Ray's apartment, huh? He's another one who never wised up. Hey, aren't you tired of always being broke?"

There was once a time, thought Mark, when all of us thought we could do it all.

*　*　*　*　*

A car screeched outside and Mark gave one of Paul's cynical chuckles. Once I always hoped for the best, he thought. Now look at me wishing for a crash, to knock off a few more jerks. He paced back and forth through Raymond's apartment, studying revenge -- he swindled Weel out of everything he owned, spurned Pearl in dozens of devastating ways, humiliated Paul before all their old friends, searched his memory for other future victims.

A salesmanlike knock at the door interrupted these gloomy fantasies. Reb, straight and sober, in a brand new three-piece suit, pin stripes, blue silk shirt, fashionable tie, and new

If it is true that the typical Britisher never knows when he has lost, it is true of the typical

black Oxfords. "Hi. Congratulations, Mark. That's fantastic. Getting all that bread out of Weel. That's some victory, huh? But listen, I bring you word from EZ Beazly."

"Come on in. I can hardly believe it. You look great!"

"I'm cured!" Reb laughed, a robust laugh from his belly, a healthy, hearty laugh. "It's astonishing, I know, but I'm cured. Just like that, as you say. I got busted in the zoo for exposing myself to the monkeys, and they sent me to this referral program for the mildly criminally insane, where they were doing an experimental program with a brand new drug. It worked. Worked on about half of us. Straightened me right out. Felt it right away, and after a week I was the best I'd felt since I was maybe four or five. I know -- it's incredible. But look at me. You saw me before."

"It's true." Mark was humbled. "You seem completely transformed. What did they give you?"

"Don't you want to know about EZ? He's over at Sam Francisco's. He says to tell you that the charges against Salugi have been dropped, on a technicality."

"Oh? I'm glad to hear that," Mark said, thinking Grool was probably off the hook.

"And EZ says you should get in touch with him at Sam's, that he's ready to leave immediately, if need be, and no later than the day after tomorrow.

"It's a mono-amine oxidase suppressant. The brain produces MAO to clear its synapses, so you can think new thoughts. But if you have an excess of MAO, your thinking gets muddy and disconnected, nothing adds up. Like I was. They think that's what happens in the depressive phase of the manic-depressive cycle. So the drug they were testing was an MAO suppressant. It's amazing. I'm cured. I feel great. Listen," Reb said in a lower voice, "the pills are very heavily controlled, but since I'm such a classic success and they want to use me to help them get new funding for the project, I can get them. Now, I'm not into dealing them, but if someone who has tried to help me, like you, felt they needed some to help pull them through a difficult period, I could probably give you a few, for what I paid for them."

"You've got a great sense of timing," Mark told him.

gamesman that his opponent never knows when he has won.

—*Stephen Potter*

*   *   *   *   *

Sam Francisco was a big dealer, a dealer who had, as his clients, other pot and coke dealers who themselves had other dealers as their primary clientelle. EZ was one of Sam's smallest accounts. Normal business practices would have been to cut EZ loose long ago, and have him deal with Salugi's friend in Santa Rosa. But, although Sam Francisco was a hustling, money-oriented businessman, he did indulge himself in a few concessions to fancy, and EZ was one of them. Sam sized up EZ as being just as capable as he was of getting rich dealing dope, but EZ was fonder than he was of the spaces between the deals, the parties and such. Sam Francisco lived to turn each occasion into a deal and every party into a marketplace, while EZ lived to turn every story into a joke and every deal into a party. They appreciated each other.

"How goes it?" Sam was a bit reluctant to have EZ meet Mark there. Not that he thought Mark uncool, but rather that he thought him a pathetic intellectual.

"Not so hot," Mark said. "My depression is the only thing I have left. It's all I can count on."

"You still hung up about that pussy?" EZ, the blunt but accurate. "Don't be such a chump. You can't lose what you never had."

Changing the subject, Mark asked EZ, "Have you seen Reb? It's a miracle. He's a changed man. I swear. He was in some experimental program where they gave him some new pills, and they straightened him right out."

"Of course I've seen him. Remember, I sent him over to give you a message. Really blew you away, did he? Did he offer to sell you some of those incredible pills?"

"At cost."

Sam roared with a wheezing laughter. "What do you think Reb was doing before he came out here?"

Mark recalled a prior conversation. "Wasn't it running a cherry-covering chocolate machine?"

In the first place God made idiots. This was for practise. Then he made school boards.
— Mark Twain

226

Sam shook his head no. "Not exactly. I will tell you what
he did. As you know, Reb's brother Teddy is my partner, so
I got the inside track. Reb's last place of employment was a
high-class bar in Nashville. He worked with six women who
regularly worked the bar -- three waitresses, two hookers,
and a local would-be movie queen. Each of the women
would let it slip to any man who expressed a personal interest in her that Reb was the world's most incredible lover.
He could stay hard for three days, coming continuously, or
something to that effect. And she'd let it slip that she
thought it had to do with those sex-pills he takes. Well, the
sex pills were colored tabs with very light doses of acid,
which Reb sold at some pirate's price as being dessicated
billy goat semen. In the end, some of his disgruntled
customers came looking for him, with the intent of cutting
off the boy's personal semen supply system, and that, in
fact, was the immediate circumstance which moved Reb to
head west."

Mark was stunned. "Do you mean, the whole insanity . . . that was just . . . this was all a con, just to sell
some phony pills?"

"Your grasp of the obvious is improving," Sam encouraged. "Which is not to say the boy is sane. Not even
close."

"He's in the wrong line of work," EZ inserted.

"Yeah. I keep telling that to Teddy," said Sam, "but
what can we do?" Sam explained to Mark, "You see, he
works himself up to a state of craziness, in order to pull off
these insane con-games he specializes in. But since he's
flipped out to begin with, he gets carried away, past the
point where he can tell whether or not he's putting it on or
really nuts."

"I can't believe it. I couldn't really believe his
recuperation, so I guess it's no harder to believe this than
that," Mark said. The recognition hit: "The town! He's
probably bilking the town, or planning on it. Sam, can I call?
I'll bill it to my home phone."

"You don't have to bill it. Call direct. I'll write it off to
charity."

Mark misdialed, dialed again. "Tom? Yeah, I'm still in

Some circumstantial evidence is very strong, as when you find a trout in the milk.
— Henry David Thoreau

the city. Yeah, I heard. That's great. I know, that should be a
crucial breakthrough. Of course I'm happy about it. Tom, will
you shut up and listen for a second! I called to tell you
something. Listen, Reb's a phony. Yeah, right, a *phony*. I
know, but listen, he's trying to hustle these bogus pills. Did
you *buy* any? . . . Well, of course I think you could spot a
phony like that a mile away Tom, I just thought . . . a
dozen, huh? What?'' Mark, grinning, told EZ, "He says
Joanie says Pearl bought a bottle of 150." Back to the
phone, "OK. I'll be back tomorrow or the next day. See
you." Hanging up, he demanded to know of Sam and EZ
why Reb hadn't picked a fatter town to fleece. "We don't
have enough troubles without sending up con men to pick up
the loose change?''

"Hang on," Sam said. "If you add up all the profits
from the pills, you'll find it won't come to much."

"Then why did he go through all that trouble?"

"I don't know. Look, I told you, the boy's perturbed.
Talk to Teddy if you want the kid's biography. I've had my
fill of him, if you want to know the truth. I've got to finish
this story I was telling EZ about this ridiculous bust in South
City.''

"Right," EZ helped. "So it's two in the morning, and
the cops send everyone home except for you and Richie and
the dude from Hayward."

"Yeah. But the cops just wait there," Sam went on,
"like they're really expecting someone to show up in the
middle of the night. Well, around four-thirty in the morning
this dude in a tuxedo, right, pulls up in a Cadillac. One of
the cops says, 'That's Mr. Big.' Just like on television. So I
say, 'Are they gonna get Mr. Big?' And Richie goes,
'Nobody *ever* gets Mr. Big.' Three of the narks go flying
through the door, they're gonna get Mr. Big. The dude
in the Cadillac sees them coming, jumps back in the car, takes
off. The narks go after him in the nark-car, this is at 4:30
man, I mean that was the only sound in South City, these
two cars zipping around the streets, screeching -- and then
there was the most incredible series of crashes, one after the
other, big ones, never heard anything quite like it. Lights all
over the neighborhood go on. Dig it -- both cars plus four

. . . tell the man of pleasure your secret wants, cares, or sorrows, and you will find that he

parked cars racked up, one cop blinded for life and another with a broken arm. The guy in the tux turned out to be a doctor who was having an affair with his nurse, and he thought the narks were some heavies his wife hired to rough him up.''

Mark was still thinking about Reb. Reb -- the mad trickster. The drunken demon god Coyote, swindling the tribe out of a dozen chickens for some of his phony medicine. The con game. Character as the sport of masquerading -- playing the man who is not what he appears to be. Except Reb doesn't know when or who he's playing.

has given up the delicacy of his passions to the craving of his appetites.

—Steele

Kali Yuga

Bell and Hammer

15

"When the world is reduced to a single dark wood for our four eyes' astonishment -- a beach for two faithful children -- a musical house for our pure sympathy -- I shall find you."

—*Rimbaud*

Mark and EZ left for the country, in the morning, stopping at the supermarket in Gumperstown, on his way home. There he had the misfortune to meet one of the last people he wished to see -- a dreaded, shrewish ex-lover named Shirley. He was able to get out of her demand for a dinner date only by agreeing to take her for coffee immediately, at Gumper's Corners.

Across the Formica table, Shirley complained to him, "Why are they so incredibly slow in this place?"

"How's it coming, Martha?" Mark called to the waitress-cook.

"Coming along."

"She says it's coming along."

"Yes. I heard. There is absolutely no way to make a living around here. You, you don't care if you live like a bum. I'm not like that, though. I'm moving back to San Francisco. What's to keep me around here?"

He shrugged. Sure wasn't him.

"If I stay up here I'll get ulcers worrying where my next meal is coming from. In the city I'll be paid well. I always am. I'm very good at what I do." Her fingers drummed like ice picks on the Formica. "How do they work the phone? If I transfer my phone to San Francisco, they'll probably hit me with a bunch of transfer charges, intercounty, but of course if I don't they'll make me pay the deposit over again. I will

229

get the other one back, though. I'll call them.''

Involuntarily, he snickered. He had tried not to listen, but she was only three feet away.

"I hate it when you laugh when I talk about money."

"I haven't seen you in months."

"That has nothing to do with it. It makes it worse."

Plump and sweaty, Martha arrived with Mark's soyburger, French fries, and potato salad.

"I refuse to believe that. She forgot me entirely."

"What did you order?"

"You don't remember. That's because you never listen to what I say."

"Where did you learn to talk like that? Your mother?"

That gave her pause. "I ordered soup."

"How's the soup coming, Martha?"

"Coming along. Maybe fifteen minutes."

"Fifteen minutes." Shirley was livid. She reached for a French fry.

"I didn't realize they gave you all this potato salad with the soyburger." She popped another fry into her mouth.

"If you'd like, you can have *all* the potato salad," he said.

She spat both pieces of half-chewed fries onto the table, snarled, "If you don't want me touching your fucking French fries, tell me."

"Hey Martha, forget the soup. The lady has to leave."

She did. The cowbell clapper crashed so hard against the glass door that Martha came out to see if it broke it. "Sorry I took so long."

"Just as well."

* * * * *

Mark drove to Lido Grande, to watch the river from the bridge.

"Hi! What's new?" It was Joanie.

"Nothing. Ever."

"You're depressed? How can you possibly be depressed? Your plan worked. We beat Weel. Lone Buck Bay is in the money."

"I know." Mark looked glumly at the sky. "I've heard this

. . . the sage desires not to desire/And does not value goods which are hard to come by.
— Lao Tzu

is earthquake weather."

She offered him half of a Bavarian apple strudel from the bakery in Gumperstown. Reluctantly, he accepted. "Read any good books lately?" she asked.

"Yes." Mark inhaled, braced for the effort. "I read. I write. I play games. I drink coffee. I smoke pot. I wonder why. Your basic idiot. Read." He wobbled on his axis. "I read this bizarre set of messages by Katzanzakis, 'Spiritual Exercises,' and in a letter to his wife from that period he writes, ' . . . I am become lost amid rows of alphabetical letters, I give my heart paper to eat as though it were a goat.' I can, as they say, relate to that."

She took his hand. "Come with me," said Joanie. "Come on -- any port in a storm, and all that."

He watched her in her kitchen, her reflection in the window, washing dishes at the sink, and when he bobbed his head to the music, an imperfection in the glass wiggled her ass as Pearl would but Joanie would never do. She called him from the kitchen, asking him to dry, and he rolled her reflected face grotesquely through the glass's wrinkles.

"What's on your mind?"

He considered.

"Don't stop drying while you think."

"The past." He dried.

"Remember Orpheus, and Lot's wife."

"Not to mention Satchel Page, whose sixth rule for healthy living was 'Don't look back, something might be gaining on you.' But as The Essex sang, 'Easier Said Than Done.' If I wasn't so stubborn, I'd go crazy."

"Don't be silly, Mark. You've barely begun. Don't you understand it, yet? You're on a long descent into an absolute but never completely attainable Perfect Hell, which you are doomed to endlessly approach but never quite reach. Who're you thinking about?"

He felt warm, realizing how close and comfortable he felt to her. Though there were no brass rings on their little merry-go-round, he still liked going round and round with her. "My fifth-from-last old lady, the one that raises attack bees in Fulton." He laughed, surprised himself that he could, and felt Hope, cruelest of illusions. "Hey, what do

Be patient with everyone, but above all with yourself.

— *St. Francis de Sales*

you think of Pearl? Personally, I mean.''

Joanie put on her kitchen mitten, performed some operation on the baking casserole and came into the dining nook. "I have two kinds of feelings about Pearl. When I'm with her and there are men around, I get this tremendous sense of being on guard, because one of the things she's best at is competing with other women for the attention of men.''

"Competing with men, too, for the attention of men. That kind of rivalry is one of the things the women's movement struggles against.

"Part of her's still back there with the old-time floozies who refused to talk to people who didn't have cocks. But there is a part of her that's trying to be independent, independent of men -- 'herself' -- even though she can only express it by demanding the freedom to flirt and fuck whom she pleases. So it's a mixture, a background of sisterly compassion overlaced with a sincere dislike. I've always been mystified that you stayed involved with her so long. Well, love is a mystery, of course.''

"What do you think of Tom and Dorothy? Is that this spring's true and perfect love?''

"It's too romantic.'' She returned to the kitchen, removed the dish and set it to cool. "They'll drive each other up the wall trying to live up to it. Did you know that Angela was seeing Larry?''

"No.'' Score six points for chaos. Mark moves back three squares. "I hope I'll be able to eat, Joanie. I have a stomach ache.''

"So? The way you eat, you must get them all the time. What do you think the cumulative effect of all those rotten meals you eat is going to be?''

"Eventually, they'll surely kill me. Life is invariably fatal.''

"And death?''

"Unthinkable.''

* * * * *

"Hello.''

A play is fiction -- and fiction is a distortion of fact into truth.

— Edward Albee

"Hi, Joyce." Home again, alone with his loneliness, he had to call someone. If only to make sure his phone still worked.

"Mark?"

"Yeah. Hi. I was wondering if you wanted to come up and visit with me for a few days?"

Dead space. "You know what I wanted to ask you? I forgot when you were down here. Have you seen that cigarette ad, it's in all the glossies, with the mustachioed sophisticate who supposedly knew the ways of worlds most men never see, playing a game of *go* with this old Japanese dude. And in the background there's this foxy Asian lady bringing them tea? But if you look at the board, you realize this guy is getting completely wiped out!"

"Yeah. I saw that. I thought of you when I did. Are you still seeing your advanced student?"

"Nah. He's the type of guy that doesn't seem to have much going for him when you first meet him, and after you get to know him better you realize your initial hit was right."

"Can you come up?"

'No. But I'll talk to you, if you come down here."

"I can't. I have a few days work-for-pay to do. Printing numbers on raffle tickets."

*   *   *   *   *

The Methodist raffle was all right, 1,500 sets of two numbers, run three up, no trouble. And the K of C raffle, 2,500, one number, run four up, that was fine. But the Pythian Sisters raffle, for the whole damn Northern California Regional Sisterlode, two colors (on a goddamn raffle ticket), one for each number, run one at a time. The new can of cobalt blue, from that other company, gummed up the numbering machines, after the red run was all done already, so he called Peterson at four in the morning, and the boss told him to wash up and put the old kind of cobalt blue on the press, run the rest with that stuff, go back and do the blues that are screwed up, wash up, finish the red

Live with men as if God saw you; converse with God as if men heard you.
— Seneca

run on the new blues. He did, he slept, he finished printing, he slept, he cut the raffles, collated them, covered them, stiched them-- the Methodists, the Knights of Columbus, the Godalmighty Pythian Sisters, and sometime in a late afternoon, days later, he finished, took his check, and headed home.

He peered as though across a great distance when a shape beside him, at Crotchky's store, called his name. It was Angela. He hadn't seen her in weeks. She told him that her father had footed the bill for her to return to college, and she had. She loved it, said she felt like a big kid in a little kids' playground, told him, "Someone like you, who's been in cold storage for a while, would love it. The sense of relevance, and competence, the immediate feedback."

"Yes," Mark replied, "I'm sure it's very ego feeding. I'm still hoping to accomplish something on my own."

"You? *You* are?"

* * * * *

He slept, dreamt that Angela was his lover again, she was smiling at him, cupped his head in her right hand and drew his face close to hers, and cut a big chip off his right ear with the scissors she had hidden in her left hand. It hurt. It bled, she had cut him, through his ear, she had cut him!

He awoke furious.

* * * * *

He looked for a sign. No sign came. He looked for a sign that no sign would come. None did. He looked for a sign that that was a sign. He looked for a sign that he could take the world itself for a sign.

The electricity went dead. Mark, with a whoop, hit a thirty-foot jump shot at the buzzer, in the dark. All was OK. He had outlasted his darkness, had made no drastic changes.

"Meaning" is something mental or spiritual. Call it a fiction if you like.

—Carl Jung

The power returned, the refrigerator hummed, the lights, music. Yuga point and Kalpa set. It began to rain. He slept.

*   *   *   *   *

Mark recognized the landscape. He kept returning to it. There were others: the hilly crossroads in a small New England town, the school (the staircases, auditoriums, halls, and classrooms), the subways and their stations and the airports. And this one, the city at night. Not downtown. A neighborhood. Sometimes Broadway and 231st Street's mix of candy stores, kosher butchers, and Irish bars; sometimes like Fordham Road, blocks on end of retail stores; sometimes like Borough Park's aging apartments. This time, it was like Sedgwick Avenue, or Tremont.

Larry was walking across the street, heading the other way. Mark called to him, but Larry seemed not to hear. Mark glimpsed his life and Larry's as being parts of a greater body, a snake's body, which contained them and others. And each moment of each life was like a lozenge on the snake's skin, and although they sometimes seemed to pass each other heading in different directions, they were in fact following the same head's single will, uncoiling, circling back, moving on. The street itself, crisscrossed with clotheslines, lined with apartments and their garbage pails, was also drawn into the snake's body, moved as one with Larry and Mark. Suddenly, a mighty laughter burst upon the street and shook it as though The Snake Of Us All Himself was laughing. Mark looked up, to face the sound, and there, on the roof of the apartment house across the street, stood Bill Beauragard, the laugher of the laugh.

"Bill!" Mark ran to the building to find the slippery patriarch, to ask him what was really going on, and why and who and how and what if and so forth. But no sooner did Mark enter the old tenement (unpretentiously named "Immediate Ocupancy") than he met. Pearl, a young and innocent Pearl, the one he had always wanted. Here she was. The lobby of the apartment had a decorative waterfall.

Beauty is just the beginning of terror we're still just able to bear.
— Rainer Maria Rilke

and Pearl, young, dressed in a green toga, with a flower in her hair, was rubbing the fall's stones with a piece of chamois. "What are you doing?"

"Smoothing out the creek's bed."

"Will that make it run faster?"

Pearl giggled girlishly, "I hope not. It's always running as it is."

"Will it make it more comfortable?"

"I don't think it ever isn't."

"Then why do you do it?"

"Because I love to."

Mark's blood raced like a white-water river. He reached to embrace her, but with a toss of her head she ran for the steps.

He followed at once, but was stopped by two elderly men seated behind a desk at the foot of the steps. The red face with the cigar rooted largely in it, like a redwood, demanded, "Where's your papers?"

"My what?"

"He looks all right," said his companion.

"Now listen," a red finger wagged, "I ain't giving you the OK to go upstairs until I see your papers in writing!" The big blimp travelled from one side of his red set of lips to another, and back again.

Mark handed over the papers.

"Listen, you son-of-a-bitch," snarled the big cigar, "I've been sitting at this bargaining table since 1944, and I can say without fear of contradiction that this is the most insulting piece of trash I've ever seen."

The other old man at the table cocked his head and winked, nodded for Mark to go on.

Twelve steps up, the stairs turned at a landing. Lily, looking even more vulnerable than she did at her most vulnerable, sat there on the floor, holding a telephone like a hope, saying, "Hello? Wrong number. They should have called by now. God forbid anything should have happened. Hello? Wrong number. Where are they? God forbid."

At the top of the stairs, an incredibly tanned woman of indeterminate age, who exuded health the way most people exude frustration, asked Mark if he knew who the party's

. . . chess is particularly the game of the unappreciated, who seek in play that success

host was. Mark said he didn't know.

The blind man said, "It's Barnaby's party."

"There's no such thing as Barnaby," the cynical young man sneered. "And this party doesn't have a host. Just victims."

"You just haven't met the host, yet." said the blind man.

Mark made it as far as the door to the next room. There, a shadowy businessman scolded Mark's buttonhole, "You better wise up and fly straight before it's too late, instead of fiddling away the best years of your life on this Barnacle jazz. It ain't worth nothing. It's just a fad."

Mark slid quickly into the next room, and his eyes took a few seconds to adjust to the bright lights of this parlor. What he saw, when they did, was that this was Pearl's Parlor. She was its center and animating spirit. The red textured wallpaper, the white fur rug, the Louis XIV table and chairs, the semicircle of a half dozen male admirers at her feet, the sumptuous red couch upon which she reclined, the soft yellow fabric that clung to her skin -- and Pearl herself. She was telling the assembled multitudes, "One day I want to cover a big bed with red satin sheets and blue velvet blankets, and get fucked so I stay fucked, fucked so I never have to get laid again, fucked so when I die I can say, 'I have known what it is to be truly fucked.' "

The fawning suitors approved and flattered. She spotted Mark, who didn't. "This one here," she pointed, "is so possessive it's ridiculous. He's probably wondering right now if I spent the afternoon with Francois in a thirty-three position." The men at her feet laughed. "You will never understand a woman like me."

Mark felt no desire for her. She saw that, grew self-conscious, smiled vulnerably at him. He did not care. Characteristically, that stirred Pearl's ardor. She batted her eyes, her cheek blushed, her small nod invited.

Mark left.

The next room was lit by one large overhead light, set three feet above the round card table. A big, rich, seven-card stud game was in progress. More money on the table than Mark earned at Peterson's in a year. Everyone

which life has denied them.

— *Richard Reti*

dismissed him at once with amused shrugs. Bill Beauragard set them straight by booming, "Howdy, Mark. Let me warn you, before you get any bad ideas, that this game we're indulging in here is way out of your league, both in terms of skills and in terms of chips, so if I was you I'd shuffle on through into the next room, through this here door, and join in the freebie game that Pepe's running in the next room."

"Get your ass in gear and deal!" a loser hurried Beauragard. "I want to win back what I lost."

Beauragard began to deal, "Now let me give you an invaluable piece of poker wisdom, free of charge. You may win later, tonight. You may even come out ahead for the night. But I assure you, my friend, you will *not* win back what you've lost."

Mark moved on. "Hi, have a seat," the Master Scribbler greeted him. Two candles in the far corner of the room were the only lights, and Mark could barely make out where the seats were. Mark seated himself between Grool and Tom Roebuck. "We're playing pass it along," Pepe told him, and opened the game by whispering, too loudly, to Grool, " ' . . . a place in the ear.' "

Grool whispered to Mark, "I am not your key."

Mark looked around, could see no one. He suddenly felt as though a pill he had forgotten taking was beginning to come on.

He whispered to Tom, "Thirty's not old."

Tom read softly to Pearl, "The pathos, the laughter, and the tears."

Pearl whispered to Joanie, "Foxy, though, isn't he?"

Joanie walked over to Mark, and whispered, her lips in his ear, "No, love."

Pepe whispered to Mark, "We're playing Pass It Along."

Pearl whispered to Mark, "You'll never understand."

Pepe whispered to Mark, "Beauragard and I want you to meet us at the fire. Go through this door and through the long hallway. The fire's all the way at the other end."

Above him, framing the entrance to the hall, old chiseled letters in the well-tended and recently washed marble announced: The Hall of Manqués. Mark entered. The

...the reason he is called The Sky is because he...will bet all he has, and nobody

exhibition cases were filled, not with waxworks or cloth dummies, but with stuffed people: The Lamont Cranston Manqué; The Betty Crocker Manqué; The Man From St. Ives Manque, with his six wives and 43 cats; The Grool Manqué; The Italian Blue Team Manqué; The New Age Hippy Manqué; and, at the very end, The Manqué Manqué, which was a stuffed Mark, surrounded by pieces of paper, reading something apparently bone-shaking from a huge book.

Mark climbed on the sill of the display case, so he could peer at the book The Manqué Manqué Mark was reading. He did, but couldn't make out the words.

Pepe, the Master Scribe entered the exhibit, and removed the book The Manqué Manqué held, and beckoned for Mark to follow, pointing to the hall's door.

Through the door, the fire, off in the distance, by the sea, on the beach. As he neared the beach, he saw the two fire-watchers -- Pepe and Bill Beauragard.

"Feed it, fuel it, fan it," the gambler in grey-felt chanted. "These days, they throw in candy wrappers, plastic gimmicks, stuff that pops or flares up for a minute. Without fuel that has some duration, it doesn't get hot enough to melt, or forge anything."

"Are you, then, my dreams?" Mark questioned like a good little clown.

"No! You are our body!" boomed Beauragard.

"It's like the commutative law of arithmetic, a plus b equals b plus a," Pepe elaborated. "Pass it along, all along, all along the line. This is as real as it ever gets. From our vantage point, you the living are the ephemeral phenomena, and we the dreams are the perennials, the enduring spirits of the species. Individuals are the looms upon which we weave our larger tapestries." Pepe, scribe of the vertiginous.

"But if I wake, you vanish."

"Don't be an idiot. We've been here all along." Pepe smashed the suggestion with the snap of one finger, as he would a fly.

"Did you say you were having trouble with your Abraxis?" Bill mocked.

can bet more than this.

— Damon Runyon

"What time is it?" Mark was grasping at straws.

"The changing of the gods," Pepe replied.

"It's a two-way street," Beauragard tried to explain.

"It's in the nature of time," Pepe went on. "Man masters matter, and is enslaved by its law. The idealist enters politics, and dances to its jigs. We conquer evil, and absorb it. It's all in my book, you know." He tapped the leather bound tome he had carried from the lap of The Manque Manque. "Very little is brand new; practically nothing that's human."

"Let me copy out the book."

"It can't be done."

"Let me read it, then."

"That's not the way."

"What is the way?"

Pepe tossed the book into the fire. Mark jumped to retrieve it, and Beauragard restrained him. The paper vanished in an instant, but the ink burned like hardwood.

Pepe then handed Mark a book identical to the one he had just burned, but when Mark flipped through its pages he saw that it was blank. "No mistakes in it," Pepe recommended, in parting.

Turning, feeling a desperate loss, Mark seized upon Bill's staff Azoth as the sole hope of restoring what had been incinerated. "Is it true that the pictures on your staff tell all the stories that were in Pepe's book?"

"Consubstantial," read the letters glowing on Bill's stick. "You, too," he added.

"Show them all to me, I'll copy down what I see."

"It would take forever, and even then it would not be the way. You'd take the play out of it." He tossed the stick into the fire, gave Mark a straight branch. "Carve a new one." And then he left, leaving Mark alone.

Mark woke. The moon was full in the window. Its patterns formed into solid shapes, the shapes shifted, circled, spun faster and faster. The moon was breaking up! Jagged sections began to come loose, small ones flew into space, and then the large chunks of it. And the moon was gone. Mark screamed.

His scream frightened him into half-waking up. He had

In the long run, men only hit what they aim at. Therefore . . . they had better aim at

only dreamed about waking up. His eyes were still shut.
Now he opened them. The moon shone full in the window.

something high.

— *Henry David Thoreau*

The Unreasonable Man

bowling

16

" . . . tell me, what is new? What profundities have you discovered? What mischief have you perpetrated? What beautiful women have you seduced?

— *Jean Varda, to Alan Watts*

She called while he waited for his coffee to finish brewing. "Want to come over for dinner some night soon? Like tonight?"

"No. I can't see you, Pearl. I'm allergic to you. You give me amnesia. Besides, by now everybody's heard how we've broken up again. If we start up again, what will people think?"

"The worst, I hope."

"No. No. We shouldn't. One must always try to choose one's dates and mates on the basis of what one's friends think. Isn't that what life's about?"

He coffeed up, put himself unwillingly to work. What was true was true whether or not he felt good, whether or not it was of use to himself, or anybody. He spent the better part of a morning with a long strip of thick index paper, some odd-sized leftover trim from Peterson's, doodling a Klee-like erector-set construction of arrows, ovals, and scalene triangles in the bottom right corner while he contemplated the blankness above it. He was full of indistinct anxieties. He threw the 59th Hexagram -- *Dispersion* -- his sixth-in-the-fourth leaping off the page at him. It was just the *season*, he felt.

Ought to check back with Larry, Mark thought, and get moving on that idea of a chess program for the problem

243

boys he works with.

By mid-afternoon he was working well on his old notes about the three phases of play. First, play is play for play's sake, child's play. Little children play a nongame called Just Running Around -- it has no rules, no purpose, no winners and no losers. You just run around for the fun of it.

George Herbert Meade wrote that a child makes a crucial development when he progresses from playing play to playing games. When a child begins to play games, he learns to put himself in an active and purposeful relationship with others -- opponents, teammates, officials. He learns compromise and accommodation. This is Phase II. The traditions are imitated and the games are all played by rules. Franz Kafka said, "In the struggle between yourself and the world, always take the world's side." The world requires that we succeed, and achieve, and avoid the penalities for failure. The Vince Lombardi trap: "Winning isn't the main thing, it's the only thing."

Adult life involves us in so many Phase II games that we may confuse ourselves into behaving as though our lives were games to be won or lost. But life, like love and music, is its own realization, an experience to be appreciated for its intrinsic values, as well as an energy to be harnessed. The present moment is more than some future moment's past. In the processes unfolding in the advancing present, we are alive; the outcomes and payoffs are merely facts.

This is the secret of the goose that lays the golden eggs -- if you feed the live process, it creates riches as byproducts; but if you cut it open to seize the gold, you destroy the process, and get nothing.

Mark did some knee bends, made more coffee, ate two oranges, continued:

Phase III is play as the creative context, work and play. It is the nature of intelligence to want to play, even in crisis situations. (TA's creative child in the hands of the nurturing parent.) Piaget calls play the opposite of imitation -- imitation is the process by which the child adapts his life to the social reality; play is the way the child adapts his experience of the world to himself.

Shaw wrote, "The reasonable man adapts himself to the

. . . religions like Christianity and Buddhism are desparate strategems of failure, the

world; the unreasonable one persists in trying to adapt the world to himself. Therefore, all progress depends on the unreasonable man.''

Mark grew tired, thought of how the sixties and the founding of the town were like child's play, with all the costumes, ceremonies, acting out, visions of Forever After. And all that had been smashed, and changed into a life-and-death struggle with Weel, a must-win game. And now he was moving into Phase III. That's all. He had worked all day long, and had become so tired he was beginning to catch himself falling foward, nodding.

* * * * *

He woke at three in the morning, went for a walk. He recalled an old friend who wrote, ''Wherever you may wander, / Wherever the wild winds whine / I will be your valentine.'' A hobo named Bozo -- used to pencil his poetry on pieces of paper he kept in his pockets while he went camping and swimming. The quips and cant were always in various stages of disintegration and invisibility, from the plainly readable deathless couplets through lines that winked in and out of objective reality, which Mark and Bozo would try to guess (Mark's imagination being as acceptable to Bozo as his own ventilated memory). At the back of Bozo's sheaf were seawashed pages, devoid of even the ghost of a letter, which he would then move to the front of the stack and begin anew. Like Han Shan, tossing his poems to the wind, and then raking them into the fire with the leaves.

Who said, ''Time stays, we go''? I'm thirty years old, and soon enough I will be dead. Henry Austin Dobson, he recalled.

I don't know. I never knew. I'll never know. And then, there, in the furthest reaches of the darkest, and most hopeless cul-de-sac . . . what? Will I really find, sitting serenely within me, a million-year-old man whose faith has never flagged and who has always known what to do?

Doubt and certainty, like those octopus experiments. Learning as a neurological process which is subjectively experienced as the irregular alternation of doubt and cer-

failure of men to be men.

— *Cyril Connolly*

tainty. Doubt, the feeling generated by a groping mind, exploring unfamiliar territories, wary and tentative, weighing the wear of the possible; and certainty, the feeling of seizing the answer, holding it, delighting in it, recording it, plugging it into the net of its immediate associations. Doubt was not a weakness, but a prelude. It was meaningless because prior to meaning, coming from never where no thoughts come. Fluid and protean as the Old Man of the Sea, reveiled and revealed. The Significance of all things.

What the hell ever happened to that guy me and Peterson were supposed to do those posters for? With the picture of the stegosaurus walking past a broken church steeple with a clock in it. Shrink it down a little, put it on some light index stock; shrink it down even more, for that matter, and make postcards out of it. Never came back, though.

The oscillations between cultivation of self and community activity, contemplation and service, were no longer as wrenching. The cycle was as natural as the moon's, if not as grand and regular.

"Hey!" It was Wince, the Mumbler, inelegantly but comfortably snuggled under a wheelbarrow ramp at a small construction site, a summer house, north of the town. "You got a cigarette?"

Mark told him he had stopped, decided not to bother asking Wince how he came to rest where he was.

Wince obliged anyway. "I'd been sleeping in my car, but the CHP impounded it. This ain't bad. People think living like I do is hard, but it's easy. It's easier maintaining when you don't have much to maintain."

"You know how to play Oh Hell?" Mark asked. "It's a card game. You win by taking exactly as many tricks as you bid -- no more, no less. And the smart strategy is to bid low because it's easier to throw away winners than it is to parlay losers into winners."

"Yeah. That's right. I bid very low. And as long as you make what you set out to do, it comes out about the same. Right?"

"Not for me. Oh Hell's not my game."

The walk back took only a moment. And home felt

If by eternity is understood not endless temporal duration but timelessness, then

unusually good -- his playpen, his cell, his rocketship. He turned on the radio, found the popular and insipid version of Pachelbel's Soporific Kanon. Heaven help us to be appreciative of small miracles, he prayed to the night. This is still so much better than what usually comes through radios-in-general that we have to admire its retarded popularity in the 1970's.

He slept, had a nightmare: He entered a great and stately library. With malicious glee, two of the librarians were tossing pieces from Mark's best chess set into the fire, one piece at a time.

He woke in the middle of the day, wondered how far low-cost computer technology had come, how long it would be before he could afford a desk terminal that would enable him to type out, retrieve and alter his notes on a cathode-ray screen, and all that that kind of information-handling facility might yield.

The phone. Pearl? Should I take the damn thing off the hook again? "Hello?"

"Hi, Mark."

"Tom." So they weren't dropping his friendship after all.

"Want to have dinner with Dorothy and me tomorrow night?"

"Sounds great. Sure."

"You ought to drop in on some of the planning sessions going on these days. This is a tremendously exciting time for us, with all that money at our disposal. Not only can we plan big, we can afford to make the plans happen. You'd love it, Mark, the brainstorming, the nit-picking analysis, all the wild possibilities . . . We miss you there." Tom waited for Mark to answer, and when he didn't he added, "Well, maybe we'll kick some ideas around when you're over. Tomorrow night, then."

"Right. See you then."

Mark pumped up his bicycle's rear tire, and took off, heading inland. Even with the wind at his back, he felt so out of shape and weak during the first two miles he was sure he'd have to quit early. But by the fourth mile he had tapped into his reservoirs of vitality and knew he could go a

he lives eternally who lives in the present.   —*Ludwig Wittgenstein*

hundred miles, if he wanted.

The first time round with Pearl, she had seen him at his very worst. Well, so what, he was now able to say. The risk-taking's part of it. Love is not the absence of pain. That's Hinduism, not romance.

Up Moscow Road, along the river to Lido Grande. He stopped for an ice-cream cone, was reminded by the periodical rack of Mencken's point -- nobody ever lost money underestimating the American reading public.

Two miles out of Lido Grande, near Gumper's Corners, Mark slid to a stop. He turned his ten-speed acoustic chopper around, to confirm what he thought he saw. The shunned goddess, the wondrously beautiful black-eyed girl from the dance in Lido Grande, when he took Pearl and went home with Martha.

He circled.

She looked away.

"Hello."

She gave him a shy glance, and then quickly and firmly looked away.

"Remember me?"

She looked, tentatively. And remembered.

"From the dance."

"Yes."

That didn't give him much to go on. He still didn't have a clue as to whether she was a goddess or only another piece of silly prettiness; but he was beginning to realize that she was neither, but rather a young woman. The age-difference, of course, made anything significant hopeless. How could he be sure? What did he know about it? Joyce was heavy into games, too, but it didn't help them, did it? The right differences would be better than the wrong similarities. All this whipped through him in the first moment. He began to consider whether or not he should go on talking to her, or just scoot on along. He decided not to decide by thinking about it, reasoning that impetuosity had been at least as good a selection-mechanism of women for him as rationality. Besides, what was needed here was not a precisely tied double bowline with a half hitch, but a fast granny knot. Inexactness was less likely to hurt him here

Man only plays when in the full meaning of the word he is a man, and he

than inaction. "I didn't want to stop dancing with you, but . . . it's complicated, but I felt obligated to leave with somebody then. I hope you weren't offended.

"Think nothing of it," she replied, pert and unrufflable. Then, without the slightest change in her portrait-studio expression, she removed from a pocket a hand in a hand-puppet of a bespectacled professorial type in frumpled clothing. The professor beckoned to Mark, took a quick and nervous look back to the poker-faced girl, and stage-whispered, "It freaked her, as they say, *out*, my good man! Cad!"

Mark was amazed. What came out was, "You must hear this a lot, but you're beautiful."

"Sweet of you to say so," she responded properly. Another hand from another pocket animated a pig-tailed schoolgirl puppet. "She doesn't hear that at all, to tell you the truth. Ain't that just the way of this blind, ungrateful world."

Her name was Beth and they went to her house in Gumperstown because her folks were not home. They could make themselves a lunch, and she agreed to get her bike and join him for the ride back to Lone Buck Bay.

Her parents lived in a lower-upper-middle-class ranch-style house, predictably furnished but situated sensationally on a hilltop overlooking Gumper's Redwoods State Park. Here and there, in the Good Housekeeping outer rooms, were some intriguingly dissonant overlays by Beth: the three-foot doll of Lao Tzu; the carved trim on the bric-a-brac shelves, swarming with faces and shapes like bugs under a rock; and the gallon mayonnaise jar filled with a homemade oat and nut and coconut cereal. It looked good to him. "Can I have some of this?"

Beth looked dubious. "Well, we'll consider it." She was beginning to trust him enough to play with him without her puppets. "Maybe just a flake or two."

He realized, when she said that, that the one glint of artificiality he had sensed in her -- a smile that looked a little forced and rehearsed -- looked the way it did because she had done live theater, and had learned to adjust her face like clothing.

is only completely a man when he plays.

— *Friedrich Schiller*

She showed him her room, a workroon filled with
puppets and toys, and mostly with dolls. A few paintings;
not unlike Angela's in style and subjects, although not as
developed. "You paint, too?"

"Not much. It's too two-dimensional for me. I don't see
things that way."

"I love your room."

"I want to get my own place."

"How come? Actually, it's probably obviously the best
move."

"Well, it might be different if things were different
around here. How were things decided in your home?"

He thought back through his homes with women, to his
family, which is what she must have meant. "Usually we
discussed it. There was a pecking order and all that, but
there were also compromises and accommodations. How are
things decided here?"

"In this house," Beth said with emphatic seriousness,
"Daddy speaks."

"What does that mean? Nobody else gets a say in it?"

Her eyes wide and grave, she repeated, "Daddy spoke!"
What more was there to be said? What was there to discuss
or dispute? *Daddy* had spoken. That was final, in the way
that thunder is, and as obviously beyond appeal.

"What does your daddy think of your puppets?"

She shrugged. "He thinks I'm trying to avoid growing
up."

"Tell him dolls and toys help you grow up."

"Daddy won't buy it."

"Tell him about the kachinas."

"Never mind him. Tell me about the kachinas," she said.

"Kachinas are traditional dolls, very stylized, used by
The Native Americans of the Southwest, like the Hopi. For
teaching. They show children the particular life quality each
kachina embodies -- health, fleet-footedness, wisdom,
whatever it is. And, with the help of the dolls, they pass on
the tribal values, the human qualities prized by the tribe."

Now it was Beth's turn to wonder at him. "Have you
studied this?"

[*Child's play is*] *the infantile form of the human ability to deal with experience by*

"Some." He told her briefly of ludics, and of Professor Ross and Huizinga. "But schools and colleges are places where play and games are dissected, and become fodder for dull foot-noted papers. I need to *play* play. Studying play is not playing. The Zen master Suziki makes that kind of distinction between Zen and a system of thought about Zen, saying that Zen can't be contained within a system of thought because Zen is what makes thought possible. In college, I was learning some theories about play. Free of the limitations of Academia I can actually play."

"Did you ever see Professor Ross again?"

"Once. During the period when my marriage was breaking up, and the excitement of working alone, free of supervising authority was beginning to wear off. He was marvelous. He asked me how my work was going, and I said, 'You mean my job?' And he snapped at me, 'Not your job; your *work!*' "

* * * * *

Puffing, sweaty and ruddy, they got off their bikes to rest at Austin Creek. Its water was bright and clear, fed by mountain springs. They took off their shoes, splashed themselves and each other. Upstream, a quartet of junior high school boys and girls ran berserk, giggling. They were loosely chaperoned by a college-age duo, who were far too involved in making out to pay attention to the revelries of their pubescent charges.

"Tell me a poem?" she asked him.

"A short one. Do you know Byron?"

"We were never intimate."

" 'Stanzas written on the road between Florence and Pisa.' "

"Is that all of it?"

"That's only the title."

"I hope it gets better."

"Me too."

"Well, how does it go?"

"Just lovely. How's it going for you?"

creating model situations and to master reality by experiment and planning.
— *Erik Erikson*

"Are you ready?"

"I'm not sure, now."

"Well, grab onto a branch or something. Here goes:
'Oh, talk not to me of a name great in story;
The days of our youth are the days of our glory;
And the myrtle and ivy of sweet two-and-twenty,
Are worth all your laurels, though ever so plenty.' "

She had listened. "That was nice."

"Now it's your turn."

"For what?"

"Don't give me that innocent Sisters of Mercy look. I saw you stuff some of your little stooges into your backpack before you left. Now fetch one of them out, and make her do a little dance."

"Pick one." She zipped open one pocket of her pack.

Mark's hand drew out a puppet of a handsome young black man, nattily attired in a black leather jacket with thin zebra-skin trim on the pockets. He pointed at Mark, and began, "Let me ask you a personal question, friends -- Did you ever wish you could sing the blues, but knew you couldn't because you were white?

"If so, then you may be suffering from the distressing symptoms of white racial guilt known as The White Twitch.

"But don't despair, friends. Babagreela Lalagroondo's Black Pills are here! Yes, just two of these amazing little pills, taken daily, will kink your hair, blacken your skin, and give you that extra special spark us *real* bloods call Soul.

"Of course, if being black right away is a bit too much for some of you bourgeois beginners out there, you can start off with our Intermediate Chicano pills, or our Elementary Polish line. Only $5.98 for three dozen, in our handy sleek new zebra-skin carrying pouch."

* * * * *

They pedalled west into the head wind, and rested again at the coast, just outside of Jenner, before starting north into the hills. Beth propped her head on the grassy rise by

As God plays with the time of this outward world, so also should the inward divine

the roadside as though it were her familiar pillow. A black and scarlet bird, jeweled against the blue sky, passed by. He watched her close her eyes, and knew she was a sign from Aphrodite that the goddess had lifted her curse on him.

They reached the town at sunset. Beth did an extended theatrical farewell to the sun's setting, with flourishes and curtsies, blown kisses and ritual sobbing.

"Do you do this every evening?"

"No," she confided, "every one is different." She shook her hair into the sky.

The first five minutes she was in his house, she said nothing, looked, stared about at . . . "What's that? The music."

"Concerto in C Major for Three Harpsichords and String Orchestra, by Johann Sebastian Batch. Every scratch a memory."

"It's magnificent."

"Did you ever read a story by Damon Runyon called 'The Idyll of Miss Sarah Brown?' The small time sport who narrates the story describes this Miss Brown as having 'eyes like I do not know what, except that they are one hundred percent eyes in every respect.' "

Beth asked, "Is there a point to your little tale?"

"Yes. I haven't gotten to it yet, but I will." He added, "It's easier when you don't care."

"What is?"

"Saying something. Doing something." He could not then explain to her that when he cared as he did then, he needed some kind of sign from the woman -- just a smile, perhaps, or something in the sound of her voice.

They talked, about reincarnation, and whether it was literally true or true simply as a valuable metaphor for the changes of personality through a lifetime, and for the journey of the personality of the human species through history.

Then they talked about themselves, until it was easy to kiss and cuddle. And by the time they actually did go to bed they had both put their shyness behind them, and they both

man play with the outward in the revealed wonders of God . . .
                                                          — Jakob Boehme

knew they both wanted each other.

* * * * *

After they made love, and held each other, and made love again, she made them a chamomile, pennyroyal, and peppermint blend she had brought. He felt as he had not felt in a long time, caring for someone who cared for him. She looked wonderful to begin with, and was looking better. She could make staying home very easy to do -- her puppets, her intelligence, her sensitivity, her intuitive sense of play.

She's so young! he reprimanded himself. Hell, after my last three -- Queen Hippolyta, Madame Curie, and Mata Hari -- girlishness ought to be a gas. "Why don't you call your parents in the morning, tell them you'll be staying another day?"

She pursed her lips, then smiled, "All right."

"Want to stay the month? We can play house."

She shook her head. "That's too fast. I don't know what to say." Not only had his question caught her by surprise, but she surprised herself by sensing that she would seriously consider it. "Are there other people like us in this town? People I could actually talk with?"

"Yeah. There are twelve of us. We got a gang called the Jo-Jo's."

* * * * *

Since he was a child, Mark had suffered from being a favored food of mosquitoes. During the most heavily infested summer-camp season of his childhood, he led all the afflicted with a peak count of 163 bites. And now, while Beth slept soundly, unscathed, he had been bitten a dozen times.

Beth rolled over. Mark caressed her legs beneath his blue flannel pajamas. They were adorably huge on her. He watched her breathe. How beautiful. Sleeping with her felt not only brand new, but like an old truth reappearing after having been obscured. He remembered his thoughts about dead pieces coming back to life. He reminded himself that it

. . . that moment when even sleep closes her eyes and dreams begin to dream . . .
— Yeats

was usually easy during the first easy sweep of an affair. Who can know if it's going anywhere? She stretched.

The muffled, "Whomp" of his feet hitting the floor woke her. Drowsily, she asked, "How come you're up?"

"I was being bitten to death."

"Not by me."

"No. By mosquitoes."

"Didn't get to me at all."

"Yeah. I always get bit more. The story of what passes for my life."

"Vitamin B complex deficiency," she diagnosed.

"Beer drinking's supposed to keep them away."

"Brewer's yeast in it. That's why."

"Yeah. Only I don't like beer much." He kissed her. "Don't go away. I'm going for a walk." He took his clothes into the kitchen. Miniature mosaic chimera mottled Mark's waking vision: the kitchen's bright yellow bulb and too yellow table, yellow-green walls, the visionless spaces that faded as his eyes adapted to the light.

Itchy, itchy, itchy.

The clock was wrong. Must have been a blackout during the night. He called the time-lady on the phone, corrected the clock. Today was Tuesday. He felt a humorous intimacy with the day's name. How many Tuesdays in thirty years? With the aid of his $10 calculator it took only four seconds to compute 1,560 plus maybe one or two for leap years. *Tuesday* -- he could taste it: thin and reedy, tan, light. When he was a child, in the moments just before and after sleep, like this one, he would spread out all of the days of the week before him like the feathers of a fan, and each had its particular shape and texture, each had its distinctive color.

Those three dreams! Pepe and Beauragard throwing the book and the staff into the flames, the librarians burning his chesspieces in the fireplace, and Pearl tossing the dirt into the pond. It was obvious that they had parallel shapes. Yes. Well, so what? What did that tell him? Nothing? Or is the dream its own interpretation? Who's that? Jung? No, Buber. Where's my jacket?

Everything proved his point. Fire is at the core of the apparently slow, cool material world. There is a family

. . . vital properties are never entirely realized, though always on the way to become so.
— Henri Bergson

resemblance to fire. Science theorizes that we grew naturally out of the whole life process on this planet, and that life grew naturally out of the chemistry of the planet itself, and the planet was the natural consequence of the condensation of the same swirl of gases that, at its center, became the sun. We're made of the same basic stuff as the sun, and the stars.

Mark needed more than a job and leisure -- he also needed a long-range plan. Like Chaucer's "Many smalls make a great," or the counsel of the *I Ching* that accomplishing something genuine requires *using* time, and subordinating many small tasks, the work a man can do in a day, to a greater task, a concentrated labor of years. The organization of independently insignificant details into an organic entity, the hunting and trapping of undomesticated truths.

There may be some minor goals to thought, but there is no end point for all thought. The goal of thought is free-thought, free to roam wherever it wishes, free from the one-dimensionality of finding *the* solution. How does Kant say it? "It is difficult to speak the truth, for although there is only one truth, it is alive and therefore has a live and changing face."

Offshore, puffs and towers of fog, like torn cotton, floated off the ocean. Everything proved his point. The wind freshened his face, and the first slim brilliant sliver of the sun rose in the apricot skies over the inland hills.

He looked back, at the cusp that led into the season now ending -- his resignations and reorientations, all the ethical turmoil, and his own inertia. He had willed a change. It had come about. He looked back at that corner from the next, leading to the passageway beyond.

And he looked down that passageway, and the next and the next, spanning time, and saw a future ludicist, himself or another, calculating with scientific precision the nature of the relationships between phenomena now linked only in music and fiction, if at all. The future ludicist raised a glass of wine and toasted Mark for having broken ground in what would then be fruitful vineyards. And then the future

. . . some of necessity go astray, because for them there is no such thing as the right

ludicist turned and raised his glass to a figure even further in the future, hidden from Mark.

path.

— *Thomas Mann*

APPENDIX

Chapter Numeral Diagrams

One: The *go* diagram illustrates the *fuseki* (opening moves) of a 1926 game between Kaoru Iwamote, now one of the grand old masters of *go*, and the immortal Honinbo Shusai (White), one of the greatest players of all time.

Two: Seven piece *tangram* is an ancient Chinese visual game of rearranging the seven simple shapes (no overlaps, no pieces left out) into silhouettes. Over 1,600 different silhouettes are now in the literature. Legend says the game was discovered when a man named Tan dropped a square tile and it shattered into seven pieces.

Three: *Monopoly* was invented in 1933 by Charles Darrow. Parker Brothers rejected the game, at first, for having "fifty-two fundamental errors," but later purchased the copyright. Parker Brothers has since sold eighty million sets in twenty-seven countries.

Four: *Hopscotch* is also known as Potsie. It is a sidewalk game of physical dexterity. The winner is the first to hop through the hazards of onesie, twosie, threesie, foursie, fivesie, sixsie, backwards fivesie, backwards foursie, backwards threesie, backwards twosie, and backwards onesie.

Five: *Pong Han K'i* is a Cantonese and Korean children's game. White and Black try to trap each other into a position where the opponent has no moves.

Six: *Skelly* is a sidewalk game played with bottle caps (called 'checkers'). Each of the numbered squares, in turn, have to be landed in, like golf. A checker landing in a Skel square (directly or knocked there by another checker) goes back to the beginning.

Seven: This Navajo *string figure* depicts the vertebral column, and is from the same family as the familiar cat's cradle figures.

Eight: The American *football* diagram illustrates an offensive play in which two wide receivers run a crisscross ten yards out and the tight end runs a button hook.

Nine: The *Chinese chess* diagram illustrates the opening position. The center rank (without files) is the dividing river. The pieces are generals, mandarin officers, elephants, horses, chariots, catapults, and footsoldiers.

Ten: *Tennis* court.

Eleven: The Agent-Respondent grid is from *Transactional Analysis'* parent-adult-child diagrams of personal interactions.

Twelve: The *chess* position illustrates the exception of the bishop pawn -- a key point in endgame theory. White can draw because he can abandon the pawn by retreating into the corner, and if Black takes, White is stalemated.

Thirteen: The deal in a five-card stud *poker* game.

Fourteen: The illustration is of the five-up variation of *dominoes*. West led the double-blank, North scored with the blank-five, East played the blank-four, South scored with the five-six, West played the blank-ace, and North ran the score up to 30-0 with the ace-five.

Fifteen: The *Bell and Hammer* card is from a German gambling game of the same name, played with special cards and dice.

Sixteen: A frame from a *bowling* scoresheet.

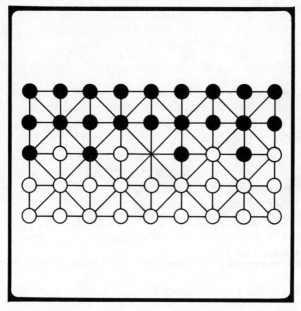

Fanorona is still played in its native land of Malagasy (formerly Madagascar), where it was developed about 1680 by doubling the size of the board and the number of pieces of the older game of Alquerque. The diagram illustrates the opening position.

Stephen Minkin broad-jumped 20' 6½'' and played third-board (chess) for Brooklyn Tech and won the Eastern Regional Teen-aged Championship of the American Contract Bridge League in 1962.

His postal-chess/love story ("Natural Numbers") will be anthologized in Hugh Fox's collection of contemporary prose. His work has appeared in many publications and on local television, and includes an illustrated comic poem for *Flash* magazine.

He's edited a literary magazine (*"Paper Pudding"*), a Maryland county newspaper, and co-edited a newspaper covering a north coast California county.

The author lives in Sonoma County, California, where he has pioneered a chess program at a residential home for allegedly emotionally disturbed boys.

The fervor of his devotion to the Golden State Warriors remains unparalleled.

This is his first novel.

P-QB4.

Christopher Swan is the co-author, illustrator and designer of Sierra Club's *YV 88,* an unusual mix of theory and fiction that details a blueprint for the reclamation of Yosemite Valley. Chris also designed Lenny Lipton's superb film handbook, *The Super-8 Book,* and co-authored and illustrated *Cable Car.*

He is currently refubishing an old ranchhouse overlooking the Sierras on the North San Juan ridge, and writing a science fiction adventure and an essay on water.

Chris is working, both in his life and in his art, toward the achievement of consonance between the way we choose to live and the environment in which we live.

For a complete catalog of Monday Publications write *Back Roads*, Box 543, Cotati, Calif. 94928.

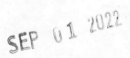